WHERE OBLIVION LIVES

BY T. FROHOCK

Los Nefilim

Where Oblivion Lives

In Midnight's Silence (novella)

Without Light or Guide (novella)

The Second Death (novella)

Miserere: An Autumn Tale

WHERE OBLIVION LIVES

T. FROHOCK

This is a work of fiction. Names, characters, places, and incidents are products of the author's imagination or are used fictitiously and are not to be construed as real. Any resemblance to actual events, locales, organizations, or persons, living or dead, is entirely coincidental.

HarperCollins books may be purchased for educational, business, or sales promotional use. For information, please email the Special Markets Department at SPsales@harpercollins.com.

FIRST EDITION

Designed by Paula Russell Szafranski

Decorative frame © 100ker/Shutterstock

Library of Congress Cataloging-in-Publication Data has been applied for.

ISBN 978-0-06-282561-2

19 20 21 22 23 LSC 10 9 8 7 6 5 4 3 2 1

For my dear friend and mentor,

Lisa W. Cantrell

AUTHOR'S NOTE

A quick note on the spellings used: the accepted spelling of the word is *Nephilim*. However, in Spanish the "ph" sound is replaced by the "f," hence *Los Nefilim*.

This novel is primarily told from the points of view of my Spanish characters, so whenever I needed to use the generic term "Nephilim" to indicate the species of Nephilim as a whole, I use the spelling "nefilim" (the lowercase *n* is intentional for plural "nefilim" as well as the singular "nefil").

I also needed a way in which to distinguish the various nationalities of nefilim within the Inner Guard. Whenever you see capitalization—Los Nefilim, Die Nephilim, or Les Néphilim—I am referring to the different nationalities of Inner Guards—the Spanish, German, and French, respectively.

—T

25 August 1932

it begins with an attack

[1]

CATALONIA, SPAIN
THE TOWN OF SANTUARI

Diago played a rapid series of staccato chords on the worn piano keys. The upright shuddered under his assault.

"Come on," he muttered. He performed another fast run but stopped abruptly, barely resisting the urge to slam the fallboard on the keys. "Damn it." Glaring at the musical notations penciled across the staves, he reconsidered the heavily revised intro.

The arrangement wasn't working. *It's still too clear. Too bright.* The composition lacked the dissonance thundering through his dreams and leaving him battered and beaten each dawn.

He erased his last notation from the score and transposed the minor chords, assessing the change with a critical eye. Somewhere in that profusion of markings and erasures lay a song—one he had to master.

And soon.

Otherwise, he had little hope of stopping the psychic attacks causing his nightmares. Re-creating the composition wasn't his preferred method of hunting, but it gave him a chance to uncover the composer's unique signature—a leitmotif of sorts—that could lead Diago to a name.

And if I learn their name, I'll send them a nightmare they'll never forget. He placed his pencil on the stand, picked it up, and then set it down again. It was a ritual that had become the equivalent of a nervous tic.

Of course, the best method was to follow the music's siren call to its source. *Pack a bag, find a ride into Barcelona, and get on a train to . . . where?*

He thought for a moment and then decided, *North, yes, north into France.* That felt right.

The mantel clock chimed eleven, jerking him out of the fantasy. Bound by his oath to Los Nefilim, one of the groups that monitored daimonic activity for the angels, he wasn't free to leave Santuari on a whim.

So I improvise. He turned his attention back to the score. Reaching for the pencil, he caught himself before he could pick it up and folded his arms across his stomach.

If he intended to succeed, he had to relax and reconstruct the dream. *Lucid dreaming. That's what I need to do.*

Closing his eyes, he took several calming breaths. Swathed in darkness, he listened for the opening passage. Just as he teetered on the verge of sleep, he caught the violin's distant strains teasing their way into his brain.

It's my lost Stradivarius—I know its voice like I know my own.

The music gained resonance as the composition took form. *It's written for a violin and begins with an attack and punch against the strings—three quick jabs of the bow—strike, strike, strike—followed by a pull to slur the chords—*

Now he had it. If he affected a portamento, he might avoid the nightmare while holding on to the nocturne, but then . . .

The front door shut, startling him out of the dream. As he straightened, his arm knocked the sheet from the upright's music stand.

The page fluttered across the floor to land in the foyer in front of Miquel's dusty boots. A predawn phone call had sent him on some errand for Guillermo, and he hadn't taken the time to shave, so a shadow of stubble darkened his face. The summer sun he loved so much had deepened his skin to a smoky brown full of warm undertones. Curls as black as his eyes gave him a carefree look that wasn't mirrored by his expression. Although he was almost a full century younger than Diago, neither of them appeared to be a day over forty.

It's our memories that make us old, Diago thought as he struggled to awaken from his impromptu nap. He rubbed his eyes and muttered, "You're home early."

"It's after noon, sleepyhead." Miquel knelt and retrieved the paper.

"It can't be, it's only"—Diago turned to the clock—"noon," he whispered. *Where had the hour gone?*

"Diago?" Miquel scowled at the score.

"Hmm?"

"What is this?"

"It's something I'm working on."

"You're supposed to be working on the composition for the Key. This is . . ." He glanced at the page and winced as if hearing the discordant song in his head. "Jesus, I don't even know what this is, but it's not the Key."

Diago looked away, hating the guilt he felt when Miquel caught him shirking his responsibilities to Los Nefilim. "Do you really believe nefilim will ever open the dimensions as the angels do?" He stood and reached for the page. "The Key is our Philosopher's Stone, Miquel—it's a fable. It doesn't exist."

Miquel lifted the score out of reach. "How can you say that? You found it once already. You unlocked the path between the realms."

"We *think* I did in a past incarnation," Diago was quick to point out. "None of us recall the details of what happened in that life—not until the right trigger revives our memories, and I haven't found my catalyst for that incarnation, and until I do, I'm working on this." He snatched the sheet from Miquel's hand and slammed it on the piano's top board with more force than he intended.

Anger ignited in Miquel's black eyes—there and gone so quick anyone else might have missed it, except Diago knew his husband's moods as clearly as his own. Nor did he fail to note the warning in Miquel's voice. "You're not on your own anymore, Diago. You can't just drift through your days like a rogue. You took an oath to Guillermo, and the job he gave you was to compose the Key. At least pretend like you care."

The sharp words worked like a slap. *Christ, what's wrong with me?* Diago struggled to calm himself. *One of us has to back down or we're going to fight.* And he hated fighting with Miquel.

Taking a steadying breath, he worked hard to moderate his tone. "It's not that I don't care." He forced himself to meet Miquel's gaze. "I do."

"Even though it's a fable?"

"I didn't mean that." *Or did I?* How many incarnations had they chased that secret song only to fail again and again? *Too many. And still we cling to the hope of composing it.*

But he didn't say that. Instead, he went to the couch and sat, pressing the heels of his palms against his forehead to block out the world. "It's just some days it feels like busywork . . . like I'm chasing smoke . . . when there are more important things to do." *Like finding the musician who tortures me with my own violin.*

For several moments, the only sound was the ticking of the clock. Then the soft tread of Miquel's footsteps moved to the couch. The worn cushions sank beneath his husband's weight.

"We've started badly today," Miquel said gently. "And that's my fault."

"I didn't help the situation," Diago admitted, and as he did, he felt the tension ease between them. "I'm sorry. I'm just so frustrated."

Miquel placed his palm on Diago's back and drew him close. "I know the nightmares are bad, but there is something else going on with you. What is it? Talk to me."

Diago dropped his hands and stared at a coloring book that their son, Rafael, had left on the table. *Magic Words* was the title. He wondered if Miquel's magic words—*talk to me*—were in the book.

They should be. No one else possessed the skill to pry Diago from his black moods like his husband. "I can't concentrate on the Key, or on that composition"—he gestured at the piano—"or . . . anything. The nightmares are part of it. I mean an occasional bad dream is normal, but a fortnight of them? It's unprecedented . . ." *Even for me.*

Miquel took his hand. "Guillermo has his people searching for the violin." He kissed Diago's palm. "He's as worried about you as I am. Whoever is causing this, we will find them."

"And what do we do in the meantime?"

"We wait."

"Waiting isn't an option. What if they try to attack Santuari with that violin? We both know there are nefilim close to Guillermo who still don't trust me." Born of angel *and* daimon, Diago's mixed heritage made him a rarity among the nefilim. But rather than acceptance by both sides, his lineage earned him nothing but mistrust. "You realize that because this person is using my Stradivarius, any sigil they produce will carry a portion of *my* aura and magic. They could easily make it appear as if I'm attacking Los Nefilim from behind its own wards."

Miquel opened his mouth, but Diago rushed on, not giving him a chance to speak.

"Let's take it one step further." He twisted on the couch so he could face his husband. "If I'm implicated, those members who don't trust me will believe you covered for me. What will we do if we lose our places here? Without the protection of Los Nefilim, we'll stand no chance to protect Rafael against his daimonic kin. He's only seven. We both know they will twist his heart and mind to suit their prejudices, like they tried to do to me."

Miquel took Diago's face between his palms. "Diago, let's not go any more steps—"

How can I convince him? He sees no danger for himself, because he thinks Los Nefilim can protect us from every threat. "I'm just saying there is more than one way to destroy someone, and if someone is after me, they'll take you down, too—"

"—you've got to stop—"

"I'm afraid."

The admission fell like a stone between them. Diago lowered his eyes, ashamed of his weakness. "In all the centuries we've lived, we've never had so much at stake as we do now," he whispered, thinking of Rafael.

Miquel's sigh came like a calm breeze after the storm. "Oh, my bright star, I understand. Really, I do. I know you're feeling helpless right now."

"That's just it. I'm *not* helpless. If I could just leave—"

"But you can't. Okay? You just have to accept that. For once in your life, you must allow other people to do the footwork that you used to do." He bent forward until their foreheads touched. "You have to keep telling yourself that you're not alone, even if it might feel like it."

"I'm sorry." Diago grasped his husband's wrists and held tight. "I am so terrified of making a mistake that will cause me to lose you and Rafael."

"You're not going to make a mistake like that," Miquel assured him. His grip remained as steady as his words. "You do your part and work on the Key, and we'll do ours to keep the doubters in line until you've had a chance to win them. It's a balancing act we've performed before. Trust me?"

"Always," Diago breathed. The tightness in his chest eased somewhat. *Maybe he's right. Maybe I've got to learn to let other people help me.* "I wouldn't be here if I didn't."

Miquel kissed him. "Good. Then trust me when I say we're going to get through this."

Diago nodded and pulled away. As he did, he noticed

a light spray of blood on the collar of Miquel's shirt. He touched the crimson stains. "Did you cut yourself?"

"I'm fine."

Did he cut someone else? "Is something going on, Miquel?"

"Yes, and that's all I can say right now."

Diago suddenly paired the blood with the predawn phone call—Miquel had obviously been summoned to arrest another nefil. *And if Miquel was called in to make the arrest, it had to be someone important and nearby. But who? And why?*

Cautious now, Diago asked, "What's happening?"

A note of warning touched Miquel's voice. "Don't ask questions. I can't say anything yet. Not until a few people in Guillermo's circle have been informed. Once they know, you will know."

Before Diago could figure a way to pry the information from him, the phone rang. He leaned over Miquel and picked up the handset. "Yes?"

"Diago?" It was Guillermo's secretary, Suero. "Don Guillermo wants you to come to his office."

"Me? When?"

"As soon as you can get here."

"Why? Suero? What does he need? Don't hang up—"

"Salut!"

"—on me."

The line buzzed in his ear.

"What's the matter?" Miquel asked.

"He hung up on me again."

Miquel shrugged. "He hangs up on everyone. You should be used to that by now."

"I'm used to it. I still don't like it."

"What did he want?"

"Guillermo wants to talk to me." He watched Miquel's reaction carefully, but his husband didn't seem disquieted by the announcement. *I'll take that as a sign that I'm not in trouble.* Unless Guillermo wanted a report on the composition for the Key. *Then I might be in trouble.*

"I'll walk with you." Miquel rose and followed Diago outside. "Because I want you to see Juanita while you're there." Guillermo's wife saw to Los Nefilim's medical care, attending their unique physiology with her treatments. "You can't keep going like this."

Diago balked at the suggestion. "I have to be in a lot of pain to see Juanita." And he wasn't quite sure he'd reached that level of fatigue yet.

"Your pain is my pain, and right now, *I'm* in pain, because I'm worried about you. So you will talk to her. Maybe she can give you something to help you sleep. Please—promise me you'll see her."

The concern in his husband's voice robbed Diago of any further arguments. "Okay, I promise."

"Good."

They walked across the grounds in silence for several moments before Diago found the courage to ask, "What if I can't remember the Key, Miquel? What happens then?"

Miquel put his arm around Diago's shoulders and drew him close. "Rafael will still love you. I will still love you. That is what will happen. We will love you if you bring the stars down on our heads."

"You are a fool," Diago muttered.

"Just for you."

[2]

They crested the knoll and reached the narrow lane leading to Guillermo's house. Stately cypress trees graced the rear corners of the home, rising past the asymmetrical roofline. Ivy-coated arcades and elegant balconies softened the severe lines that made the stone structure seem more like a fortress than a farmhouse.

Diago's gaze traveled from the house to the village. He checked his watch. School would let out at one for the midday meal, and he had no idea how long his meeting with Guillermo might last.

Miquel seemed to read his mind. "I'll get Rafael when school ends." He touched his index finger to Diago's chest, just over his heart. It was a casual gesture, their equivalent of a peck on the cheek, but it meant the world to Diago at the moment. "I'll meet you here in an hour."

"Okay."

Miquel continued on the road toward the small cluster

of buildings that composed the town of Santuari. There, the inhabitants moved about on various errands as they worked together to create a self-sustaining stronghold near the city of Barcelona.

The compound covered three hectares of land that Guillermo had gradually claimed over the centuries. In addition to giving his nefilim a place to call home, the expansive holdings allowed him to penetrate Catalonia's high society with ease.

A few mortals, indistinguishable from the nefilim, also moved through the village on business, unaware of the supernatural creatures surrounding them. Far outnumbered by mortals, the nefilim remained inconspicuous as a matter of self-preservation. They'd learned hard lessons about mortal fear and aggression during the Inquisition and similar purges.

Diago stepped onto the path to Guillermo's house and passed beneath the shade of an ornamental arbor. Insects hummed lazily in the heat of the day. Their chorus soothed him and kept time with the crunch of gravel beneath his shoes. The violin rode in on a cricket's chirrup and once more tickled the back of his mind.

The intro rose and fell before slurring into decay. The melody floated gray and soft like fog . . . *No. Not fog—the smell of cordite is too strong. It's . . .*

The barrel of a rifle blocked his path and wrenched him from the daydream. The violin's notes scattered like dandelion seeds in the wind.

He blinked at the woman holding the gun. Carme, one of Guillermo's capitáns, stood in front of him. She coordinated Santuari's border patrols and had probably come to give Guillermo a report.

"Diago, I'm glad I caught you," she said, although she didn't look pleased at all. She wore her scowl like a uniform, and between her Roman nose and overbite, today's expression rendered her face more equine than usual.

If horses had shark eyes and a voice filled with murder.

"I have an appointment with Don Guillermo," he said. The front porch lay merely two meters behind Carme. *So near and so far.* "I hope you'll excuse me."

Carme didn't move. "I wouldn't worry if I were you. Don Guillermo is tied up with reports from Madrid. You'll probably have to wait for him."

As long as you're not there. "Still, I don't want to be late." He started to move around her.

She extended the Mauser's barrel to block him a second time. He briefly considered sidestepping the obstacle. *Then again, she'll have her say, either here or in a more private location.* Twice now she had caught him alone and tried to provoke him into a fight. *And twice, she has come close to success.* Thus far, he'd controlled his desire to strike back, but a breaking point would come, and when it did, he wanted witnesses.

"What do you want, Carme?"

"Valeria"—Carme tilted her head toward another nefil at the base of the drive—"said she saw wolves in the western fields this morning."

They lived in the country; wolves came with the territory. Curious about where she was going with the information, he held his peace.

"You might want to keep Rafael's little cat inside until we take care of the situation. We're also telling the children not to play out there. It helps if the parents reinforce the warning. Probably best if everyone stays out of the western fields. You know, until the wolves are gone."

Her meaning finally resonated with him, and a needle of fear returned to prick his heart. The western fields held more than wolves. An old stone finca that was little more than a two-room shed occupied one corner of the isolated field. Guillermo used it for a gaol, where the screams of the interrogated couldn't be heard by those in Santuari.

"Wolves," Diago repeated numbly.

She watched his expression closely in an effort to gauge the effect of the news on him. It was an old trick to spring the information on a potential suspect and then observe their reaction. A flicker of concern, a scent of fear, or even a flash of anger might indicate a deeper association with the prisoner already in custody—a connection that could lead to the suspect's arrest for an interrogation of their own.

Unfortunately, Carme's attempt to unnerve him had succeeded, but not for the reasons she intended. Miquel had returned home reeking of blood and secrets.

Cold now, Diago asked, "And these wolves, are they roaming Santuari or Barcelona?"

"You never know," she said. "They travel in packs and range wide."

Movement behind Carme distracted him. Suero had ventured to the edge of the porch. The younger nefil was blond in the way of the Spanish, with light eyes and a slight build.

"Diago." He lifted his hand. "I thought I heard you. Let's go. Don Guillermo is waiting."

Apparently those reports from Madrid weren't as time-consuming as Carme thought. Diago pushed the gun barrel aside and stepped around her. He felt her eyes on his back, but he didn't turn until he entered the foyer.

Suero lingered at the door, watching Carme's retreat. "Is she giving you trouble again?" he asked.

Diago shrugged. "With Carme it's always hard to know whether she's picking a fight or just doing her job." He appreciated Suero's concern, though, which took a slight edge off his abrupt phone summons.

"Let me know if it becomes the former." Suero closed the door on the August heat. "She's been warned to back off."

"That's good to know," Diago said as he allowed the younger nefil to take the lead.

They moved deeper into the house, where the cool white of the entrance hall gave way to bright splashes of color. Talavera tiles accented the baseboards and risers on the various stairways. The inlays were decorated with glyphs, which to the mortal eye were nothing more than the profusion of motifs seen in Spanish architecture. But if one looked closer—and knew *how* to see past the distractions of the vibrant patterns—they would find Saturn's sickle, Mars's shield and spear, or Jupiter's thunderbolt alongside Enochian sigils of protection embedded in the flowering designs.

Likewise, the ornate railings—wrought by Guillermo himself—also contained those same symbols, cunningly hidden by the curls of iron and artistic embellishments. For now the glyphs lay dormant, but the vibrations of a specific song would activate their explosive magic to protect Guillermo and his family.

From somewhere nearby, a radio announcer introduced a listener's request to hear Carlos Gardel's rendition of "Mi

Noche Triste." Someone in the kitchen sang along in a clear high voice.

I could tell them something about sad nights, Diago thought as they reached a set of stairs leading into a square tower. The inlays guarding these risers carried different sigils than those in the main living areas. A mortal might mistake the tiles' radiant sparkle as flecks of quartz catching the light. To the nefilim, however, the bright flickers indicated the wards were active.

Thus, as they climbed, the kitchen's music grew muted until it was finally silenced by the power of the glyphs. Nor would anyone below be able to hear what transpired in the tower's second level, which housed Guillermo's offices.

The antechamber was just off the landing and resembled a war room. A conference table commanded the floor and was piled with files along with a couple of ancient grimoires. To the left of the entrance, a large map of the world covered one wall.

Scattered across the map were pins with colored heads. Blue represented angelic activity and red the daimonic. While the Inner Guard monitored daimonic activity for the angels all over the world, each country was assigned to a special unit. In Spain it was Los Nefilim, although Guillermo kept his eye on other countries as well, because the borders of mortals meant very little in a supernatural war.

Diago approached the map and noted a new color had been introduced into the mix. A black pin pierced a town on the German side of the Rhine near Offenburg. Before he could get close enough to read the town's name, the teletype machine in the far corner burst into a staccato rhythm.

The clacking keys brought Guillermo from the inner sanctum of his office. He was a big man, built like a bull with broad shoulders and narrow hips. Like most Catalonians, his skin was lighter than the Spaniards from Diago's home in Andalusia. A smattering of freckles sprayed across his nose and cheeks. Sun washed through a high window, touching his auburn hair and beard and merging with the fire of his aura to implode in violent shades of gold and orange.

Guillermo hesitated on his way to the teleprinter and removed the cold cigar from his mouth. His eyes narrowed as he scowled at Diago. "Still not sleeping?"

"It's getting better," he lied. When the bigger man's expression didn't change, Diago hurried to reassure him. "I'm going to see Juanita on my way out."

"That's good. She'll fix you up." Guillermo turned back to the machine and rapped the teletype's metal casing with his knuckles. The signet ring symbolizing Guillermo's authority over Los Nefilim flashed red and gold, once more dazzling Diago's vision.

"Have you seen this?" Proud as if he'd invented the teletype himself, Guillermo didn't wait for an answer. "It's the Creed Model 7. It has an absent subscriber service so we don't need a receiving operator anymore. This machine"—he warmed to his topic—"can give us around a hundred hours of continuous operation. It's top of the line and frees up my people for more important work." He shook his head in wonder. "The twentieth century is amazing. I love the speed of information."

Suero rolled his eyes. Obviously he'd heard the merits of the machine one time too many since its arrival.

Diago couldn't help but smile, either at Suero's boredom, or his friend's enthusiasm. No matter how old Guillermo became, he retained the excitement of a child when it came to gadgets.

Suero went to his desk and retrieved a slim book. Diago caught Federico García Lorca's name on the cover. From the well-worn pages, Diago assumed it was a personal copy. As one of the lesser nefilim, Suero was a child of the duende, the dark spirit of inspiration, which left the artist wounded and bleeding unlike her gentler sister the muse. The duende was an oft-mentioned theme of Lorca's work, which made him Suero's favorite poet.

Suero asked, "Do you need anything else before I go to lunch, Don Guillermo?"

The teletype finally ceased its racket and Guillermo ripped the sheet free, scanning the information quickly with a practiced eye. "No, thank you, Suero."

Suero left them alone.

Guillermo read the paper with a frown.

"What is it?" Diago asked.

"The jury reached its verdict in General Sanjurjo's trial."

Now that *was* news. In early August José Sanjurjo, a mortal general, had attempted a coup d'état against Spain's fledgling Republic with a small following of officers. Poorly planned and badly executed, the entire fiasco had been defeated in short order.

"They found Sanjurjo guilty of treason," Guillermo said as he pulled an ashtray close and crushed his cigar against the amber-colored glass. "We've been watching the trial closely."

Diago expected no less. Since the nefilim's affairs often moved in tandem with those of the mortals, the members of Los Nefilim kept a keen eye on the trial and its verdict.

Recalling Carme's talk of wolves, Diago asked, "Do you think this means one of your officers is conspiring against you?"

"Someone is always conspiring against me." Tossing the paper to the conference table, he went to his office. "Come on. I've got something to show you."

Curious now, Diago went to the door and looked inside. The container on Guillermo's desk could easily be mistaken for an infant's coffin except for the handle, which was set squarely in the center of the lid and indicated the container's true purpose. It was a violin case from the nineteenth century.

My *violin case.*

Ivory inlays of decorative glyphs adorned the edges and glowed in the semidark room. The sigils still hissed with Diago's magic, like the lyrics of a song long gone and half remembered.

But not forgotten, Diago thought as he hurried to the case. *Was this why the song had seemed so near lately? The violin was on its way home?*

A quick examination showed the walnut finish had been polished to a high sheen. Someone had scraped most of the rust from the latches, probably a store owner in an attempt to make the case more attractive to a modern buyer. While the silver handle had been recently polished, the leather hinges were cracked—wounds so long neglected, amputation and replacement were the only cure.

Better than any drug, relief flooded his veins in a rush of euphoria. *Miquel is right . . . I'm not alone.* "How did you find it?"

"We haven't. Your Stradivarius isn't in there."

Diago's elation crumbled. *Steady.* He attempted to maintain a neutral expression. A glance at Guillermo told him he'd failed miserably.

"I'm sorry, Diago."

"It's okay," he whispered. "It gives us a clue."

"That it does." Guillermo withdrew his lighter from his pocket and rubbed his thumb over the case. "It was discovered in a secondhand store in Strasbourg, France."

My instincts were right this morning when I thought the music was coming from the north. "Someone stole it from me in that area."

"During the Great War, right?"

"Yes."

"Open it."

Mindful of the broken hinges, he carefully lifted the lid. A creased photograph rested against the brushed red velvet. It was a publicity shot of a handsome young man, wearing formal attire. He held a violin.

My violin. Diago lifted the photograph. "Was this here?"

"Tucked into a side pocket. We almost missed it."

Diago studied the photo. The young man possessed a square face and full lips. His pale hair was swept to one side, and he treated the photographer to a sublime smile. At the bottom of the photo was a caption in German.

Diago read it aloud. "'Joachim Grier, Concertmaster of the Berlin Philharmonic.'"

"Do you recall him?"

"Something about his face is familiar, but I can't place where I've seen him. Could he have been in France during the war?"

"Possibly. He fought for the Germans."

Diago frowned. "Where does he live now?"

"Joachim is dead, but his sons inherited his estate. It's not far from Strasbourg, on the German side of the Rhine."

Diago took another kick to the gut. *The violin might as well be on the moon, then.* A cold war seethed between Los Nefilim and Ilsa Jaeger, the queen of Die Nephilim, Germany's Inner Guard.

It doesn't matter. If the Stradivarius was on the moon, Diago would find an angel to fly him there. *At least the trains go to Germany.* He met Guillermo's gaze. "I have to retrieve it."

"*We* have to retrieve it."

We. Diago's heart sank. *I have to convince him to let me go after it.*

Guillermo kept talking as he returned to the antechamber. "What's happening to you is extraordinary. I can't find a single case where a nefil's instrument has been used against them like this." He went to the wall map. "Come here. See the black pin?"

Diago joined him. "Blue for angel, red for daimon, black for . . . ?"

"The unknown. Sabine Rousseau's Les Néphilim reported strange music in the Strasbourg area, near the Rhine. Rousseau sent her people to canvass the French side of the river, but they found nothing. On a hunch, she sent three Néphilim into Germany. The music was the strongest here"—Guillermo's blunt finger moved to the edge of the Black Forest—"about six kilometers northeast of Offenburg in the municipality of Durbach."

Diago considered the area. "Let me guess: the Grier estate is also in Durbach."

"You would guess correctly." Guillermo tapped the map once more before he lowered his hand.

"Could we be dealing with broken glyphs from the Great War?" Diago asked.

The massive shelling had been like dropping a boulder in a lake. The sound waves had shattered old glyphs and damaged newer wards. Although the war had ended fourteen years ago, Red Zones of broken magic existed all over Europe. Unlike the French's slow cleanup of the mortal Zone Rouge, the nefilim had no way to know which glyphs had broken until supernatural activity erupted in an area.

Guillermo scowled at the map. "It's possible, especially if it's an older ward. However, Jaeger claims there is nothing going on. She is still furious that we assisted France during the Great War while the Spanish mortals declared neutrality. We took her off guard and she is bent on revenge."

"You think she's hiding something?"

"I don't know, and I can't push her too hard for information. Rousseau's Néphilim were spying, so they were never in Germany, if you take my meaning."

"I do."

"Then you know we need to find out what's going on."

"What do we know about the Griers?"

Guillermo flicked the lid of his lighter. "Joachim quit the orchestra shortly after his wife's death sometime in nineteen twenty-eight. He moved his two sons"—Guillermo grabbed a file from the table and read the notes—"Rudolf, who is seventeen, and Karl, who is twenty-four, to the family estate at Karinhall."

"Named for his wife?"

Guillermo nodded and flipped through the file. "Rousseau's spies found that the older boy, Karl, has applied to be a member of Ordo Novi Templi as a Server, which is the lowest rank, reserved for those who are"—he turned the page—"either under the age of twenty-four, or less than fifty percent racially pure."

"'Racially pure'?"

"They base their theology on the writings of a mortal occultist"—Guillermo dug through the files to retrieve a bulkier folder—"who calls himself Jörg Lanz von Liebenfels." He located a thin book tucked within the file. "You're going to love the title: *Theozoology, or the Science of the Sodomite Apelings and the Divine Electron.*"

Diago's lip curled. "Even for mortals that is so . . . offensive."

"It'll make for some fun bedtime reading for you." Guillermo found an empty briefcase and inserted the files along with the book.

Diago's heart skipped a beat. *He's sending me after my violin. He wouldn't be briefing me if he wasn't sending me.* He barely kept his excitement from creeping into his voice. "Can you summarize it for me?" he asked, referring to the book.

"In a sentence? The blond races interbred with the dark races, and in doing so, they diluted the Aryans' paranormal powers, which can only be rediscovered through selective breeding."

"That's ridiculous. Their race has nothing to do with their psychic powers." For mortal magic, it wasn't a question of race but rather a matter of possessing enough willpower to bring their desires into manifestation.

Angels and daimons had recognized this exceptional ability early on and took corporeal bodies in order to mate with the strongest mortals. The nefilim were born of these pairings, combining the magic of the supernatural entities with the more mundane power of the mortals.

Guillermo tapped the briefcase. "The point is that if Grier buys into this nonsense, he will see you as one of the 'Sodomite Apelings' and believe you are inferior to his superior German intellect and breeding."

Diago didn't need a mirror to know that Guillermo referred to his olive skin and Berber features. "It wasn't what I wanted to hear, but at the same time, knowing this in advance helps me secure a plan of action. So what's our next move?"

"We're going to play Grier's game and see where it leads. Suero placed a call to the brothers earlier today, and the housekeeper said Karl would be in touch this afternoon." Guillermo inserted two more files into the briefcase. "I'm pretending to be a buyer for the Stradivarius. If they bite, and I think they will, I'll send you as my appraiser before making an offer. I just need to find someone to send with you."

"No."

Guillermo frowned and withdrew his lighter. Two clicks of the lid and then, "What?"

"I need to do this alone."

"You've got nothing to prove, Diago."

"The hell I don't," he said with perhaps more heat than he intended. "I know you've got people close to you who still don't trust me. If you send someone with me, regardless of your intentions, you're signaling that I need to be watched. This is precisely the kind of chance I need to prove my worth to Los Nefilim. Help me earn their trust. Let me go alone."

Guillermo caressed the lighter with his thumb and considered the issue. "Okay, tough guy, you go alone. Find the violin, get whatever information you can, and get out. But"—he lifted the briefcase, holding it just out of Diago's reach—"if you need help, pull out, and call for reinforcements. Understand?"

"Yes." Diago grabbed the briefcase before Guillermo could change his mind.

"If Grier follows through like I think he will, I'll set things up with Rousseau to get you into Germany under Jaeger's nose."

"You forget that I spent most of my life as a rogue." His longtime refusal to join Los Nefilim was not unusual among the nefilim. Many others, belonging to the ranks of both the angel- and daimon-born nefilim, roamed outside the martial confines of the Inner Guards and either worked as mercenaries or abjured the supernatural wars altogether. "I know how to circumvent the Inner Guards."

"And you forget that those days are gone. You're now a member of the Inner Guard and officially linked to Los Nefilim. Rousseau is an ally, and we want to keep our relations with her on good terms. So we follow her lead and make sure nothing trickles back to her side of the border, or down to ours."

"Understood." Playing by the Inner Guards' terms of engagement made his job more difficult, but not impossible. Diago glanced into Guillermo's office. "What about the violin case?"

"I'll send it to your house later."

"Anything else?"

"Yes—you and Miquel and Rafael will have lunch with us today. Don't say no."

"Will Lucia and her viperish tongue be in attendance?" The governess for Guillermo's daughter, Ysabel, made no secret of her hatred for Diago, and by extension, Rafael. "I don't ask for myself, because I can sling barbs back at her, but she has taken to insulting Rafael, and that I will not tolerate."

"Ah. Lucia is on business elsewhere. So now you must say yes."

"Then I say yes."

"Excellent." Guillermo steered Diago toward the landing. "So tell me: any progress?"

"With?"

"The composition for the Key. How is it coming?"

The eagerness in Guillermo's voice almost robbed Diago of his ability to answer. *The truth. Tell him the truth.* He took a deep breath. "I haven't been working on it. At all. I can't seem to get focused."

Guillermo toyed with his lighter, thumbing the lid up and down for two beats as he considered the confession. His disappointment was palpable, and Diago felt sick.

Three heartbeats passed before Guillermo asked, "Any reason why?"

Diago fumbled with the briefcase's straps, not wanting to mention the nightmares for fear Guillermo would change his mind about sending him alone. "I feel overwhelmed, and I don't know . . ."

"Trapped?"

"Yes." He exhaled the word as a relieved sigh, because it was true. "Yes, I feel trapped by Los Nefilim, the Inner

Guard, codes of silence I barely understand"—unable to meet his friend's eyes, he looked away—"by fatherhood. Isn't that a horrible thing to say?"

"No. It's not," Guillermo said. "Rafael is a good child, eager to please, but he also came to you with problems of his own. Those issues use your mental energy the same way working on a composition might."

Exactly. And there's more, of course. "He wants his mother. He always wants his mother." *But his mother is dead, because everything dies, even the angels.* "It's the one thing I can't give him."

"That'll never change. He'll always want her." Guillermo didn't reassure him with platitudes. That wasn't his way.

Diago winced. "Couldn't you lie to me just once?"

"I'll get you a dog. Dogs always love you."

"I don't want a dog."

"Then you get the truth. Look, none of this is your fault," Guillermo hurried to assure him. "But the fact remains that you missed some formative bonding years with Rafael. You didn't find him until he was six. You're working hard to make up for lost time and help him accustom himself to life in Santuari, just like *you're* learning to adjust. So I understand, it's just—"

"We need that composition." Diago finished the thought for him. "I know that, and I'm frustrated because I haven't found the triggers to stimulate the right memories. And maybe it's because I need to ask for help."

"You tell me what you need and it's yours."

"Well, we were in our last incarnation together. It could be that you'll remember something I've forgotten. So once I've returned from Germany, maybe we could collaborate?"

Guillermo locked the office door and clamped his hand on Diago's shoulder. "Nothing would please me more than to compose with you again."

"Yes, it'll be just like we used to be before . . ." Diago caught himself before he completed the sentence with *before we destroyed each other in our firstborn lives when you were Solomon and I was Asaph.*

In that firstborn life Asaph had sworn his fealty to Solomon only to betray him. They had been like brothers until the daimons drove them apart with lies. Pride and a desire for revenge had turned their final days to ashes.

But that is the past, and the past is as dead as Solomon and Asaph. We're in an incarnation far, far from those dark days.

Guillermo seemed to feel the same way. "Before we grew apart?"

Relieved, Diago whispered, "Exactly."

[3]

Lingering over wine and empty plates, a pleasant silence fell over the two families—at least until Ysabel nudged Rafael. Diago absently wondered what she had put him up to now. Over the last several months, Guillermo's daughter had adopted Rafael as the sibling she'd always wanted, and the two had quickly become friends. Unfortunately, that also meant Rafael was often dragged into Ysabel's many schemes. Neither acorn fell far from the trees that spawned them.

"Go on, ask him," she whispered.

"Okay, okay." Rafael chased the last almonds of his dessert around his plate with his spoon. "Papá, may I play fútbol with Ysabel after lunch?"

"That depends on Don Guillermo and Doña Juanita."

Guillermo traded a calculating look with Juanita. "I don't see the harm in it." Before Ysabel could move, he pointed at his jubilant daughter. "But it had better be fútbol and not that spy game you've started playing. No more of that. I don't want you creeping around the compound listening under windows. Do you understand me?"

With her round face and thick auburn curls, she was an eight-year-old version of her father, right down to the way her face belied her guilt when caught flat-footed in a scheme. "How am I ever going to be a proper nefil if I don't learn how to gather information?"

"If you want to be a proper nefil, you'll follow orders and I've just given you one."

Ysa showed no sign of letting the argument go, however. "You said you learned on the streets when you were younger than me."

"That was a different time."

"Not that different," Juanita said.

Guillermo's cheeks flushed pink. "Whose side are you on?"

As cool as her milk-pale skin, Juanita rested her chin on her hand and met her husband's glare. "It's not about sides. If she was a boy, you'd be complimenting her on her acumen."

"That's not fair," Guillermo shot back. "I give my experienced female Guards the same respect and assignments as I do the males."

Ysabel seized the opening. "How did they get their experience?" She didn't give him a chance to answer. "By doing the work."

"They weren't eight years old."

"I want to learn, Papá."

Seeking to help his friend, Rafael said, "Ysa is really very good at it, Don Guillermo, and she is very careful."

High praise indeed, given that Rafael spent his first six years on the streets. Nonetheless, Diago touched his son's arm and whispered, "Be still."

Miquel, meanwhile, lit a cigarette and developed a sudden keen interest in the Picasso hanging on the opposite wall.

Guillermo ignored everyone but Ysabel. "This has nothing to do with your gender. You're my daughter. If something happens to you, my heart will die."

An appeal to the emotions. Nice save, Diago thought, taking mental notes in case Rafael developed a sudden interest in proving his value to the Inner Guard through espionage. Fortunately, his son seemed more intent on picking the almonds off his plate with his fingers.

Ysa stood her ground and retorted, "I'd be in a lot less danger with your guidance."

And touché. Diago wondered what prompted her to challenge her father today. A quick glance at Juanita told him that whatever the reason, she supported Ysa's cause, because she assessed her daughter's attitude with the eye of a maestro watching her student deliver a master performance.

Guillermo sighed and reclined in his chair, studying his daughter, who didn't flinch from the examination. Reaching for a cigar, he took his time preparing it. The only sound in the dining room was the snip of his cigar cutter, followed by the click of his lighter's wheel.

Once the cigar was lit, he puffed a cloud of blue smoke over the table. "I'll think about it."

Her eyes narrowed. "That means the answer is no."

"It means I'll think about it."

"Today?"

He enunciated each word slowly to make himself plain. "When I get time."

Stalemate. Diago took Rafael's napkin from the boy's lap and nodded at his sticky fingers.

Getting the hint, Rafael licked his fingers and then wiped them with the napkin.

Diago frowned but said nothing this time. *Definitely no spying for him until we get his table manners under control.*

Ysabel glanced at her mother, who gave an almost imperceptible shake of her head.

Ysa's disappointment was palpable, but she followed her mother's advice and retreated. "Okay, Papá."

A wise move. Pushing Guillermo into a corner was never a good idea.

"Good. Now go play," said Guillermo. "You want to grow up too fast. Be a child while you can. You have a guest"—he nodded at Rafael—"be a good host."

She reached over and tugged Rafael's sleeve. "Come on, we'll go—"

"To your room," Juanita finished for her. "Rafael is still in his school clothes. You can play fútbol later."

Diago folded his son's napkin. "Go on. We'll call you when it's time to go."

"Okay." He put his arms around Diago's neck and whispered in his ear. "She's going to be mad now."

"Be a good friend to her then," he murmured back and then kissed his son's cheek.

When Rafael drew alongside her, he took her hand and gave her fingers a gentle squeeze. Diago noted that Guillermo watched his daughter's back with equal parts trepidation and admiration.

After the children were out of earshot, Juanita said, "She has your craving for knowledge, Guillermo, and she is ready to begin learning about the family business."

Guillermo's cheeks reddened again, but this time from

chagrin rather than anger, because everyone at the table knew Juanita spoke the truth.

She continued, "Besides, she's right: it's better she work under your supervision rather than running amok on her own."

"I said I would think about it." Guillermo waved his cigar in Diago's direction. "Do Miquel and Rafael gang up on you like this?"

"All the time."

Miquel crushed his cigarette in the saucer. "Not all the time."

"And you stand your ground, right?" Guillermo asked.

"Actually . . . um . . . they usually win."

Guillermo bit down on his cigar. "You're not helping me."

Diago shrugged. "You have to admit, Ysa handles herself exceptionally well."

Guillermo raised his hand for peace. "Okay, okay. I'm thinking about it. Now if you two will excuse us, I need to talk to Miquel in my office."

Diago glanced at his husband. Whatever it was, Miquel wasn't surprised. In fact, he appeared relaxed, even a little excited about the meeting, so the conversation probably bore no relation to wolves and the gaols in which they were kept.

"Take your time," Diago said.

"I will. You talk to Juanita." Miquel leaned close. "Like you promised."

She tilted her wineglass to him. "I am at your service."

Diago forced a smile to his lips. He hoped it didn't look as painful as it felt. "Wonderful."

Miquel stroked the back of Diago's hand as he rose. "Did you think I was going to forget?"

"I had hoped." *In vain*, he thought. *We know each other far too well.*

Miquel tipped him a wink before he followed Guillermo out of the room. Once they were gone, Diago leaned back in his chair and stared at the ceiling. "He knows what you're saying is true." He glanced at her. "About Ysa, I mean. He'll come to terms with it soon."

"Don't be so sure about that," she said with more resignation than anger. "This isn't the first time I've had to give him a strong push in the right direction regarding her upbringing."

An easy silence fell between them. Juanita was the first to break it. "You look like a man in need of a nap," she said.

"Between the esqueixada and Guillermo's wine, it shouldn't be hard. Unfortunately, I have to delay my sleep in order to talk to you about my inability to sleep. But I may fall asleep doing it." He raised his glass. "A paradox."

She smiled at him as one of the cook's assistants entered the room and began stacking the dirty dishes.

Juanita stood and tilted her head toward the door. "Let's go to my office."

Diago didn't argue. If Carme hunted traitors, even the most innocuous comments had a way of becoming incriminating when passed along as hearsay.

Juanita waited until he joined her in the corridor, and they walked together to her clinic. When she closed the door of the examining room, he said, "This doesn't have to take long. I just need the proper dosage of Veronal, or some other barbitone, to drown the dreams."

She unlocked her office door and went inside. Having

never seen her inner sanctum, he satisfied his curiosity with a peek. Her desk sat between a sideboard and a bookcase filled with medical texts, which all seemed very mundane until he noted some of the titles were in ancient Greek. Along another wall was a divan with a chair beside it.

"Why is your first suggestion a mortal remedy?" she asked.

Diago lingered at the threshold. "Because I hate you prying around in my head."

Juanita went to the couch and gestured for him to sit. "I love you for your honesty, Diago. However, your reliance on mortal remedies cripples you."

"How so?"

"Come in and close the door."

"I thought we were just going to talk."

"We are." She patted the divan again. "And then we are going to see if we can solve your problem." When he still didn't move, she lowered her voice. "I'm not going to strong-arm you into this, Diago, but I need your cooperation. If you don't want my help, then we can tell Miquel we talked and couldn't find a solution. That's all."

Except that would be a half-truth, a lie of omission, and how many of those had caught up to him over the years? *Too many.* Miquel deserved better. *And I promised him that I would let her help me.*

"Okay, okay, you win." Whether he meant Juanita or his conscience, he wasn't sure. Determined to see the procedure through, he summoned his courage, shut the door, and went to the couch. As he sat, he asked, "Now I get my answer: How have I crippled myself?"

She brought him a pillow. "The dreams are a good example. Your first impulse is to drown them with drugs, instead of using your abilities to probe deeper into their meaning."

"I see you've been reading Freud again."

"Freud is a quack. Jung is closer to the mark."

In spite of his nervousness, he laughed.

"Now lie back and let's talk about these nightmares."

"I can talk sitting up."

"Work with me, Diago."

"I don't remember them," he said as he reclined. "The moment I awaken, the images are gone."

"And the music?"

He thought back to this morning's exercise on the piano. "I recall a few chords, but even those are distorted."

She sat beside him and combed his hair from his forehead with her fingers. "The first thing I want to do is diagnose why you can't remember. We need to see if there is some supernatural reason, or if you're subconsciously blocking an emotionally painful memory. What I will do is open the channel between the subconscious and the conscious, so that you can recall the nightmare. Then you should be able to interpret the significance of the images."

"This is the part where you go into my brain, isn't it?"

"Only with your permission. But yes, I do want to establish a mental connection with you." As she spoke, she allowed her glamour to slip and wore her mortal body loosely. The light filtering through a window shimmered around her three sets of wings.

His answer remained locked in his throat. Juanita wasn't simply Guillermo's wife. She was his angelic adviser and as such also reported directly to the Thrones, those otherworldly creatures that commanded the lower angels, the Messengers such as Juanita.

What if these nightmares mean I'm damaged in some way? Broken? No longer useful to Los Nefilim? Will she tell the Thrones? And then what will they do? He considered asking her, but he feared the answers would be worse than his uncertainty.

He opted for humor. "The last time an angel sought a connection with me, I wound up with a son."

Her expression didn't change.

"That was a joke."

"Ah."

"I'm not doing this well. I'm sorry. It's not that I don't trust you. In my head"—he touched his brow—"I know you wouldn't hurt me."

"But here"—she touched his heart—"you are anxious." The compassion in her gaze made him ashamed he took so long to respond.

He swallowed around the lump in his throat and nodded. "And that is why it has taken me so long to come to you. I'm sorry."

"You have nothing to apologize for. I understand. You have suffered terribly under angel and daimon alike, but this is a simple spell. I'm going to place sigils, here, here, and here." She touched the center of his forehead and then each temple. "These will connect our souls so I can evaluate your condition as you dream. I'll see what you experience. That way, I'll be able to diagnose if there is an external spell that makes you forget the images upon awakening. That is all."

I'm being foolish. Regardless, hearing the explanation

eased his nervousness. *Just as she'd probably known it would.* "Okay. Let's just get it over with."

"Relax," she whispered. Her finger raised chills over his flesh as she designed first one glyph and then the next. When she completed the lines of the final ward, she sang an ethereal note. The midnight fire of her song flashed through all three sigils in hues of blue and black.

Diago's scalp tingled from the indigo crown that now encircled his head. He found it hard to keep his eyes open. *But that is what she wants.*

As Juanita hummed, the azure of her irises seeped into the whites until her eyes resembled twin orbs of lapis lazuli. Thin veins of gold indicated her mood by swirling lazily through the blue.

"This is similar to hypnosis," she murmured. "I will take you down into sleep by adjusting my voice until I find the vibrations that best affect your brainwaves." Her timbre changed as she elucidated through one set of vocalizations and then another. Diago could tell by the subtle variations that she utilized all three sets of her vocal cords. "When I find the correct pitch, you will begin to dream, and then I will follow you into your subconscious. Now close your eyes."

It wasn't hard to obey her.

"Think about the music you hear when you sleep. Try and conjure the song."

Engulfed by darkness, he listened. Silence met him, as deep and impregnable as the void. Then, from far away, he caught the first isolated notes of the violin. It was his Stradivarius.

Louder now, as if sensing his presence, the music drew near. The bow attacked the strings *(Diago recalled making those quick jabs: strike, strike, strike, followed by a smooth pull)* before slurring the chords into decay. The intro descended into pallid notes, gray and soft like fog *(no, the smell of cordite is strong in the air . . . it is not fog but smoke)* drifting over the muddy ground.

The dream solidified, taking him deeper into his subconscious. The faint outline of a château appeared behind broken *(burned)* trees, shrouded in fog . . .

"Smoke," Juanita whispered.

Smoke.

The song's tempo slowed to become a dirge. Diago walked the scorched field. Lumps of clay *(bodies)* littered the ground. In the distance came the steady percussion of drums *(bombs)*, shaking the earth with furious thunder.

Squinting through the smoke, he perceived a shadowy figure pushing a tram filled with corpses. The arms and legs trembled as the wheels jittered along on the hastily laid tracks of war. One hand opened to release a silver disc that sank into the mud.

Then the bow resumed its attack and punch against the strings *(quick jabs: strike, strike, strike)* and the night came down and the world went black and silence descended quick and hard, like the stillness that follows the falling of a bomb.

Diago opened his eyes. His heart pounded and for one wild moment, he thought of Guillermo's Creed Model 7, churning out messages in staccato beats. He became aware of Juanita's strong hands, pinning his shoulders to the cushions.

"You're safe." She eased her grip and caressed his cheek. "Take a deep breath. In through your nose, out through your mouth, slowly, slowly." She gentled him until his terror subsided beneath her touch. “There.” She wiped the sigils from his brow. “Are you okay now?”

He fumbled for his handkerchief and sat up, wiping the sweat from his face. “Yes. No.” A shaky laugh escaped him before he could stop it. “I’m not very helpful, am I?”

“You did fine.”

The phone rang, and someone picked up an extension elsewhere in the house.

Juanita went to the sideboard and filled a glass with two fingers of liquor. She put the drink in his hand, and he threw back the shot.

“Was that the music you hear each night?” She took the glass and placed it on the table.

“There are subtle variations, but it’s more or less the same each time.”

“I sensed a presence, but it was distant, diffuse, neither angel nor daimon. I’m not sure what to make of it.”

The black pin is in my brain. He rubbed his eyes.

Juanita continued. “However, there was no spell to prevent you from remembering your dreams. Does the imagery mean anything to you?”

“It’s a memory from the Great War. I was on that battlefield.” But not the house . . . no house had been on that field.

Juanita touched his shoulder. “It’s not unusual to be tormented by past engagements. Nefilim suffer from prolonged battle stress just as mortals do. Did anything noteworthy happen during that fight?”

“Noteworthy,” he repeated dully while rubbing his forehead. He found it hard to keep venom from seeping into his words as he answered her question. "Aside from the sheer magnitude of the death toll?" A sudden image flashed through his mind: *huddling in a trench as shells exploded around them. Cold and wet and eaten alive by lice, he'd shut his eyes against the mud falling like rain and when he opened them again, someone's scalp landed at his feet . . .*

"Diago?"

He jerked himself free of the memory, uncomfortably aware of his clammy palms. "I don't know what you want from me, Juanita. After so many days of battle, they all seemed the same." *A never-ending misery.*

She sat beside him and mercifully didn't pursue the issue. "Don't push yourself too hard. You should remember any new dreams now. More details will come to you. It might be tied to a past incarnation."

That's something I can deal with. Too, her words brought up something he'd always wondered about and gave him a convenient way to shift the conversation from himself. "Why can't we see clearly into our past lives?"

"In spite of your supernatural nature, your brain is organic. It can only hold so much information. You've been reborn what? Five times since your firstborn life?"

He nodded.

"Can you imagine if all those memories came crashing down on you at once?"

He saw her point. "It would be overwhelming."

"Precisely. So your brain gives you the facts necessary for your immediate survival and supplements those facts with newer memories when they're needed. It's the same way you didn't recall much of your firstborn life as Asaph until you met Guillermo. You were wary of each other without knowing why, but the longer you interacted, the more memories surfaced."

"Do you think that is what this is? Another broken relationship from a past incarnation?"

"It could be."

Someone knocked at the door.

"Just a moment," she called, but she made no move toward the door, keeping her attention on Diago. "Since your memories of your firstborn life as Asaph are almost complete, I would guess this is the result of a more recent incarnation, maybe even the previous incarnation to this life. The answers to those questions are inside of you."

"Okay." He nodded. "I think I understand."

"Good." She went to the door.

Miquel stood in the corridor. "Everything okay?"

"Yes." Juanita smiled at Diago. "I think we made some progress."

Diago summoned a smile of his own. Judging from his husband's expression, it looked as ghastly as it felt.

Miquel hesitated as if he might say something else and then thought better of it. "I'm going to get Rafael. You finish here."

"I'll be right out." Diago stood. "Thank you, Juanita."

She kissed his cheek. "Don't wait so long before you come to me again."

"I won't." It was an easy lie. He almost believed it, and he was pretty sure she almost did, too.

Guillermo rapped his knuckles against the door. He held the briefcase in his other hand. "I hope I'm not interrupting."

Diago pocketed his handkerchief. "No, we're done."

"Good. That was Grier on the phone. He wants to play. You're going to Germany, my friend."

Diago went to the door. "When?"

"Monday."

Three days. "Why so long?"

"I need to arrange the details with Rousseau." He handed the briefcase to Diago. "Meanwhile, happy reading."

[4]

Later that evening, Diago finished tidying Rafael's room and admired his son's art while the child finished his toilet. Colorful drawings of their life in Santuari covered the walls: Guillermo's bulls in the pasture, Ysabel's hair flying behind her as she chased a fútbol, Miquel playing guitar, and Diago kneeling beside Rafael, teaching his son the daimonic art of shaping stone.

In each illustration, the sun or moon possessed an angel's wings, which flowed downward to encircle the various scenes. *And that is how he sees his mother*, Diago thought as he noticed the draft of a new drawing on Rafael's desk. *The sun, the moon, the stars . . . he thinks she is always watching over him.*

Diago touched the bright yellow disc in the drawing and thought of Candela with her dark, dark eyes. She had promised to give him a song to bring peace to the angels and the daimons, a song only he could understand, and she had. If only she hadn't resorted to rape to get her way, he might have found something other than shame for their time together.

From down the hall, the toilet flushed and the bathroom door squealed open. Within moments, Rafael entered the bedroom, dragging one leg behind him. He chided his little white cat with laughter in his voice. "Stop it, Ghost."

Ghost hugged Rafael's ankle and held on to her prey. Rafael giggled and yipped when her sharp teeth tweaked his tawny skin. "Help me, Papá, she's got me."

The sight of them coaxed a smile to Diago's mouth. He snapped his fingers. "Ghost, be good."

The cat responded to the noise and twisted away, scampering out of sight, only to come running back, bounding across the bed at full speed. Without pausing, she launched herself at Diago. He caught her midair and cradled her in his arm, stroking her fur and humming until she calmed.

"You do that really good, Papá."

"That's because it's time to get quiet," he whispered. Settling the cat on the bed, he turned to his son and noted splashes of water soaked into his pajama top. *At least the weather is still warm. He'll dry off in no time.* "You washed your face?"

"And my teeth, too." He bared his teeth. "Will Miquel be home soon?"

"Maybe. Don Guillermo needed him to work late this evening." Diago didn't elaborate. Miquel had driven toward the western fields at sunset. The less their son knew about those activities, the better Diago liked it.

"Who is going to stay with me when Miquel has to work late and you're gone?" That was the third time he'd asked a variation of that question in as many hours.

Diago hadn't considered how worried Rafael would be about his leaving. *Nothing to do but keep reassuring him.* "Eva will come and stay with you. You like Eva, don't you?"

"Oh yes! She is very nice. We play fútbol and she says I am so good that I should be able to play for Barcelona someday. Do you think I'm good enough to play for Barcelona, Papá?"

Relieved the conversation had shifted to fútbol, Diago smiled. "You've got a long time to think about whose team you want to join."

Rafael went to his nightstand and retrieved a small box. Resting on a bed of velvet was a carmine stone about the size of a marble. It was an angel's tear, all that Candela had left to the child before she had abandoned him to the care of the nuns in the lunatic asylum.

Placing the tear between his palms, Rafael knelt beside his bed and recited the prayers the nuns had taught him. Diago watched in silence, glad Miquel wasn't there. Privately, his husband encouraged Diago to find a way to stop the ritual, but Diago refused. When Rafael outgrew the custom, he would release it. Meanwhile, the child found comfort in the motions and the words. *What harm can come from it?*

Rafael finished and kissed Candela's tear. He held the stone up for Diago to kiss. Instead, Diago clasped his son's small hands between his palms and pressed his lips to Rafael's forehead.

For a long moment, as he did every night, Rafael searched Diago's face. "Do you think you will ever love Mamá?" he asked.

Someday I may forgive *her*, Diago thought. To his son, he said, "Maybe."

"Was she mean to you?" He put the tear away.

Unsure how to answer the question, Diago turned back the covers, avoiding his son's eyes. How could he explain Candela's enchantment without making the boy doubt his mother's love for him?

I can't. That is the answer. I cannot. "It's complicated," he said and consoled himself with the fact that Rafael was too young to understand. "One day when you're older, I'll explain it to you."

Rafael climbed into bed. "Father Bernardo says that all nefilim reincarnate and that we're born over and over again. Is that right, Papá?"

"It is."

"Will you always be my papá?"

"Yes." Diago sat on the edge of the bed. "This is why our firstborn lives are so important. Our angelic or daimonic parents make us supernatural. When we die, our spirits fly free to seek a mortal womb in which to grow a new body, and from there we are reborn. So because I helped create you in your firstborn life, I will always be your father."

"I know that. But will you always be my papá like you are now? Here to teach me. And Miquel. Will Miquel be my papá when I'm reborn?"

"Ah, I see." He considered the question and realized he had no idea how to answer that either. "I don't know if I will be your father again. I do know that the attachments we form in our firstborn lives are the strongest and often bring us back to one another in similar ways. Don Guillermo, Miquel, and I have encountered one another in each incarnation, but being a father is a new experience for me. I hope I am your father again." *Because you have changed my life.*

"I do, too. Ysa says she wants her papá again, too. She still loves him even though he won't let her be a spy."

Diago resisted the urge to ask Rafael what precipitated Ysa's debate with her father. While Rafael likely knew Ysa's side of the story, Miquel would have all the facts. "First she has to learn to follow orders."

"Do you follow orders?"

"Yes. I work harder than most nefilim at being a good member of the Inner Guard."

"Because we're half daimon?"

"That's part of it. Others have cause to distrust me, because I acted badly in my firstborn life and they remember. I must now prove to them that I've changed."

"How do you do that?"

"With my behavior." Diago kissed his son's forehead. "It is time for sleep."

Rafael wiggled his arms free from the sheet for a hug. "I love you, Papá."

"I love you, too." He hugged the boy and shut off the bedside lamp. At the door, he paused. "Oh, and one more thing, you never play in the western fields, do you?"

"No, Papá. Even Ysa won't go there. Don Guillermo said he would be very, very mad."

"Good. That's very good. That's one order you never disobey. Good night, Rafael."

"Good night, Papá."

He closed the door and stepped across the hall to the room he shared with Miquel. As Diago dressed for bed, he listened to Rafael recount his day's adventures to his cat. Each night he talked himself to sleep as if silence left him too much room to think.

Tonight Rafael must have been tired. The child's voice faded earlier than usual.

Unlike his son, Diago was wide awake. The drowsiness that had dogged his day was gone. Excited by the prospect of the assignment, he withdrew the briefcase Guillermo had given him earlier in the day and found the tattered copy of *Theozoology*.

Opening the book to the first page with its primitive drawings, he leaned against the headboard and tried to absorb Lanz's reasoning, searching for a way into Karl Grier's head. He took a few notes and didn't notice the time until he heard Miquel's truck rumble into the yard.

The front door opened and shut. Moments later, Miquel entered the room. He closed the door and kicked off his shoes. Climbing into bed beside Diago, he thrust his head between Diago's nose and the book. "How do I smell?"

"Like Juanita's shampoo." Diago tugged one damp curl.

Grinning, Miquel sat back and snatched the book from his hand. "What are you reading?"

"*Theozoology, or the Science of the Sodomite Apelings and the Divine Electron*."

He wrinkled his nose and thumbed through the pages. "What is it about?"

"It's an assimilation of biblical scriptures, apocrypha, and archaeological findings all mingled together with Jörg Lanz von Liebenfels's racist theories. His gnosis is that the blond and dark races represent good and evil, respectively. He also believes that the blond races interbred with the dark races, and in doing so, they diluted the Aryans' paranormal powers."

Miquel's already black gaze darkened even more. "So what does that make me?"

Diago caressed his husband's cheek and smiled mischievously. "Between the sheets, you are the devil incarnate."

Grinning, Miquel leaned over Diago's lap to drop the book into the open briefcase. "Enough work. It's time to play."

Diago didn't want Rafael stumbling onto the documents, so he closed the briefcase and locked it.

When he looked up again, Miquel held a jewelry box between two fingers. "Something for you."

A moment of panic ensued as Diago tried to remember what occasion he might have forgotten. It wasn't their anniversary, or a saint's day. "Have I missed something?"

"Nothing at all," Miquel assured him as he pressed the box against Diago's palm. "It's a very special gift that I commissioned for you and it was just finished today. I thought about saving it for Christmas, but given your upcoming journey, I decided to make it a going-away present."

"You spoil me."

"I know."

Diago lifted the lid to find a silver ring. The wide band, adorned with sigils carved into the metal, accented a crimson angel's tear marred by jagged streaks of silver that glittered hard as sorrow.

"Prieto's tear," Diago murmured as he tilted the ring to catch the light. The angel, who called himself Beltran Prieto, had given Diago the tear last year. Caring nothing for Prieto or his gifts, Diago had placed the tear in his bureau and forgotten about it.

Apparently Miquel had not.

"Guillermo made the band for you, and Juanita designed the sigils of protection." Miquel took the ring from the box.

Diago automatically clenched his fist and fought to keep

his voice low. "Prieto used us as pawns to further the angels' war. He is just as bad, if not worse, than his sister, Candela. I want nothing of his." He turned from Miquel's steady gaze. "I'm sorry. It's not that it isn't beautiful, but every time I look at it, I'll think of Prieto."

Miquel took Diago's right hand and massaged his wrist. "I want you to listen to me." He ran his thumb over the skin of Diago's missing pinkie and kissed his knuckle. "I didn't do this to bring you pain."

"I know that, but—"

"You can't listen if you're talking."

Diago sighed and bit his lip.

"The other nefilim will only see that you wear an angel's blessing. This"—he held up the ring—"is a sign of celestial favor, and it was a gift to you, Diago."

"I didn't say it—"

"Ay, ay." He shook his head and pressed one finger to Diago's lips. "Listen. An angel's tear carries a portion of their magic and it's a powerful token. Why do you think Candela gave Rafael her tear?" He didn't wait for a response but answered his own question. "Because like you, he is part daimon and she wanted him to be accepted unconditionally by the angel-born. Prieto gave you his tear for the same reason. You say he used you, but he was under orders. He took a bad situation and gave you a chance to save Rafael. You did that and so much more."

Miquel slid the ring onto Diago's finger. "He was grateful to you and this is your reward. Do you know how hard it is to win an angel's gratitude?"

Diago said nothing, nor did he remove the ring. While he disdained Prieto's motives, he wasn't so obtuse as to completely disregard the angel's position. Miquel was right. Prieto couldn't have simply refused an order. To do so would have jeopardized his life. Instead, he'd applied his wits and mitigated the damage, and in doing so he enabled Diago to save his son.

Whispering now, Miquel slid close, the smell of his musk overriding the scent of lavender in his hair. "If you openly wear Prieto's favor, the others will be confident, not just of you, but that you are instructing Rafael in accordance with Los Nefilim's values. In this way neither Rafael's place nor yours will ever be questioned." He pressed his lips against Diago's palm. "Bad things are happening, my star. We need to be very careful."

Diago recalled his conversation with Carme. "Is this because of the wolves in the western field?"

Miquel's grip tightened and his eyes went dark. "Who have you been talking to?"

"Carme mentioned that we should keep Rafael out of the western fields. Has someone accused me of being unfaithful to Guillermo?"

"No . . . ," Miquel said. "Not yet."

"But they could."

Miquel nodded.

Diago whispered, "Someone with a grudge."

"Someone who wants you out of the way."

Someone close to Guillermo. Swiftly on the heels of that thought came a name. *Lucia.* She was Ysabel's governess and had her own room in the main house. She never missed a meal with the family.

And she loves Miquel.

She believed that he would love her if only Diago would

disappear from their lives. The facts finally clicked into place. *She's the wolf at the western finca.*

"It's Lucia, isn't it? She's being interrogated."

"Yes."

"How long has she been there?"

"Since dawn."

Diago recalled Guillermo's quip about Lucia being on business elsewhere. *And what a bloody business it will be.*

As far as the leaders of the Inner Guards went, Guillermo was more lenient than most, but he would not suffer a traitor, especially one who endangered his daughter. "Was Lucia caught by Ysabel playing her spy game?"

"Yes."

Now Guillermo's reaction to Ysa's demand to be a spy made sense. If Lucia had caught the child eavesdropping, Ysa might have suffered an accident—a deadly one. *Guillermo is scared. He'll also make an example of Lucia so that others don't follow her path.*

"Was Rafael involved?"

"No, but we've increased security on both of the children just the same."

Relieved, Diago exhaled and looked down at the ring. It was going to take more than the symbolism of an angel's tear to prove himself to certain members of Los Nefilim. *Then I have to demonstrate that I'm above suspicion, not just for my sake, but for Rafael's as well. And that is why a successful conclusion to this assignment in Germany is so important.*

Even so, he didn't discount Miquel's concerns about the ring. "If I wear Prieto's tear, will you relax?"

The relief in Miquel's eyes told him the answer before his

lover breathed, "Yes. Because these wolves, they are not just in the western fields. They are everywhere."

Diago remembered Carme's warning. *They run in packs.* Which meant Carme and Miquel were looking for a cell of traitors within Los Nefilim's ranks. "Okay. I'll wear it for Rafael."

"For you," Miquel murmured. "Wear it to protect *you.* Because if you die, you will take my heart with you, and if you take my heart, how will I live?" His lips brushed Diago's earlobe.

Diago caught his breath as a shiver went through his body. "For us then."

Miquel left a trail of kisses along his throat. "For us," he whispered before he covered Diago's mouth with his own.

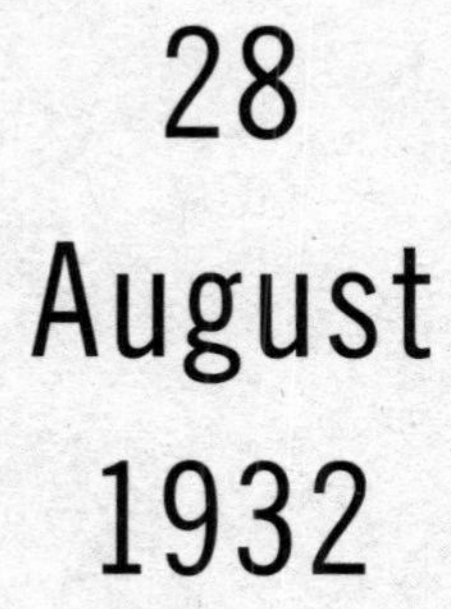

28 August 1932

chasing dragons

[5]

BARCELONA
CARRER DE LA RIERETA 31

In El Raval the sun went down on the slums of Chinatown, where the last thin rays of light did more to deepen the gloom than expel it. Three addicts conferred in the recesses of a doorway. Mere shadows in the vague twilight, the men showed no overt interest in the tall stranger with red-gold hair, who stood before the narrow gate at Carrer de la Riereta 31.

Jordi Abelló had no doubt the men had marked his presence. He kept them in his peripheral vision. They might be mortal, they could be nefil. Nothing was ever as it seemed in Ciutat Vella, the old city. If they were mortal, so be it. But if they were of a supernatural realm, then evasive measures would be necessary. He couldn't afford to be caught here by Guillermo's Inner Guard.

A few meters down the street, one of the addicts giggled. His companion shushed him, glancing at Jordi as he did. The third blew a cloud of cigarette smoke into the air while feigning the studied calm of a predator.

Jordi's left hand twitched, itching for the feel of a pistol grip against his palm. He found himself hoping the three men *were* nefilim. A fight would do him good, release his tension and clear his mind, but the addict's eyes neither reflected the last of the day's light nor absorbed the darkness of the shadows—they were indeed mortal and hardly worth his time.

He opened the gate and stepped inside the building. The corridor was dark and the wooden steps sagged beneath his shoes as he climbed. On the second floor, the reek of mortals clotted his sinuses. Voices murmured from behind the doors. A baby wailed with loud angry sobs.

The stairwell constricted like a throat. At the third floor, he stepped off the landing and went to the second door, the one that was red.

Jordi knocked.

Someone shuffled forward and two locks turned before an eye peered through the crack. The door opened.

Jordi stepped inside.

Salvador Muñoz glanced into the hall before shutting the door. He was a wiry nefil who looked more at home slinking through the brush than waiting in an apartment. "You're late."

Jordi didn't like the insolence in the other man's tone; such impertinence was a sign of lax leadership. *That will change when I've regained my place as Los Nefilim's king.* For now, though, he let the comment slide. He needed Muñoz.

"Don't you listen to the radio?" Jordi snapped back. Ever since José Sanjurjo was sentenced, rumors abounded of a second monarchist plot to overthrow the Republic. The entire country was on high alert. "The mortal police and the Civil Guards have patrols everywhere." He didn't need to mention that Guillermo had members of the Inner Guard embedded in both.

"We have other problems," Salvador hissed. Moving away from the threshold, he drew Jordi to the center of the room before he spoke again. "They've taken Lucia to the gaol in the western field."

"Goddamn it. How did it happen?"

"No one knows."

Jordi moved to the window. "Has she talked?"

"Not yet. Or if she has, Guillermo is waiting until he gathers all the names before he makes more arrests."

"No, he won't risk them disappearing in the night." Jordi knew his half brother's tactics well. "He'll move swiftly."

"She'll break. Lucia isn't as tough as she wants us to think."

"Kill her."

"I can't. Two nefilim are with her at all times. They radio in every hour on the hour. Both guards have to be killed, or they'll raise the alarm. Once the guards are dead, then I'll have to deal with the wards surrounding Lucia's cell. It will take time to neutralize those glyphs."

Jordi didn't doubt Salvador's assessment. Whatever sigils guarded Lucia's cell would be strong, and while Salvador was angel-born, he was merely in his second-born life, lacking both Guillermo's and Jordi's experience with complex glyphs.

Salvador continued, "Alone, I'll never get out of Santuari in time, and I'll be the gaol's next resident. I need a partner."

"Poison her."

"Please," he said, sneering. "All her food is monitored and Juanita prepares her meals herself. Guillermo is leaving nothing to chance."

Fuck, fuck, fuck. And everything had been going so well. Jordi rubbed his brow and looked down onto the street. From here, the alley seemed empty. Then another cloud of cigarette smoke emerged from the doorway where the addicts stood.

"Did you just come to me with problems, or do you have a plan?" Jordi drummed restless fingers on the sill.

"I'm in charge of the wards in that sector. I can take them down long enough for another nefil to slip through. We can meet at the finca on the hour, but this is where the timing gets tight. The moment after the guards radio the base, we must take them. That will give us at least thirty minutes to weaken the glyphs, so that one of us can slip inside and kill Lucia. We'll also need enough time to get away from Santuari before the bodies are discovered."

It did sound tight, but Jordi had worked under harsher circumstances. "We can't afford to have this botched. I'll send her into her next incarnation myself."

Losing the spies he'd embedded in Guillermo's ranks would burn, but if he didn't move fast to pull the other three, he'd lose experienced nefilim as well. *And those are more precious than gold right now.* "Did you bring a map?"

Salvador went to the room's sole table and spread a heavily creased piece of paper across the scarred surface. "Here"—he pointed to a gray line—"is the trail that leads behind the property, and here"—he pointed to another area about a kilometer away—"is the finca."

Jordi calculated the distances. "When are you on duty again?"

"Tomorrow night."

Monday evening. Now that Sanjurjo's trial was over,

Jordi had planned to leave for France in the morning. *I've already pushed my luck by staying in Madrid for the duration of the proceedings*. But the mortal was a necessary component to Jordi's long-term plan to regain his rightful place as Los Nefilim's king, just as Lucia's capture represented the potential destruction of that objective.

Jordi really had no choice in the matter. He'd have to delay his return to France for another day. "All right, I'll play mother bird and find some way to draw Guillermo's attention to me. That should give our people time to cover their tracks. Tell them to abandon Santuari and move to safer ground. We'll regroup in Portugal."

"I'll put out the word." Salvador seemed relieved.

"When should we meet at the gaol?"

"The best hour to strike is at four in the morning. We can be in and out by five. By the time we reach Barcelona, we'll be able to blend in with the morning workers so Guillermo's people in the city won't notice us."

"Then it's a plan." Jordi nodded. "Any other news?"

"They're sending Diago to Germany."

"Do you know why?"

"They found his violin, the Stradivarius he lost during the Great War. It belongs to a pair of mortal brothers named Karl and Rudolf Grier. Diago is going to retrieve it."

"Do you have an address?"

"Durbach, Germany. That's all I know. Diago leaves tomorrow morning."

"Estació de França?"

"Yes. The six o'clock train."

Jordi had no idea how the information might prove useful, but gathering every stray fact was how he'd managed to stay ahead of Guillermo so far. "Get me more details if you can but don't jeopardize yourself." *Not until we've taken care of Lucia.* "Anything else?"

Salvador shook his head. "That's all I have."

Jordi folded the map and tucked it into his breast pocket. "Once we're done, get out of Spain."

"I'll contact you again once I'm safe."

"Good, I'll see you in the morning." Jordi didn't wait for an answer. He went to the door and left the building. Church bells rang as he reached the street. The addicts were gone.

It was a nice evening, so he walked, keeping his head low. If he chanced upon another nefil, he didn't want them to see the preternatural light in his eyes.

At the Hotel Colón, he slowed when he saw two policemen strolling by the front doors. They continued past the hotel and stepped around the corner.

Jordi hurried across the street and checked the lobby before entering. A few mortals chatted with one another while others sat and read the newspaper. No nefilim were in sight.

The desk manager perked up when he saw Jordi coming. "Señor Abellio," he called, using the alias that Jordi had registered with the hotel. The manager waved one hand and then smiled the ingratiating smile that he must wear to bed.

Jordi swerved to reach the desk before the man could call more attention to him. "Yes?"

"A package arrived for you." He went into the office behind the desk and returned with a small box wrapped in plain brown paper.

The address on the wrapper was to the Avignon apartment Jordi shared with his lover and confidant, Nico Bianchi. The label was addressed to Sir George Abellio. Jordi didn't recognize the handwriting.

On top of the box was a white envelope with the name George Abellio written in Nico's distinctive slant. *But why had Nico forwarded it here?*

Jordi tipped the man and walked toward the elevator, a sense of urgency adding length to his stride. The lift attendant stared impassively at the panel when Jordi barked his floor number at him.

At his floor, Jordi stepped off and went to his room, tossing his key to the desk before he closed the door. Placing the box beside the key, he opened Nico's envelope first.

> J,
> The package arrived by courier, who said the contents were for your eyes only and quite urgent. I sent it via a trusted friend on their way to Valencia.
>
> Yours,
>
> N

Jordi doubted the "trusted friend" was on the way to Valencia. Nico was far too careful to give away a tactical position in a note.

Glaring at the package, Jordi removed his coat and loosened his collar. Nico's apartment was known among many rogues as a contact point for Jordi, so it wouldn't be unusual for Nico to receive mail for one of Jordi's aliases.

But why that one? And why Sir George? Sitting at the desk, he turned the nondescript box over. No return address, but several postmarks stamped the package's route to Avignon.

Sir George Abellio. The name resurrected a memory. *Sir*

George. He was known as Sir George in his last incarnation, during the twelfth century.

Could this be from a nefil from that past life? Perhaps a rogue seeking to reconnect with Jordi? And if so, were they friend or foe?

Better safe than sorry. Jordi traced a sigil of protection over the box and hummed a chord. The red and gold vibrations of his aura charged the glyph. Only then did he feel safe to use the hotel's letter opener to pry the wrapping free.

Behind the paper was a plain white jewelry box. Lifting the lid, he removed the wadding to find an identical pair of silver brooches wrapped in tissue paper. One was polished to a high shine while the other was black with tarnish.

Despite their conditions, they both depicted an intricately carved angel standing over a lyre. Unlike other angelic drawings from the period, this angel possessed three sets of wings and the feet of a raptor—an accurate depiction of a Messenger in his true form.

The angel on the brighter pin held gemstones set within the silver: jacinth in the right hand and an emerald in the left. The stones sparkled brightly beneath the room's electric light.

The other brooch had sustained damage deeper than tarnish. An indentation in the center made it appear as if someone had struck the brooch with a blunt object. Both the jacinth and the emerald were loose in their settings. Neither stone had clarity.

The banner over the angel's head in both pieces bore the inscription: Amor vincit omnia.

Love conquers all.

"Love tokens," Jordi murmured. He caught the scent of fire and metal from a blacksmith's forge. A hammer struck the anvil with a measured rhythm, like the slow steady beats of a heart. The fires silhouetted a giant of a nefil. Jordi recalled those blunt hands and questioning whether the smith possessed the finesse to craft jewelry. *Evidently he did.*

Shifting through the tissue paper, he found a typewritten card at the bottom of the box. The note said: *Wear your pin so that I will know you in this incarnation. We will judge the traitor in vehmgericht. Watch for me.*

Jordi scowled at the word *vehmgericht*. The vehmgericht were the secret trials the nefilim once used in Germany to root out traitors to the angel-born. Mortals had eventually adopted the word and the custom during the Middle Ages to protect their feudal rights.

But in the beginning, vehmgericht belonged to us.

Jordi scanned the note again for any clues. The signature was nothing more than a hand-drawn symbol composed of a vertical line with two more lines branching upward to the right to make the rune Fehu.

"The letter F?" Why use such an archaic symbol in place of a signature? Jordi reached for the wrapping paper again. The package was sent from Offenburg, Germany.

Salvador mentioned Durbach. Jordi rose and grabbed his bag. Rooting through the side pockets, he found three maps: Spain, France, and Germany. He opened the German map and searched for Offenburg. Within moments, he found Durbach—six kilometers northeast of Offenburg.

Picking up the brooches, Jordi held them side by side. *Whose name might begin with F?* He kicked off his shoes and drew his feet onto the bed as he turned the pins first one way and then another. Nothing came to him.

"Christ burning in shit, but I hate riddles."

The quickest way to discover the meaning behind the incarnation would be to read the stones. Unfortunately, the ability to divine the history of jewels was a daimonic skill, and Jordi didn't trust the daimons in Barcelona. Any one of them would sell him out to Guillermo for a peseta if they saw something to gain from divulging the information.

Good thing he didn't need them. An ingenious nefil always found other avenues to the same destination. Being more resourceful than most, Jordi had experimented with various substances until he found that opium quickly led him into lucid dreams.

Time to chase the dragon and see where he leads, Jordi thought as he opened his bag again. Beneath a false seam was a metal case next to a small tin of cocaine. Jordi removed both and placed the cocaine on his nightstand before taking the case to the desk.

He opened the lid and laid his equipment on the blotter: a stubby candle, a pin, some foil, and a paper straw. The foil and straw always left him feeling cheap and dirty, like a street addict chasing a high.

Exceptional times call for exceptional means, he thought as he selected a small brick of opium. *Love tokens sent across distance and time qualified as extraordinary.*

With practiced moves, he lit the candle, and then daubed a piece of opium about the size of a peanut from the brick with the pin. He transferred the opium onto the foil. Picking up the straw, he moved the foil over the flame. As the opium vaporized, the liquid oozed across the foil's surface, writhing like a snake. White smoke rose into the air. Jordi followed the smoke with the straw, inhaling the drug deeply.

The sweet taste of opium filled his mouth. He repeated the procedure four more times before he blew out the candle. Knowing just when to stop was what separated him from the addicts.

He waved the foil gently and when it had cooled, he licked the last of the opium from the blackened surface. Once he had returned everything except the candle to the metal case, he adjusted the pillows and sat on the bed with his back against the headboard.

A feeling of peace and well-being suffused his body. As he moved the tarnished brooch to the nightstand, the jacinth fell free of its setting. Jordi caught the gemstone and placed it beside the brooch.

His memories lay behind the brighter pin. He was sure of it. Cradling the shining silver brooch in his palm, he shaped a glyph over the design and hummed a tune. The opium darkened the edges of his song, deepening the amber vibrations to brown.

Concentrating on the angel's face, Jordi felt the room drift away. *The angel's smile.* So serene, loving . . . loving . . . *he was my adviser, my lover . . .*

Jordi remembered his previous incarnation when he was known as George . . .

George and the angel burrow beneath the quilts and furs to escape the cold. Drowsy from their lovemaking, they are on the verge of sleep when the music finds them.

Light notes drawn from a stringed instrument with a bow travel over the night and through the shuttered window. A distant voice joins the instrument, a tenor singing in another language. It is the third night the enchanting musician has serenaded them from the town's tavern.

"Arabic. He sings in Arabic," whispers the angel. "Last night it was Italian. And his voice . . . I have never heard a nefil with such range. He is the one we need. Find him."

"In the morning," George murmurs. He has no desire to leave the bed to go wandering through a night made brittle with cold.

The angel, who calls himself Frauja, isn't dissuaded. "Have I led you wrong yet?"

No. No, he hasn't.

"You said you wanted the Key," Frauja murmurs against George's ear.

And he does want that song—*needs* that song—because now that he carries the Thrones' blessing as king of the Inner Guard, he must shut his brother Guillaume into a prison realm, one where he can never again reincarnate in the mortal world. Then there will be no other nefil strong enough to challenge George's rule.

"You know I want it."

"Then I need his voice." Frauja strokes George's throat. "The whisper of his darkness to merge with your fire. No other nefil will do. Bring him to us."

The request irks George. The initial arrangement between them required no other nefil, but George doesn't argue.

If the Thrones discover he is hiding a fallen Messenger, he'll be driven from his post as king and Guillaume will once more win sovereignty over the Inner Guard. George is playing a dangerous game and they both know it.

Secrets are like chains, George thinks as he slides out of bed and awakens his mortal manservant with a kick. "Find that musician and bring him to me. Take the guards with you. Don't come back without him."

The man stumbles from the room half awake. Another servant enters and adds wood to the fire. Candles are lit.

The covers of George's bed lie flat. The angel is gone. No one sees him but George.

An hour passes before the manservant returns and leads an unfamiliar nefil into the room. At a gesture from George, the manservant backs into the corridor and shuts the door.

The stranger places his bag at his feet and cradles an instrument's case in his arms. His clothing speaks of no country, of all countries: a surcoat of black with seams threaded in yellow covers a cote dyed a rich dark green. The loose pants, favored by the Hungarians, are tucked into his worn boots. Long black hair falls beneath a stylish chaperon popular with the Italian merchants, and it suits him well. His eyes are dark and green, surrounded by lashes so thick and black they resemble kohl in the chamber's half-light.

George remains by the fire and glares at the flames. "Who is your liege?"

"I have none." The stranger speaks the language with an accent that is impossible to place because, like his clothes, it belongs to no single country.

"You are a rogue?"

"That is your word, but yes."

"What is your word?"

"I say I am free." He meets George's stare as an equal.

The impunity of the act angers George, but he doesn't admonish the stranger. Until he is certain of the angel's game, he will move in a judicious manner. "Play for me." It is a command.

The stranger seems unperturbed. "Will we exchange songs?"

It is a reasonable request and a matter of professional etiquette that when one nefil plays for another, they exchange songs. In doing so, they are able to gauge the strength and color of one another's souls.

George isn't feeling reasonable. "Perhaps."

The stranger seems to intuit George's mood. His expression is serious as he retrieves a nearby stool. He brings it close to George's chair and sits. From the wooden case, he removes a Byzantine lyra and its bow.

"What is your name?" George asks as the stranger adjusts the instrument's pegs.

"Yago."

"Where are you from?"

"Nowhere, everywhere."

"Where did you begin?" George snaps the question like a lash.

"Córdoba."

Balancing the lyra on his thigh, he draws the bow across the strings, testing the sound, and then he measures George with a critical eye. "Is there something in particular you would like to hear?"

"You choose."

He chooses a love ballad and renders it with heartbreaking skill. His voice is as much an instrument as the lyra, and he progresses through chords no mortal and few nefilim will ever sing. When he finishes, the final clear notes of his tenor shade the air in viridian hues the same color as his eyes.

The angel appears behind Yago. "Don't move," he whispers.

Yago stiffens at Frauja's sudden presence, but he doesn't turn.

Reaching out to twine one slender finger in the black of Yago's hair, Frauja pronounces, "He is the one."

The angel's touch is intimate, his smile more so. Worse still, he has revealed himself to Yago like he has to no other.

Jealousy grabs George's heart with sharp nails and he winces, because . . .

. . . the brooch pricked his flesh, awakening him from the opium dream. Blinking in the predawn light, he looked down at his palm, where his blood smeared the angel's lips.

The names of Yago and Frauja hit Jordi's brain like twin bullets, and the pain of his last incarnation flushed through his body. He remembered dying in white light and fire, the sun burning like a thousand mirrors and Yago's song ringing in his head.

A groan burned deep in his chest and rolled through his throat. He slid his other hand along the coverlet to grasp the cloth, bunching it in his fist.

Oh, God, yes, I remember Yago, Yago, Diago. They are the same. He retrieved the tarnished pin and the jacinth. "You worked for me. We were a team."

The angel's eyes gleamed from the pin as if to say yes.

"The Thrones refused to give me an angelic adviser, but I found Frauja." *And now Frauja has returned*, Jordi thought as he recalled the note's signature rune.

Or has he? If Frauja knew where Jordi was, why hadn't he come in person?

Jordi rubbed his forehead as if he could massage the

memories into his brain. The answer had to be the obvious one: because he can't.

Guillaume and his nefilim had done something to lock Frauja away from the earthly realm. *Yago and I died trying to save the angel.* Yes, that definitely felt right, but there was something else, something he wasn't remembering.

Struggling past the opium clouding the fringes of his consciousness, Jordi reached for the tin of cocaine. Two quick hits drove the last dregs of the opium from his mind.

Alert now, he turned the brooch over in his hand. Frauja had somehow found a way to send Jordi a trigger.

But why two brooches? The answer came immediately.

Because Diago needs a trigger.

Heart racing, Jordi rose and began to dress. He and Diago had encountered each other in this incarnation, but their interactions had been few and fleeting. *That's because neither of us remembered our past together.* "The second brooch is the key to reigniting his memories. Once he recalls our life together as George and Yago, he will leave Los Nefilim." Then, along with Frauja, they would judge Guillaume in vehmgericht and bring him to ruin before the Thrones.

Jordi glanced at the clock and grabbed his coat. Salvador said that Diago's train left at six. He had just enough time to get to the station.

29
August
1932

a terrible sound that is no sound

[6]

AV. DEL MARQUÈS DE L'ARGENTERA, BARCELONA
ESTACIÓ DE FRANÇA

The train station's majestic ceiling loomed over the crowds bustling between the ticket gates and platforms. As Guillermo led their small party through the mass of humans, the mortals parted before his bulk like schools of fish clearing for a shark.

Diago and Miquel followed in his wake, keeping Rafael between them. Although they had risen before dawn to reach Barcelona, they had only a short time before Diago's train left for France.

A man in a fedora bumped into Diago. "Excuse me," he muttered as he hurried past.

Rafael's fingers tightened around Diago's, and though the boy said nothing, Diago sensed his fear. The press of bodies was suffocating enough for an adult.

And children are small, easily broken. No one knew that better than Diago. Without stopping, he leaned down and lifted his son into his arms. Guillermo must have caught the movement from the tail of his eye, because he turned and took Diago's bag. Miquel put his palm on Diago's back, giving their small family an anchor in the heaving mass of bodies.

Guillermo led them to a small alcove near the entrance to the platforms. In the oasis of quiet, Miquel held his arms out to Rafael, but the child wasn't quite ready to release his father.

Rafael hugged Diago's neck. "Do you really have to go?"

He felt his son's heart pounding against his chest. "You know I do."

"Don't come home beat up. Every time you go away without us, you come home beat up. Tell him, Miquel."

Miquel drew near. "No fighting. You upset Rafael when you do that."

"I'll be careful. I promise."

Rafael's eyes narrowed, and Diago knew the suspicious look well—he'd worn it enough times on his own face. "Okay. But if you come home beat up this time, I'm going to be very angry."

Diago whispered, "But you'll still love me, right?"

"You know I will," said Rafael. "And Miquel will still love you, too."

"There we go," said Miquel as he took Rafael from Diago. "He'll be home before you know it."

"Tomorrow?"

"Not tomorrow," Diago and Miquel said in unison.

Diago sighed. "A week."

"Just promise you'll come back."

Diago took his son's face between his hands and acknowledged his fear. "I know you're scared because your mamá said she would come back and she didn't. Right?"

Rafael nodded.

"I will come back for you. I will not leave you."

Rafael's lip trembled, but he didn't cry. "Okay."

"Okay." Diago kissed the boy and turned to Miquel. Although they had said their good-byes at home, he wished they could have another moment alone. "Take care of each other."

Miquel leaned close as if to whisper. Instead, he brushed his lips against Diago's cheek. "Take care, my star."

Diago's heart pounded until he heard nothing but his pulse. *What if someone saw us?* He lowered his head and glanced around. No one seemed to pay them the least attention.

Miquel gave him a sly wink.

Exasperated with his husband's antics, Diago fussed with his bag so Miquel wouldn't see the flush warming his cheeks. He should have seen the kiss coming. Miquel loved to push society's boundaries just to test how far he could go with their affection in public.

Guillermo put his hand on Diago's shoulder. "I'll walk you to the train."

Relieved to be moving again, he followed Guillermo for a few steps before he made the mistake of glancing over his shoulder.

Rafael waved, his face already clouding as he fought back his tears.

Unprepared for the guilt crushing his heart, Diago whispered, "Wait, Rafael needs—"

"Don't look back, keep going, he's going to be fine." Guillermo grabbed Diago's arm and propelled him forward. "He needs to get used to this. And so do you."

“I know, but I just need a min—”

The whistle blew.

“I’m taking your last minute before you get on that train.”

Disregarding Guillermo’s advice, Diago looked back again. Miquel whispered something in Rafael’s ear and the boy laughed through his tears.

The constriction in his chest eased somewhat. *Guillermo’s right. They’re going to be fine.*

The bigger nefil redirected him back toward his goal, guiding him through the crowd. “How are you sleeping?”

“Better.” That was a white lie, but if Guillermo knew the truth, he might end the assignment before it began. *Too much is riding on my success.* “The music is still there, but it’s not as intense. Maybe because of the protection in Prieto’s tear?” He held up his right hand, where the ring protruded beneath the leather of his glove.

“Maybe.” Guillermo didn’t seem convinced, but he didn’t argue the theory. “Just in case it’s not, though, stay on your guard. Call us if you need anything. Everyone has been instructed to accept all charges.”

“I will.”

“Your French contact will meet you at the station in Strasbourg.”

His contact would be a cigarette vendor, wearing a red bow tie. “We’ve planned for at least four different contingencies, all of which seem to be more in line with soothing Rousseau’s nerves than getting me over the German border.”

“Doesn’t matter. If Rousseau is comfortable that all the protocols have been followed, we keep our ally. Leave her no cause for complaint.”

“I’ve done this before, you know.”

"Not as a part of our organization you haven't."

"So you keep reminding me."

"That's my job. Questions?"

"No."

They paused beside the hissing train. The boarding call went out across the platform.

Guillermo offered his hand. "Be safe, my friend. And trust me to take care of matters here."

"I will." Diago shook his hand, feeling the strength of Guillermo's grip complement his own. "Watch for me."

"Always."

They released each other, and Diago boarded. In the aisle, he was forced to squeeze past a couple in the process of exchanging an ardent parting embrace. A sudden pang of envy clouded his eyes. He wondered what it would be like to openly kiss Miquel in public and not disguise their gestures as whispers.

Ducking his head so no one would see his jealousy, he brushed past them and took a seat at the back of the car. Once he had settled on the bench, he touched his cheek where Miquel's kiss lingered against his skin. Just as the members of Los Nefilim were forced to live discreetly among the mortals, so was their love.

He consoled himself with the thought that like Los Nefilim, their love thrived.

The engine exhaled a gust of steam and gave a little jerk, pulling him from his melancholy thoughts. The train moved away from the station as if already exhausted by the trip. As they rolled past the city, brittle sunlight leaked through the grimy windows and caught the dust motes swirling through the air.

Barcelona faded into the distance.

Diago shifted his weight in the seat and felt something prick his hip. Unable to remember what he might have placed in his pocket, he reached into his jacket and removed a tarnished silver brooch.

He looked at it curiously. An intricately carved angel stood over a lyre. In the left hand, he held a fractured emerald set within the silver. The setting in the right hand was empty. The angel possessed three sets of wings and the feet of a raptor.

An accurate depiction of a Messenger in his true form.

A chill passed through Diago. Rubbing his thumb over the blackened silver, he managed to make out the inscription on the banner over the angel's head: Amor vincit omnia.

Love conquers all.

How did it get into my pocket? It didn't come from Miquel. While his husband often showered him with gifts, he would never give Diago something so ruined.

So then who? Running his finger over the delicate engraving, Diago thought back to his walk through the station. A man had bumped into him.

Did he follow me onto the train? Diago surveyed the other passengers. Twelve mortals occupied the car with him. A woman with two small children sat opposite a pair of priests. Businessmen and people with no discernible trade occupied the benches. Engrossed with their newspapers, magazines, hushed conversations, or the view outside the windows, none seemed to notice him.

Nor did any of them resemble the man who had shoulder-checked Diago. Or did they?

Would I even know him if I saw him again? All he recalled was that the man wore a fedora pulled low over his eyes.

Why? Because he didn't want me to see the preternatural radiance in his gaze? They had brushed against each other, not hard enough to stop either of them, but with sufficient contact for the man to slip something into Diago's pocket. *And distracted with my son, I didn't see his eyes.*

Diago cursed under his breath. He had no idea where the man went after that. For all he knew, the stranger wasn't on the train. He might be stalking Miquel and Rafael at this moment. *And what if he caught them?*

Then he might be in for the fight of his life. Backed into a corner, either of them would be a formidable opponent. Besides, Guillermo and Suero were with them. What Suero lacked in power, he more than made up for in cunning.

Diago calmed himself. His family was fine. He had to believe that and keep going. Every decision he made from this point forward proved his worth to Los Nefilim. To go back meant he didn't trust Guillermo to protect his family. Others, like Carme, would see his return as a dereliction of duty.

This is a job. Focus.

Maybe the answer to the mystery lay within the brooch. He returned his attention to the pin. In spite of the grime, the emerald twinkled in the sunlight.

Juanita said he'd crippled himself with his dependence on mortal measures, and she was right. It was time to rectify that.

The gem was his clue. Whoever had owned the brooch would have left vibrations from his life in the striations of the emerald. The ability to read those patterns was a daimonic skill—one at which Diago excelled.

He removed his left glove and placed the pad of his thumb over the emerald. A whiff of meadowsweet floated through the open window. Beneath the scent of the herb came another odor so faint it was barely there, but once he recognized it, he couldn't deny the smell of blood.

Diago lowered his head. Another serendipitous glance around the car assured him that none of the mortals paid him the least attention. He removed the glove from his right hand.

Tracing a sigil of protection over the brooch, he hummed a low note. The vibrations of his vocalization charged the sigil. If someone approached him, the spell would awaken him.

Anyone passing him would see a well-dressed man taking a light nap. A few of the more sensitive mortals, lesser nefilim with a touch of the angel-born in their souls, might notice a pale halo around his body, which they would attribute to the coach's natural light.

He was as invisible as he could make himself.

As Diago hummed, a slender line of silver emerged from the angel's tear in his ring. With no effort on his part, the magic entwined with his song and supplemented his spell.

Not one to scoff at an added level of protection, he closed his eyes and purposefully kept his mind blank. Fingering the ridges of the emerald, he allowed himself to sink into a shallow trance.

The motion of the train, rolling over the tracks, lulled him even deeper. He heard nothing other than the low murmurs of the mortals in his coach.

The vision began suddenly, startling Diago with its force—

He stands in a room ravaged by his song. Frigid air chills his lungs. The drifts of snow *(parchment)* around his feet are all too real. Rushes, freshly woven into mats and sprinkled with meadowsweet, can't quash the odor of scorched glyphs tracing veins of silver over the stone walls. Tapestries lie crumpled against the floor, splashed with blood *(ink)*. A quill lands by the open window; the feather trembles like his heart.

In the courtyard below, soldiers talk as they load the dead into a cart. Their voices don't rise to his room. It is as if they stand in different worlds.

Perhaps we do . . .

The quiet yawns between them, a terrible sound that is no sound, interrupted only by the occasional crackle of dying sigils. Outside the chamber, the shrieks have ceased, but he hears more guards coming. He doesn't know if they are friend or foe. It doesn't matter, because he can't stop them. His throat is raw. He tastes blood on his lips.

The angel's sigil over his heart blazes so cold it burns. The pain brings sweat to his scalp and dampens his hair. He somehow remains on his feet. *But not for long . . . I cannot endure this.*

In the courtyard, the soldiers finish loading their wagon and push it toward the gate. A corpse's arm slips from beneath the tarp. A silver disc falls from the hand. It is a brooch. The twin to the one he wears.

The door to his room slams open. A soldier strides across the floor, kicking debris out of his way. A box ricochets off the wall and splinters in two: the lid flying in one direction, the body in another. The mirror it once contained is already broken, a million shards of light, spinning through the air.

"What have you done?" The man is hoarse with rage. With a powerful hand, he grabs the back of Diago's neck, startling him deeper into his terror. The sigil flares across his chest. He lifts his hand. The blood he smells is his own.

Then the world flushes white with a burst of agony. *Now I can die.*

But he doesn't. He screams with the last shreds of his ruined voice. Still, he does not die, no matter how he tries, he cannot die, and his cry grows higher in pitch until it becomes . . .

. . . the train whistle. The long blast wrenched Diago out of the vision. The brakes locked, adding to the shrill dissonance in his head.

Diago opened his eyes just as his body pitched forward. He clenched the brooch in his fist. The pin cut into his palm, drawing blood. Twisting hard to the right, he fell to one knee, catching himself with his forearm against the opposite bench. His gloves tumbled to the floor, and his bag struck his thigh.

The train shuddered to a halt. Mortals cried out, more from shock and fear than from pain. One of the children began to cry.

Diago knelt, his heart rapping his chest. Drops of sweat fell from his hair. The scent of his own fear gagged him.

It was almost a full minute before he wrestled his jangled nerves into submission. He snatched his gloves off the floor with one trembling hand and stood. He should have seen the owner of the brooch in that vision. *But I saw myself.*

A neighboring passenger turned to him. "Are you okay?" The man gestured to Diago's hand. "You're bleeding."

He palmed the brooch with his right hand and slid it into his pocket. Fishing a handkerchief free, he pressed the cloth against the shallow wound. "I'm fine. Yourself?"

"A few bruises. Rattled nerves."

All across the car, others rose gingerly. No one seemed to be seriously harmed.

The man gathered his loose papers, which had scattered on the floor. Diago helped him.

A porter entered their car. "Everything is fine," he said as he maneuvered down the aisle. "Please remain in your seats. A car is stalled on the tracks. They're moving it now and we'll soon be on our way."

Diago handed the last of the papers to the man, who thanked him. As he returned to his seat, he reached into his pocket and ran his finger over the brooch. The tapestries, the mats on the floor, the clothing of the men in the courtyard—all of the images indicated the twelfth century.

It's a memory of a past incarnation. Of that he was certain. Diago tapped a thoughtful rhythm on his thigh with one restless finger, like a cat twitching its tail. The image of the disc, falling from someone's hand, was present in both the vision and his nightmares.

A disc the exact size and shape of this brooch. Diago withdrew the pin and examined it again. This piece of jewelry had belonged to him in a past incarnation, of that much he was certain. Had someone worn a mate to the pin? *The man who put it in my pocket, maybe?*

Maybe. But that didn't answer the question as to how the brooch still retained so much of Diago's essence. Even if he'd owned it in the twelfth century, the brooch should have gone through any number of owners from then until now. In that case, he would have gotten a vague sense of his past life intermingled with the experiences of everyone else who'd come in contact with the pin. *But never in a vision as extreme as the one I just experienced.*

Like the nightmares, the vision had hit him with the force of an attack. *Which likely means that whoever deposited the brooch in my pocket has interests hostile to mine. And he knows I am bound for France.*

Diago swore under his breath. The last thing he needed was complications with Rousseau. He had to determine whether he was being followed before he set foot on French soil. If he found the other nefil, then he intended to extract answers from him. *By whatever means necessary.*

Diago switched trains at Girona, and then again at Figueres. Each time, he watched the crowd. At both stops he left the stations and wandered into alleys, choke points intended to reveal anyone shadowing him. By the time he reached the Portbou Station at the French border, he was certain no one followed him.

Which means the nefil remains in Barcelona, or I've lost him. As he passed a public phone, he paused and debated calling Guillermo's house to report the incident. *And what do I tell them? A man, who I cannot describe, bumped into me, and then I found a brooch in my pocket that led to a memory of a past incarnation in the twelfth century?* And once they had the information, how could they possibly advise him?

He hesitated beside the phone for another moment and then decided to forgo calling. *I've got to show them I can handle the situation.* If something of importance turned up to supplement his facts, he'd have ample opportunity to call Santuari and let them know. For now, he would remain on guard, gather more information, and complete his assignment.

With his decision made, he moved toward the desk where a handsome young Frenchman in a crisp uniform waited to process travelers through customs.

It was time to focus on the Grier brothers.

30 August 1932

the angels are falling

[7]

SANTUARI, SPAIN

Guillermo dreamed of a great marble staircase shadowed with moonlight. A hall tree squatted to one side of the entryway. Angels were carved into the mahogany; they writhed around the frame with mouths full of black.

Hanging over the hall tree were the tattered remains of a medieval standard. On a field of gold an eagle with a lyre in one talon and a blood-red cross in the other decorated the shield of arms. Three crimson fleurs-de-lis surrounded the shield.

A loud bang broke the silence. The walls shuddered with the force of the tremor. Two more ferocious crashes followed the first. From somewhere deep within the house came the slow and hypnotic beats of a death march played on timpani. Clarinets and tubas entered the arrangement. Cellos moaned—softly at first and then louder—joining the brass and timpani to rise chromatically until Guillermo recognized the composition from Wagner's *Götterdämmerung*: Siegfried's death and funeral.

As the music gained strength, veins erupted beneath the wallpaper, tracing lines from one end of the hall to the other. Fingers wormed through plaster, scrabbling to pry open the seams. With each puncture came a lick of flame and the sound of nefilim's voices, crying as they sang.

Movement at the top of the stairs caught Guillermo's attention. Diago ran onto the landing, but before he could descend, a shot rang out. He slid down three stairs, clutching at the banister and halting his fall. Blood soaked the white of his shirt.

All around them, the fire escalated with the opera's violent crescendos, following the horns with a savage roar. Smoke filled the air; it stung Guillermo's eyes and choked his lungs. He ran toward his friend. Blinded by the haze, he stumbled and fell into a bottomless abyss.

Before his eyes were fully open, Guillermo rolled into a sitting position. His heart punched his chest with one hard blow after another.

He fumbled for the pad and pencil he kept beside his bed and jotted down quick notes: *banner, eagle with a lyre, three fleurs-de-lis, gold field, hall tree/angels, Götterdämmerung: Siegfried's death, nefilim's souls, crying, fire, crying, Diago shot, abyss*. He sketched the scene in stark lines without much detail.

Three knocks echoed through his house, startling him so badly he almost dropped the pencil. As his heart settled in his chest, he realized someone was at his door.

With dreams like these, he tended to linger on the verge of slumber in order to cement the imagery in his brain. *No time for that today.* Reaching for his robe, he glanced at the bedside clock, which showed six thirty. Outside the window, the sky was dirty and gray with dawn. *Still too dark to see without a torch, but not for long.*

Juanita stirred beneath the sheets, her body caught between her angelic and mortal forms, ethereal as the night caught between the sun and the moon. In the early days of their arranged marriage, the sight of her in such disarray had unnerved him: her four-fingered hands, the crackling energy around her wings, the mysterious orbs that were her eyes. As the decades had passed, their relationship gradually shifted from mutual respect to love. She easily could have returned to her celestial home after Ysabel's birth. Instead, she had chosen to remain at his side, and not an hour passed that he didn't find himself glad. Especially on days like this, the ones that began with nightmares and predawn visitors.

"What's happening?" she mumbled as she reached for him.

He caught her hand in his and brushed his lips across her knuckles. "Go back to sleep. I'll go see."

She vocalized a soft chord in her native language and then stretched as her mortal form solidified around her. "I'll be down in a minute."

Of course she would. Like him, she knew visitors this early usually meant trouble. He tied his robe's sash and left their room, pausing briefly beside Ysabel's door. His daughter lay curled on her bed, hugging her favorite stuffed horse. Assured that the two people most precious to him were safe, he went downstairs.

At the front window, he glanced outside. Father Bernardo stood on the porch. Hairy as a black bear and almost as ugly, Bernardo posed as Santuari's priest. He raised his hand to knock again.

Guillermo reversed the ward over the lock and opened the door. He stepped onto the porch, the dread from his nightmare following him into the day. "What's going on?"

"We've lost three nefilim," Bernardo said with no preamble, gesturing toward the hulking shape of a lorry parked in the yard.

"Oh, goddamn," Guillermo muttered, following Bernardo from the cool flagstones to the rocky soil.

In spite of the weak light, Guillermo recognized Carme squatting on the tailgate. Her motorcycle leaned against the lorry. She and Bernardo must have cut the engines and coasted into the yard to keep from waking his family.

As he and Bernardo neared, she moved to one side so he could see the three bodies laid side by side on the bed. The trio was covered by tarps. Without waiting to be asked, Carme pulled back the canvas on the first body and shined the beam of her torch over the face.

It was Lucia. From the angle of her head, it was clear her neck had been broken. The binding glyphs Juanita had seared into her flesh were now nothing more than charred shadows on her throat and arms.

While her death gave him no pleasure, Guillermo likewise found no grief in his heart for her passing. She had given information to his enemies. In a final act of treachery, she had taken the names of her coconspirators into her next incarnation.

Guillermo had nothing for the passing of Lucia Urbina other than the cold rage burning in his chest. "Who are the other two?"

Carme answered him. "Valeria Soto and Enrique Rosales. It was their shift to guard her."

"Shit and bitter shit." Guillermo's stomach clenched. "There will be blood for this." Valeria and Enrique had been as loyal and trustworthy to him as they were to each other. *And right now I need nefilim like them at my back*. "What the hell happened out there?"

Carme jumped down. "We found Enrique's body outside, so he must have gone to investigate. The intruder garroted him. Then one of them shot Valeria before she could radio the situation to us."

Guillermo turned to Bernardo. "Get Miquel."

The priest didn't move. "Eva is already on her way to wake him. She'll stay with Rafael."

Guillermo lifted the tarp from Valeria's face. A bullet hole pierced the center of her forehead. Another had torn through her larynx. The shot to the head had killed her. The other was a more ancient gesture, symbolic of silencing an enemy's song. He kissed his palm and rested his hand over her throat. "We will watch for you, my good servant Valeria Soto."

It was the nefilim's prayer and served as a good-bye, or a blessing, or a curse. To watch for another meant they would search the eyes of every soul until they found each other again, either in this incarnation or the next.

He repeated the motion and the promise with Enrique's corpse while noting his severed larynx. "Our killer is bringing ancient tactics into the twentieth century." He showed the others the crushed larynxes. "We're dealing with an old nefil, one who has been through at least three incarnations, maybe more."

When he came to Lucia, he noticed her larynx remained intact. "And with this one: any doubts about her guilt should be assuaged." He touched her throat. "The killers didn't steal her voice, so we know she worked for them."

"Still, they silenced her," Carme said.

"Yes, they did." He leaned over her body and growled, "Carry my curse into your next incarnation, Lucia Urbina. You will pay for your treachery. I *will* watch for you."

He jerked the tarp over her face just as Miquel reached them. Unlike Guillermo, he had taken the time to dress.

At least one of us is ready for the day. He nodded a greeting. "Did Eva brief you?"

Miquel tossed his cigarette to the ground and crushed it beneath his heel. "We've got three dead."

"Good. We can forgo that part of the report. Now that you're here, Carme can tell us how someone slipped past our wards." He turned his glare on her.

She didn't flinch. "Salvador Muñoz was in charge of the sigils in that sector," she said. "He's missing. I found two sets of footprints around the finca. One of them is his, the other I didn't recognize. Both pairs led east. I've got my people searching the area now."

"There's an old trail there," Miquel said. "It goes from the backside of our property to the road to Barcelona." He glanced to the house. "Here comes Juanita."

Guillermo turned in time to see his wife slip out the front door. Like Miquel, she had taken the time to dress. She joined them and climbed into the back of the truck to examine the bodies. Holding out her hand, she said, "Give me the light."

Carme passed the torch to her.

She squatted beside Enrique's body and touched his chin,

tilting his head backward. "Miquel, come here and give me your knife."

He hoisted himself onto the bed and then passed his pocketknife to her.

"Hold the light for me." She indicated the open wound of Enrique's throat. "Point it here."

While they worked, Guillermo turned on Bernardo. "What is our time frame?"

"According to Alfonso, Valeria radioed in on time at four. When she didn't check in at five, he contacted Carme, and then he came to get me."

That wasn't too bad. They were just over an hour behind the killers. Guillermo checked his wrist and realized his watch was still beside his bed.

Juanita rocked back on her heels. "Guillermo."

"What?"

She held a faceted gemstone, which was about the size of his thumbnail, between her fingers. "Jacinth. And it was inserted in Enrique's larynx."

Guillermo held out his hand and she passed the jewel to him. The jacinth triggered his memory of another gem: a dark emerald with an identical cut because it was the mate to this one. *But where have I seen them?*

He rubbed his thumb over the face of the gem and slowly became aware of four pairs of eyes watching him. His people awaited his instructions. He needed time.

Time I don't have.

Clutching the jacinth, he turned to Carme. "Go to the trail Miquel mentioned and see if you can examine the tire tracks. Try and figure out what kind of vehicle the killers used. Get someone on the road and question every goat herder and farmer between here and Barcelona. If anyone saw the killers, I want their names. Understand?"

At her nod, he continued, "But I need you to stay here and double the wards. See to it personally. Set up checkpoints on all the roads surrounding Santuari. I want to know who leaves and who returns down to the minute."

"I will, Don Guillermo." She went to her motorcycle and mounted the bike. With one kick, the engine roared to life and she took off with a plume of dust trailing in her wake.

Miquel and Juanita covered the bodies again. They jumped down, and Miquel secured the lorry's tailgate.

Guillermo turned to the priest. "Take the corpses to the church. There will be no school today or tomorrow." The day had brightened enough for Guillermo to notice lipstick on Bernardo's collar. He pointed to his own neck. "Did you cut yourself shaving?"

Bernardo pulled the white tab free of his collar and examined it. "Um, I was busy taking confession when Alfonso came to me."

Miquel raised his eyebrows. "Taking confession at five in the morning? I didn't realize you were so dedicated, Bernardo."

"Maribel, she is a troubled woman." He coughed and glanced uncomfortably at Juanita's bemused expression. "I confer with her often over the nature of her"—he cleared his throat and stuffed the clerical collar into his pocket—"the nature of her soul."

Guillermo put his hand on Bernardo's shoulder and guided him toward the driver's side of the lorry. "Personally, I don't care if you're in bed with half of the village. What I do need is my spy inside the church." He opened the lorry's door and squeezed Bernardo's shoulder until the priest winced. "Sometimes mortals do come to the village, so I need for you to act with a modicum of discretion. If others see you bleeding in shades of lipstick, they might ask questions, and those questions might reach the cardinals, and then I will have to find another nefil, who I trust as dearly as you, to become our priest. Do you understand how quickly these things can escalate?"

Bernardo flushed red and nodded. "I do, Don Guillermo. It won't happen again."

Guillermo released him and patted his back. "Good."

"I'll call Esteve to prepare the bodies," Bernardo said as he got into the cab. "We'll need coffins." Still muttering to himself, he started the lorry. The stink of diesel fuel filled the air.

Guillermo rapped the driver's door. "I'll be at the church later."

Bernardo raised his hand in acknowledgment and then grinded through the gears.

A thin brow of gold peeped over the horizon. It wouldn't be long before members of his staff began to arrive.

"Come on. I should get dressed." Guillermo led the way into the house with the jacinth in his hand. Once inside, he went to the kitchen and cleaned Enrique's blood from the gemstone. Holding it up to the light, he said, "I need to know who owned this."

Juanita frowned. "It's a pity Diago isn't here. He could divine it for us."

"We can't wait for him to return. We keep taking hits." That bothered him more than anything. Centuries of hard work were unraveling before his eyes. "We've got to find a way to go on the offensive."

Miquel eyed the jacinth. "Should we call on the good condesa today?" He meant Christina Banderas, the daimon-born Condesa of Barcelona. "She's helped us before."

"Not from the goodness of her heart, though. She barters with us."

"Of course she does." Miquel shrugged. "Everything has a price."

"Her price is always more than I'm willing to give," Guillermo grumbled. "She wants Catalonia to herself and the daimon-born nefilim. I'll be damned if I'm giving it to her."

Juanita washed her hands in the sink. "I don't disagree that's a high price for the lives of three nefilim, but Christina is not unreasonable. It's one reason why we've been able to work together in the past. She knows your position. She will ask for the moon, because it's her nature, but that doesn't mean you have to give it to her."

"Juanita is right," Miquel said. "And consider this: whoever murdered our nefilim is not in their first incarnation. That means we all have a history together. We've got to have a name."

"Okay. We'll try the condesa. Tell Suero to call Christina as soon as he gets here and arrange a meeting between us. I also want him to call Sofia Corvo." Sofia coordinated Guillermo's covert operations throughout Spain from her base in Barcelona. "I want her people to canvass the local rooming houses and hotel registries for weekend guests. If anyone is using a known alias, we might be able to narrow our list of suspects."

"You think the jacinth might be a red herring?"

"I'm assuming nothing until I have evidence in front of me."

The phone in Juanita's clinic began to ring. "I'll be up to

take care of Ysa in a moment," she called over her shoulder as she hurried down the hall.

Guillermo jabbed his finger in Miquel's direction as he walked to the stairs. "Be ready. You're going with me today."

"Good choice," Miquel said. "I'll make some coffee."

"Coffee will be useful." Guillermo went to the stairs. He reached the second-floor landing and found his daughter waiting for him in the hall.

"Papá?" Auburn curls slipped from her braid and gave her a fiery halo. He noticed she'd left the comfort of her stuffed horse in her bedroom. "I dreamed of blood on the walls of the finca." A hint of fear touched her eyes. "Our sigils were broken and our nefilim were dead."

Her words sent a chill through him. His first thought—*she is too young for this*—died before it truly took root in his mind. A mortal child might not comprehend the violence of her dreams, but Ysa wasn't mortal.

With his heart sinking, he knew Juanita was right. *I've got to teach her.* Although doing so would rob Ysa of the last vestiges of her innocence. *No matter how badly I want to spare her, I can't deny what she is, or the potency of her dreams.*

"Well . . . it . . ." He caught himself before he could soften the news as he'd always tried to do in the past. "You dreamed true," he blurted. "That was Bernardo just now with the bodies."

She twisted one of the ribbons on her gown between her fingers. "I saw Enrique and Valeria . . . in my dream."

He nodded. "You are right about that, too."

She glanced over her shoulder. Her lower lip quivered. "Is it my fault that they're dead, because I told you about Lucia?"

"No." And here, in comforting her, he found his footing again. *Although the day is coming when she won't need me*, he thought with a pang.

Kneeling in front of her, he looked her in the eye and clasped her hands in his. "Never think that. The fault belongs to whoever killed them, but not to you. You saved more lives than you lost, and sometimes, Ysa, that is all you can do."

She hugged him, and as he held her, he wished he could stop time . . . just hold this moment and keep her forever unsullied by Los Nefilim's violence. Yet, in spite of all his power, he knew he couldn't, nor could he afford to shackle her with ignorance.

Ysa's voice pulled him from his thoughts. "I'm sorry for Valeria and Enrique, Papá. We will watch for them."

"That we will." He released her and she stepped back.

She seemed all right. Instead of tears, the fire of her anger rimmed her irises and turned them a deep and violent orange. "Do we know who killed them?"

Yes, he thought. *She's going to be a fine strong nefil.* Guillermo rose and answered her question. "No, not yet, but I have a clue. Now you should get ready for the day. There is no school, but your mamá will need your help."

"Is there anything I can do to help *you*?"

"Not yet. But soon."

"Have you been thinking?" she asked eagerly.

"Yes, very hard. Now go."

For once she didn't argue with him. He waited until she closed her bedroom door before he returned to his own room.

Setting the jacinth on his nightstand, Guillermo dressed quickly. When he reached for his watch, the pad caught his eye again. He reread his notes, trying to resurrect both the imagery and feelings from the dream.

Picking up his pencil, he continued the sketch while glancing from time to time at his notes. The house was old, the wallpaper dark, molded plaster ceilings overhead. *Standard, hall tree/angels*. He'd underlined the words.

He filled in the lines around the banner—the eagle, wings spread, clutching a lyre, and then the three fleurs-de-lis surrounding the eagle. Next he added lion's feet to the hall tree. Working from the bottom up, he fleshed out the angels, drawing their faces from memory. When he finished the sketch, he examined his handiwork.

The angels' mouths were open. *Open and full of black*, he remembered. While examining their faces, he had a sudden epiphany: the angels weren't rising. The angle of their wings was all wrong for angels ascending.

"They're falling," he whispered, the nightmare's apprehension enveloped him once more as he thought of Diago. "They are fallen angels defeated in battle . . . but from which war?"

The Carolingian? The Great War? Each of those conflicts involved the Thrones fighting among themselves, and the fallout had sent more angels plummeting into the mortal world. Some descended into the daimonic realms, carving out an existence within the earth itself. Others went mad and lost their ability to move between the realms; those were the most dangerous of all.

Could that be the answer to the black pin? Had he sent Diago into the maw of a fallen angel?

Guillermo lowered the paper and fixed his gaze on the gemstone. No, that theory didn't fit the facts. The nefilim had encountered numerous fallen angels in the past—both the sane and the insane—and none exhibited the ambiguous qualities of Durbach's entity.

Downstairs he heard Miquel greet Suero. It was time to go. He folded his notes and put them in his breast pocket along with the gem.

By the time Suero organized the meeting, it was two o'clock. Christina refused to meet them anywhere except at the Club d'Escorpí at four, most likely on the presumption that the timetable would rush Guillermo and prevent him from arranging an escort into the bowels of daimonic territory.

On the way out the door, Guillermo paused by Juanita and kissed her cheek. "Tell Sofia I need backup at Club d'Escorpí." He kissed her on the mouth. "I love you."

"And I you. Hurry home." Juanita picked up the phone.

"I will." He fished a cigar out of his pocket as he walked to the car.

Suero held the door open for him. Miquel was already waiting in the backseat. They stopped by the church and picked up Father Bernardo, who stuffed his bulk into the front seat. He'd left his clerical collar behind and wore a longshoreman's cap over his unruly hair. "I should be praying for the dead."

"Pray we have no more," Guillermo murmured as Suero turned the car toward Barcelona.

[8]

BARCELONA
CLUB D'ESCORPÍ

The Club d'Escorpí nestled on the Carrer dels Flassaders, a narrow street in the labyrinthine neighborhood of La Ribera. Suero was forced to park almost a block away from the club itself. The condesa had chosen her position well. Guillermo's only way in was on foot through winding alleys that begged for ambush. It was Christina's way of keeping them humble.

This was nothing new. She made sure to retain the upper hand in any encounter, and so long as his people weren't jeopardized, Guillermo allowed her to choose the rendezvous. He hoped if their fortunes were ever reversed, she would offer him the same courtesies.

Nevertheless, while he admired her—she was a worthy foe and a fierce tactician—he didn't intend to walk into her territories without insurance of his own. He scanned the street and noted the presence of Josefina Zavala, one of Sofia Corvo's lieutenants.

Dressed in a coverall and a flat cap, Josefina could be

mistaken for a tall thin man. Her hands were thrust in the coverall's deep pockets, where Guillermo had no doubt she stored an array of weaponry.

Josefina tossed her cigarette to the gutter and waited as patiently as a spider on her web.

Guillermo tapped Suero's shoulder. "Stay with the car." The young nefil gave him a sharp nod. It wasn't an insignificant assignment. While they were inside, Suero would monitor the sidewalks and be ready to move them out on a moment's notice if necessary.

"Bernardo, you come with us. Stay in the background, keep your eyes open. Miquel, you're with me."

They exited the car. Lean and lethal, Josefina fell into step beside Bernardo as they entered Flassaders.

"I have the list you asked for, Don Guillermo," she said quietly, seemingly without moving her lips.

"Good, we'll look at it after we finish with the condesa."

Despite his wariness, Guillermo walked the street as if he owned it. To show fear invited contempt, and right now he needed their respect.

The surrounding buildings brought an early twilight to Flassaders. The few mortals they passed stepped aside for Guillermo and his people. To them, he was a well-dressed man surrounded by bodyguards. That translated to either a mark or serious trouble in their neighborhood. He felt their eyes on his back as they weighed the odds of staying or finding another street to haunt.

They all decided they had business elsewhere.

Not that their presence meant much to him. Guillermo was more concerned with two scorpions that scuttled out of a drain to watch them from a gutter. A third hung from a gargoyle's mouth. He noted all three and guessed there were more. The eyes of the daimons were on them.

A poster encased behind broken glass promised an evening of jazz. Over the door were the words CLUB D'ESCORPÍ with a scorpion's tail replacing the letter *s*.

Josefina touched Guillermo's arm as she stepped in front of him. She entered the building to announce them . . . and to check for traps. She was gone less than a minute before returning. "It's clear, Don Guillermo."

The narrow hall gave way to a wider room. Guillermo stopped at the threshold.

Condesa Christina Banderas stood by the bar. Her hair, normally as black as Miquel's, had been dyed a stunning platinum blond and marcelled to perfection. Dressed for the evening, she wore a beaded dress and high heels, looking every inch a noblewoman out for a night on the town. She was stunning and well aware of the effect she had on men.

Guillermo's gaze followed her curves not out of lust but from a sense of self-preservation. He was more concerned about any weaponry she might have concealed under her dress. Although she rarely attacked unless threatened, once menaced she was like the black mamba and would strike again and again until she neutralized the danger.

Five of her nefilim occupied various tables in the room. Guillermo recognized them all as disciplined fighters. Most likely more were nearby, ready to storm the room at the first sign of aggression.

This was what a peaceful meeting looked like between the two groups.

Christina's dark blue eyes swallowed the light and threw nothing but shadows at Guillermo. She took a black cigarette holder from the bar and casually inserted a slim cigarette. "Don Guillermo . . . or should I say 'Your Majesty'?" the last coming from her mouth with an ironic lilt.

He ignored the mockery. "Let's dispense with the formalities. I'm short of time." He gestured to the threshold. "I will ask permission for myself and my people to enter your establishment so that we can negotiate."

One of the men rose, languid as a feline, and lit her cigarette. Light skinned with pale eyes, Edur Santxez was a highborn lord within the daimon-born's echelon and Christina's lover. While his features weren't exactly handsome, he was endowed with an abundance of grace and sensuality that accompanied his every move.

From behind a cloud of blue smoke, Christina whispered, "Enter."

Guillermo strode into the club, motioned to a table, and raised his eyebrows. Christina glided forward and took a seat. He sat opposite her so he could keep one eye on the exit, where Josefina and Bernardo flanked the door. Miquel took the seat between Guillermo and Christina so he could watch the other nefilim.

She acknowledged Miquel. "We've missed seeing you in Barcelona, Don Miquel."

"No, you haven't," he retorted.

She smiled.

Now that shots have been fired . . .

Guillermo cleared his throat. "I need to show you something, Condesa." Acutely aware of Christina's nefilim and their sudden attention to his movements, he slowly reached into his pocket and produced the jacinth. "I need you to read this gem and tell me who came onto my property to murder three of my nefilim."

Christina regarded the jacinth in the same manner Guillermo imagined she might appraise a turd dropped on her table. "Where is your pet rogue? I've yet to see a stone he cannot read."

She knew Diago was no longer rogue. Her comment was another dig. She meant to push him. That much he expected. How far he intended to let her go depended on his mood, and he wasn't feeling affable about delays.

"Diago is currently away on business. That left me two choices: find a rogue to assess the stone or come to you."

"And we certainly don't want word to get out that your defenses are down, now do we?"

Jab, jab, jab, he thought. *Poke me one more time, and I'll poke back*. "I don't care if you put it on the wireless the minute I walk out the door," he lied smoothly. He'd be damned if he intended to give her the satisfaction of scoring points off him. "Heads will decorate my borders when I find the culprits."

Her eyes narrowed—she knew he was serious now. "Why me?" she asked as she tapped the ashes from her cigarette into an art deco ashtray, which depicted two angels facing each other. It wasn't lost on Guillermo that the angels' heads had been removed and their wings broken.

"Rogues don't have skin in our game. You and I, we have stakes in the outcome of this reading."

"No one is killing *my* nefilim."

"Not yet."

"Is that a threat?"

"It's an observation. Another angelic war is on the horizon."

She shrugged. "Then it's in our best interests to sit back and watch you eat yourselves."

"And if my side loses? Then who gets eaten next? Hmm?" He folded his arms on the table and leaned forward. "You and I might not like each other, but we've reached détente. Yes?"

She smoked and raised one shoulder in a half-hearted acknowledgment of his truth.

Undeterred by her indifference, he went on, "Rest assured you will find no such truce with the side that hunts Los Nefilim. Based on my understanding of the events, one faction of angels wants to wipe the daimon-born from the face of the earth."

"I have only your word for that, and you want something from me."

"Check with your people. They know I'm telling you the truth."

She flicked her ashes into the tray and glanced at Edúr. He gave her an almost imperceptible nod.

Rolling the cigarette holder between her fingers, she met Guillermo's gaze evenly. "What are you offering?"

"Protection. I will bring your troops under my banner to save them. They will be treated with the same respect and dignity that I currently give to my own people."

"And if I refuse?"

"The other side will carry out their genocide. The daimon-born will find no sanctuary behind my wards, and if I am forced into exile, I will take only my people with me."

She glared at the gem. "I want our territorial lines renegotiated, and I want you to take your base of operations out of Catalonia."

He shot Miquel a raised eyebrow, the equivalent of *I told you so.*

Miquel made no sign he noticed.

Guillermo shook his head at Christina. "I'll not willingly pull my operations out of Catalonia for you or anyone else."

"That's my offer," she said. "Take or leave it."

He felt the gazes of his nefilim on him. Miquel's dark eyes were inscrutable in the dim light.

Again, Guillermo saw his dream and Diago falling. He fixed Enrique's and Valeria's death masks in his mind—*their crushed larynxes. I brought all of them to this.* He had to know his enemy's name, or he would keep flailing at shadows until it was too late, but he couldn't give her what she wanted.

"Well," he said as he scooped the jacinth into his palm. "A rogue it is, then." He stood. "But when the war comes, you and your nefilim are on your own." He gestured to his people.

Her glare turned hard as diamonds. Edur moved to catch her eye.

They were almost at the door when Christina spoke. "Wait."

Miquel stepped back and Guillermo turned.

Edur had taken his place at Christina's shoulder.

She motioned for Edur to return to his table. "If this war comes, and I'm forced to seek shelter in Santuari, I will retain my title and holdings."

"Done," said Guillermo.

"And I will retain command of my people at all times."

"Done. Once the war is over, we can renegotiate the port treaties in good faith."

She made a show of considering his counteroffer and then motioned for him to return to his seat. "I will read for you."

They took their seats again, and Guillermo returned the jacinth to the scarred surface. "We will have the terms drawn up after I have ascertained the truth of your reading. One thing hinges on the other. Will you take me at my word?"

"We have an agreement. I name Edur Santxez, Cristóbal del Granado, and Iria Mejia as my witnesses to this oath."

The named nefilim bowed to her will.

"And I name Miquel de Torrellas, Bernardo Ibarra, and Josefina Zavala as mine." He nodded at the gem. "Shall we begin?"

Christina exhaled twin clouds of smoke through her nostrils. She crushed the smoldering cigarette between the ashtray's broken angels and assessed the jacinth. "And how do I know I am not condemning one of my own?"

"The nefil who owned this gem is angel-born. I am sure of it."

With a grace that belied the difficulty of the gesture, she traced a sigil of protection over the jacinth. Humming softly, she charged the ward with the cobalt vibrations of her song.

"When I look into this stone, I will tell you all the things I see, both good and bad." Closing her eyes, she reached through her wards to take the gem, rolling it across her palm.

The silence stretched between them. A minute passed and then two. Guillermo frowned, resisting the urge to reach for his lighter. Miquel was still as stone.

Christina flinched as if she heard a loud noise. Sweat glistened on her brow. "I see rushes on the floor . . . a banner . . . an eagle with a lyre and a blood-red cross . . ."

Guillermo's heart jumped. It was the banner from his dream.

". . . a nefil with red-gold hair wears a red cote . . ."

Red—the color of kings. Guillermo leaned forward, hanging on her every word. Then a date came to him from nowhere: eleven hundred and forty-five.

Christina cocked her head, listening to a sound only she could hear. ". . . I hear voices . . . drums . . . no, not drums but bombs . . . like echoes . . . dark sounds . . . nefilim crying . . . their souls are shadows . . ."

Guillermo glanced at Miquel. A muscle jumped along his jawline. His knuckles were white.

Christina fell silent. Her hands trembled. A thin line of blood leaked from her nose. Foam speckled her lips, bleeding over her lipstick and onto her chin. A seizure gained force and rattled her body. The beads of her dress shimmered like a thousand tears as her heels clacked against the floor.

Edur rushed to her side, but he wasn't as fast as Guillermo, who reached out and knocked the jacinth from her hand. The seizure stopped the moment she released the jewel.

Edur caught her in his arms.

Miquel slammed his palm on the gemstone to prevent it from flying onto the floor.

Guillermo slowly became aware of drawn weapons on all sides. He kept his hands on the table.

"Put the guns away," he said to Josefina and Bernardo.

Neither of them appeared happy about the prospect. Guillermo repeated the order, and, slowly, they complied.

Edur murmured to Christina and traced a protective sigil over her brow.

Her eyelids fluttered. She straightened in her chair and

smoothed her dress. "Get me a drink," she whispered as she stroked his arm.

The thin line of a headache fingered its way into Guillermo's head. "You said you heard voices . . . nefilim crying . . ." He recalled his dream. "Did they sing? Could you see them?"

Christina's hand shook as she accepted a tumbler from Edur. She sipped the amber liquor and took her time answering him. "Do you understand what I mean when I say dark sounds?"

"Death-songs," said Miquel.

Christina raised her glass to him. "When either mortals or nefilim suffer a violent death, the frequencies produced by their auras manifest to become black songs, shadows that cling to the mortal realm. They are visible to certain daimons—those of us who know how to look for them."

Guillermo leaned forward. "And these nefilim who were crying . . . these were the dark sounds you saw?"

"I heard them, but I couldn't see them. They were behind a veil of gray. When I tried to penetrate to the other side, something attacked me. I've never sensed anything like it."

The black pin. "Can you tell me anything . . . a name, a place . . . ?"

"I sensed trees. Great heavy firs. If I had to guess, I would say the Black Forest."

Durbach, Guillermo thought. *She's just seen straight into the black pin, where I've sent Diago.* He deliberately avoided Miquel's gaze. "Thank you, Condesa. I'll have my man call Edur when the terms have been drawn. If there is anything I can do—"

"Don't hurry back." She tilted her glass toward the door, clearly inviting him to get the hell out of her establishment.

Guillermo took the hint. He turned and strode from the room, his people following him back onto the street.

Miquel returned the jacinth to Guillermo before he lit a cigarette. "If whatever is in Durbach can reach Christina here in Barcelona—"

"Diago will be fine," Guillermo said with more confidence than he felt. He strode toward the main avenue as if he could leave his misgivings behind. "Christina is only fifty years old and in her second-born life. She doesn't have Diago's experience. Let's work on our problem: the banner, the rushes, the cote. I remembered a year."

"Eleven hundred and forty-five," Miquel said.

"Yes. That was the trigger I needed. We were together in that incarnation. Now we've got to figure out what happened."

When they reached the car, Suero opened the back door.

Guillermo gestured to Josefina. "Come with me. Miquel, up front. The rest of you, give me a song of silence." He got into the backseat, sliding across the bench seat to give Josefina room, and waited for Miquel to take his place in the front.

Bernardo shut the door and traced a sigil of silence over the window, charging it with his song. Suero sauntered around the car as if checking the tires, creating dozens of smaller sigils and sending them shooting beneath the chassis. Soon the car was bedazzled with glyphs. Mortals who glanced their way saw an empty vehicle. Nefilim would only hear the buzz of a distant song, like a radio playing from another room.

Josefina withdrew an envelope from her breast pocket. "Look under the Colón. I think you will find a familiar name."

Guillermo scanned the list. *George Abellio. Room 220.*

And there it was: that familiar feeling of having an important piece of the puzzle ratchet into place. "My half brother has finally decided to make his move."

"We should have known." Miquel spat the words.

"Not necessarily. I've made many enemies over my incarnations. It could have been anyone."

Except Jordi wasn't anyone.

In their firstborn lives as Solomon and Adonijah, it was Adonijah who was the elder soul, the one in line to inherit command of the nefilim from David. At least until Solomon's mother, a Messenger angel who called herself Bathsheba, interceded to establish Solomon as the priest-king of the newly formed Inner Guard.

Then I let my arrogance overtake my good sense, betrayed my best friends, and died broken and alone. The Thrones had revoked their blessings on Solomon's kingship and forbade him from ever reassuming his firstborn name. For his next three incarnations, he had lived as Gilen, Guillem, and then Guillaume, either serving the Inner Guard as a soldier or living as a rogue.

It wasn't until his previous incarnation, when he was Guillaume, that he had earned the right to be restored to power. *I'll lose command again if I'm not careful.* Guillermo remained under the same probation his brother had endured in his last incarnation. He had to watch his step.

Then mind the matter at hand. He checked the dates of Jordi's stay in Barcelona. The timeline fit. He handed the list to Miquel and spoke to Josefina. "What else have you found?"

"We talked with the maids and got a general description

of Abellio." She handed Guillermo another piece of paper—this one a sketch of his brother's face.

Lupine eyes stared from a hungry face made craggy and hard. His cheekbones were high, and he wore a light beard. The sketch was in pencil, but Guillermo knew Jordi's hair was a slightly lighter shade than his own auburn curls. They shared a father; light skin and eyes more orange than brown.

Josefina continued, "He was initially scheduled to leave on Monday, but he extended his stay. So we checked with the train station. Our contact said a man fitting Abellio's description had tickets to leave Monday morning, but he came early and changed his departure date."

Early Monday morning. Christ. They were all very likely in the station at the same time. "Let me guess, he changed it to the Tuesday train."

Josefina nodded. "His original ticket was to Paris, but on Monday, he switched his last stop to Portbou at the border."

"See if you can find out which train he took in Portbou."

"We've already got people on it."

"Can you connect Muñoz to Abelló?"

"Three mortals saw Abelló enter a tenement where Muñoz has been keeping a room."

"Okay, good work, Josefina. Thank you. What about Muñoz?"

"He served during the Rif War, so we're expanding our search south. If he wants to lie low, he'll head back to the Moroccan hills. He knows his way around the area. We'll find him if we have to turn every stone between here and the Algerian border."

"You make him a priority. I want him alive and ready to

answer questions." He reached into his pocket and withdrew his lighter. "He is going to be an example to us all. Do you understand me?"

Josefina nodded. "Yes, Don Guillermo."

"Questions?"

"No, Don Guillermo."

"Get to work." He leaned back in the seat.

Josefina left the car, and the others got in.

Suero glanced in the rearview mirror. "Where to, Don Guillermo?"

"I want to go to the Hotel Colón to talk to the manager."

Suero nodded and put the car into gear. As he pulled away from the curb, the sigils blew away from the vehicle like leaves in the wind.

Shadows lengthened over the Plaza de Cataluña, where the Hotel Colón dominated the square. Suero parked the car and started to get out.

Guillermo shook his head. "You and Bernardo wait with the car. This won't take long. Miquel, come with me."

As they walked up the Plaza's stairs, Guillermo ran a soldier's eye over the Colón's façade. It took him a mere moment to realize what drew his brother to this particular hotel.

Put a machine gunner in that window beside the last O and they'll command the square.

Miquel's gaze flickered upward before he turned to look over the Plaza. They were thinking the same thing.

Guillermo paused and drew a cigar from his breast pocket. He snipped the head and took his time lighting it. "Can you get a few of our people on the staff here? Lesser nefilim if possible. Jordi will look right over them."

Miquel nodded. "Consider it done. We'll trace his movements in the major cities and find what other hotels he has frequented. If they have strategic value, we'll put them under surveillance."

"I'll leave that to you."

They continued on their way. In the lobby, the desk manager ran a practiced eye over their clothing. He adjusted his tie and offered them a professional smile. "How may I help you?"

Guillermo opened his coat and removed Jordi's sketch. He slid the page across the desk along with a banknote worth a hundred pesetas. "Have you seen this man recently? I understand he was in room 220. George Abellio."

"Are you with the police?" The manager palmed the money.

"Pretend we are," Miquel said.

The manager examined the sketch. His smile locked into place.

He knows something.

Miquel traced the sketch's hair with his fingertip. "His hair is coppery. Not as auburn as Don Guillermo's"—he tilted his head toward Guillermo—"but still a very deep red." He withdrew his hand, and as if by magic, another bill appeared on the paper.

The manager's eyes widened at the banknote. He pocketed the money and then released the sketch. "Yes, yes, I seem to remember him now. He had a rather brusque personality. He didn't tip very well at all. I recall he received a package while he was here."

Now that is interesting. "Do you remember anything about the package?" Guillermo placed another banknote onto the desk. "Big? Small? Maybe where it's from? Who it was addressed to?"

"Small enough to conceal in a pocket." The manager swiped his palm across the counter and the money disappeared. "I wasn't here when it was delivered, but it seems to me that the postal stamps were German." He frowned and stared at the ceiling as if the answer might be written overhead. "Yes, the address is right there on the tip of my memory."

Miquel rolled his eyes and pushed a fourth banknote onto the counter.

The manager's smile broadened. "I remember now. It was addressed to Sir George Abellio in Avignon, France, and the package was mailed from Offenburg."

Six kilometers from Durbach. "Thank you, sir. You've been most helpful."

He and Miquel didn't speak until they were outside once more.

Miquel said, "Our last intelligence indicated Jordi was in Belgium, but it seems he has moved to France."

"Who could possibly be sending Jordi packages from Durbach?"

"The Grier brothers? But how the hell would they know about him? Or how to find him?"

"That's a damn good question." It was a riddle. A riddle with a loose end, and he had but one clue. He fingered the jacinth in his pocket as they reached the car.

"Take us home, Suero." Guillermo got inside. He withdrew the gemstone and leaned forward, tapping Bernardo's shoulder with his knuckles. "You didn't get a good look this morning. Does the stone trigger a memory for you?"

Bernardo held out his hand and Guillermo passed the jewel to him. He turned the jacinth first one way, and then another as if he intended to fashion a bezel for the gem.

A flicker of recognition lit his gaze. “I was a blacksmith in that incarnation. I fashioned the jewelry for Sir George. He wanted two brooches.” His profile was as hard as granite. “The jacinth represented George, the emerald represented his lover.”

Brooches could be mailed in a small box. “And who was his lover in that incarnation? Lucia?”

Bernardo turned his head toward the window. “I don’t remember.”

Guillermo narrowed his eyes. *Liar.*

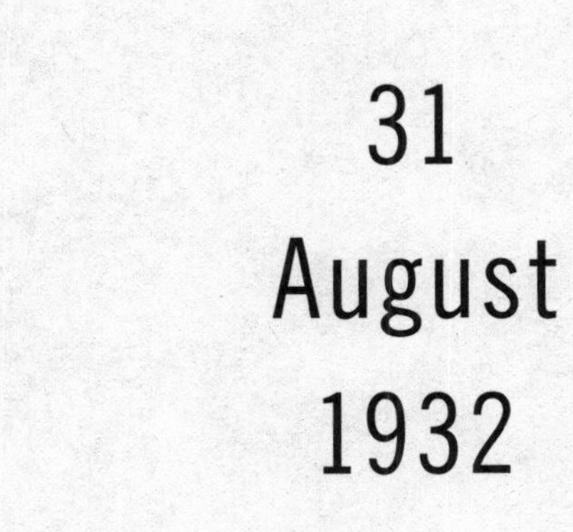

31 August 1932

and the night came down

[9]

SANTUARI, SPAIN

Guillermo and Bernardo buried Lucia in the middle of the night at a crossroad so she couldn't find her way back to them. Like crushing an enemy's larynx, it was an ancient custom, one that Guillermo wasn't sure would work, but he didn't care. An ample number of his nefilim were superstitious enough to be frightened by the act, and if that kept some of them on edge, it was worth it.

When they were done, they loaded the shovels into the bed of the lorry. Bernardo drove. As the truck rattled along the road, he said, "I remember when Jordi was Sir George and I was Bernard. Sir George came to me and commissioned the brooches."

Guillermo lit a cigar. "Go on."

"He was very specific as to how he wanted them to be designed. They had to be identical."

"What did they look like?"

"The center was a Messenger angel with open hands. I

was told to set the emerald in the angel's left palm and the jacinth in his right."

"Can you sketch it for me?"

"I think so. Probably should have young Rafael do it. He's quite the artist."

"He is very talented. We're going to leave him out of this."

"Of course, Don Guillermo."

"You said the jacinth represented George, and the emerald represented his lover."

"I remember seeing Diago wear one of the brooches. Except in that incarnation, he called himself Yago. The names are very close, so I didn't want to say anything in front of Miquel. He gets jealous."

"An astute observation on your part, but you're not Miquel's keeper. Next time I ask you a question like that, tell me."

In the glow of the truck's instrument lights, Bernardo flushed a dark red and nodded. "I'm sorry, Don Guillermo."

"You thought you were doing the right thing, and your loyalty to your friend does you justice." He patted Bernardo's arm as the priest pulled into Guillermo's yard. "Do you remember anything else about that incarnation?"

"George was king of the Inner Guard. I was in his retinue as a spy. So was Yago. He worked for you. I served as your liaison to him." He paused and thought for a moment. "That's all I can remember for now. If anything else comes to me, I'll call you."

"You do that." Guillermo got out and closed the truck's door as softly as he could. Leaving his boots on the porch, he slipped into the house.

Once in his bed, he fell into a deep dreamless sleep. He woke to Juanita bending over him. She gave him a sad smile and stroked his hair. "It's late."

He rubbed his eyes and checked the time. Nine. She'd let him sleep in. He had enough time to get dressed and have breakfast before they would have to leave for the funeral.

She kissed his forehead. "I'll fix you something to eat."

"No," he said, his voice gruff with sleep. "Just coffee. Coffee will be useful." He sat on the edge of his bed and rested his head in his hands.

After she left, he grabbed his robe and went to take a shower. The house was silent. As she normally did when such a catastrophe struck, Juanita had dismissed the staff so they could attend the funeral.

Twenty minutes later, Guillermo had donned a suit. He went downstairs to find Ysabel in the dining room with a cup of warm milk. Her unruly curls had been tamed into braids and a small black veil was pinned to her hair. Like her mother, she preferred pants, but this morning, she wore a plain dark dress.

"Let me see you," he said as he cupped her chin and tilted her face upward. *So young, yet she takes her role so seriously.* He adjusted one of her hairpins and said, "I need you to be my eyes and ears today."

She grew still beneath his touch.

"Everyone from town *should* be at the funeral. I want to know who doesn't come. Likewise, I want to know if someone attends the funeral and leaves early. Do you understand?"

A nod. "Why is it important?"

"It could mean they are making their escape while everyone else is distracted, or they might have a legitimate reason for being absent. We'll check them all to be certain."

"You think there are others like Lucia and Salvador?"

"Unfortunately, yes. This evening, come upstairs to my office and you can give me your first official report." He straightened her veil and stood back to examine his handiwork. "There. That's better."

Someone knocked at the door. Juanita emerged from the kitchen and took off her apron. Like her daughter, she wore a dress and a black veil pinned to her hair. "I'll get it."

Guillermo pointed to Ysa's glass. "Finish your milk. I'm going to get some coffee."

By the time he returned, Juanita had escorted Miquel and Rafael into the room.

Guillermo raised his cup. "Have you had breakfast?"

Miquel nodded. "Yes, thank you."

Rafael toyed with a button on his dark jacket. The child hadn't seemed this fragile since he'd first come to Santuari a year ago. *He's so lost without Diago.*

Nonetheless, he met Guillermo's gaze and offered a shy smile. "Good morning, Don Guillermo. I'm sorry your friends died."

"Thank you, Rafael. They are your friends, too. You just didn't get a chance to know them in this incarnation. They will come again. Watch for them."

Ysabel left her chair and took Rafael's hand. They were a miniature bride and groom. *Only in dark clothes, and off to mourn instead of celebrate.*

"May we walk together, Papá? Rafael has never been to a funeral before."

"Of course you may."

Ysa gripped Rafael's hand in hers and led him to the foyer. "Don't worry, Rafael. I will show you what to do."

Guillermo had no doubt she would. When he was sure they were out of hearing range, he whispered to Miquel, "Bernardo talked to me last night." He quickly relayed his midnight conversation with the priest.

Miquel winced when Guillermo mentioned Yago and George, but otherwise made no sign the information bothered him. *Of course, he's a professional to the bone.*

Guillermo continued, "You and I are meeting after the funeral. Grab Suero this morning and whisper in his ear that I want him and Bernardo to search our archives for any information they can find on the nefilim during the twelfth century. Then you and Suero meet me in my office at six."

Miquel nodded. "I will."

"We should go," Juanita said.

"Okay. Okay. I hate these things." He followed his wife to the front door, where he took his hat and put it on.

They left the house and walked toward the church, their pace slow to accommodate the children. It was a short walk and the day was pleasant with the seeds of autumn in the air. If they hadn't been off to a funeral, it would have been a lovely outing.

They soon reached Santuari's church, L'Església de la Mercè. The structure possessed none of the elegance of her Barcelona sisters, but her beginnings as a Christian edifice no longer mattered. Now she served Los Nefilim. The grottoes beneath her floors stored their relics and their manuscripts. Their guns. L'Església de la Mercè was old.

Los Nefilim were ancient.

The nefilim parted somberly for Guillermo and his family. He went to Enrique's wife to offer his condolences before moving to Valeria's lover, and then to her sister. He escorted each of the family members to their seats himself before he took his place with his family behind theirs.

After the church and graveside services, small groups lingered on the lawn. Guillermo walked among them, wondering how many more of his people were connected to Lucia, Salvador, and Jordi.

Who will be the next one to stab me in the back?

One he felt sure of in his loyalty, Miquel, wandered over to him. "I talked to Suero and Bernardo."

"Good. I don't know how late we'll be tonight. Bring Rafael. He can spend the night with Ysa."

"He'll want to bring his cat."

"That's fine. Cats are nice. They catch rats, and we seem to have a few."

[10]

STRASBOURG, FRANCE
PLACE DE LA GARE

Diago left the train in Strasbourg and stepped aside to let the crowd pass as he got his bearings. With his back against a column, he watched the mortals hurrying to their next destination. Their murmurs ebbed beneath a squall of brakes and the tick of massive engines to momentarily drown the faint ghost-music in his head.

Although his nightmares had receded somewhat, the violin still hummed in the back of his mind, reaching into his bones, urging him toward his destination. As he neared Durbach, the composition became clearer, less distorted. His desire to reach the Grier brothers grew intense. He was tempted to brush aside Guillermo's order and cross the border without wasting time with Rousseau's people. If he did, he could be in Durbach as early as this evening.

Then what will that say about me and my ability to follow orders? He steadied himself and tried to think of a plausible reason to circumvent Guillermo's directive. After working the problem from several angles, all that filled his mind was the mental image of Guillermo's disappointment.

Besides, what kind of example would I be setting for Rafael? No, his responsibility both to Los Nefilim and his son was clear—he had to play by the rules.

When the last of the crowd moved toward the station's main hall, and Diago was certain he wasn't being followed, he pushed away from the column. He needed to find his contact.

The tobacconist's shop wasn't hard to locate. Inside, a young woman wearing a red bow tie served a customer. Tall and heavy-boned, her mortal ancestry spoke more of German lineage than that of the French. She possessed long golden hair, which she had twisted into braids and twined around her head. Incredibly blue eyes were set over her ruddy cheeks. While her pupils didn't reflect as strongly as those of the angel-born, she possessed enough fire in her gaze to indicate she was nefil. Like Suero, she was one of the lesser nefilim, born of a minor spirit.

She finished with her customer, and as he exited the shop, she turned her attention to Diago. "May I help you, sir?" Her pleasant voice made him think of water murmuring over stones.

He took off his glove so she could see his missing pinkie and the ring containing Prieto's tear. "A pack of Lucky Strikes."

She gave his hand a quick glance, followed by a much longer examination of his face. "Oh, I'm sorry, sir. I'm sold out of that brand."

Diago noticed five packs of Lucky Strikes in plain view. She'd given him the correct response. Now it was his turn. "What would you recommend?"

She placed a pack of Gitanes on the counter. "On the house."

"Thank you, but I insist on paying." He gave her enough francs to cover a day's pay—part of Guillermo's arrangement with Rousseau. The Inner Guard took care of their own in more ways than one.

"Thank you." She smiled and let her gaze travel over him from head to foot. "I leave work at five," she whispered.

He nodded as he pocketed the cigarettes. Leaving the shop, he headed straight for the men's room. Choosing the last stall, he latched the door and opened the package. Inside, a sliver of a note was wrapped around the first cigarette:

Hotel Hannong.—L

He knew the place. Checking his watch, he realized they had over an hour before their meeting. Diago lit a cigarette and then burned the note over the commode. He flushed the ashes and transferred the rest of the cigarettes to a silver case before he left the stall. They would make a nice gift for Miquel.

Outside the wind carried the scent of the nearby river and tugged at the brim of his hat. After being so long on the train, stretching his legs felt good. He took an extra turn around the block before entering the lobby—both to shake loose any tails, and because it was pleasant to do so.

No one seemed to be following him.

He still had some time, so he went to the hotel's restaurant and ordered an early dinner. While he waited for his meal, he removed the brooch from his pocket and examined it again.

Further attempts to divine the stone had resulted in the same images. *Like a film stuck on repeat.* Whenever he tried to move past the vision in the tower, the ghost-music would resume, growing louder until it drowned his ability to concentrate. *Because it doesn't want me to see the truth.* Although even now he wasn't sure if "it" referred to the music or to the entity that manipulated the song.

The waiter interrupted his musings with his meal. Diago pocketed the pin and ate while watching the door. At five fifteen, his contact entered the lobby. She still wore her uniform.

He raised his hand and caught her eye. She breezed past the maître d', who did his utmost to intercept her path. He rushed behind her, but before he reached them, Diago rose and held her chair.

"I'm sorry, sir." The flustered mortal bowed and apologized. "She doesn't belong here."

Diago took several francs from his pocket and pressed them against the man's palm. "Bring the lady a glass of wine."

"Whiskey," she said as she smoothed her trousers.

"Whiskey," Diago reiterated as he passed more francs between them.

With an exasperated sigh, the maître d' nodded and gestured to the waiter.

Diago took his seat. "You have me at a disadvantage, madam."

She extended her hand over the table. "Lorelei Fischer."

Lorelei. Of course, the maiden of the rock. He took her hand and brushed his lips across her knuckles. "You are a long way from home, Lorelei Fischer."

"The Rhine is my home."

"I should have known." He released her. "Diago Alvarez, at your service." The waiter came with her drink. When he left, Diago asked, "Or are you at mine?"

She gave him a Mona Lisa smile over the rim of her glass. "How soon must you cross?"

"As soon as possible."

"Pity. I've never had the occasion to seduce one of the daimon-born."

"You don't have one now." He picked up his glass with his left hand so she would see his wedding band.

"I thought that was for show."

"It is. It shows you I'm married." Guillermo said to cooperate with Rousseau's people, but he never indicated that Diago should tarry. "So how are we crossing? And more importantly, when?"

She tossed down the shot and stood. "I have a car waiting."

"Excellent." Diago paid his bill and followed her to the street.

Her Citroën was a two-seater from the mid-1920s. A pair of Wellingtons stood at attention on the passenger floorboard. Lorelei got into the driver's seat and nodded at the boots. "You might want to save your shoes. Where we're going will be marshy."

She cranked the car, and the engine purred as if it had rolled off the assembly line yesterday.

He changed quickly and put his shoes in his bag. "How did you guess my size?"

"We didn't guess." She pulled away from the curb. "Guillermo's secretary gave it to us."

Of course he would. It was the kind of detail Suero was known for.

Once they had merged into traffic, she said, "I'll get you across the river and to your car on the other side. From there, you're on your own. There's a map in the glove box. Take it."

Diago found the map and opened it. His route was marked in red. "Durbach is about twenty-one kilometers from Kehl?"

She nodded. "When you've finished your assignment, follow the same route home. In Kehl, you'll find a pub called the Angel's Nest. Our people there will get you back into France."

"Got it." Diago tucked the map into his pocket.

Lorelei drove them out of the city and into the countryside. "Madame Rousseau said you served in the Great War."

Diago tapped a restless rhythm on his thigh. "I did," he said, hoping the curtness of his response would dissuade further questions.

He was glad he wasn't required to go farther west, where his memories would be ignited by the sights and sounds of familiar places. This portion of the Alsace-Lorraine had belonged to Germany prior to the war, so he'd had little occasion to visit. Here, he could be a tourist, a traveler, unburdened by memories.

Lorelei glanced at him and dashed any hopes he had of avoiding the subject. "What was it like?"

"I try not to think about it." And for the most part, he was quite successful. *Unless I'm trapped in a nightmare or stuck in a car with a curious youngster.*

"They say the shelling was so intense that the sound waves bent reality in some areas."

Again, Diago recalled crouching in the trench—the memory returned unbidden, unwanted. *The bombs pounded the earth around his unit. Mud and shrapnel pelted them in a hailstorm of violence. The shelling went on as one hour bled into another. The air shimmered in hues of black and gray—a bruised wave of sound crashing over them, drowning them in a cacophony of destruction . . .*

The car hit a pothole deep enough to jounce them in their seats. Diago opened his eyes. He wiped his palms against his slacks and let the wind carry the memory away.

As his heartbeat gradually slowed, he knew it was time to shift the conversation to a different theater. Lorelei wanted to talk about the war. Fine. Unexploded munitions were still a very real threat even in the areas outside the Zone Rouge.

Other dangers lurked for the nefilim.

"Speaking of the shelling, do you have any idea how severely the bombardments damaged the old glyphs on the German side?"

Lorelei considered the question. "We suspected a broken sigil was the cause of the music, but no one has gotten close enough to confirm it. The Black Forest was a bad place before the Great War. It's extremely unstable now."

"Wonderful," he murmured.

"Keep your eyes open and your voice strong." Lorelei eased the car around a family of farmers and their horse-drawn cart. "Trust your instincts. You'll be fine."

He hoped she was right. They fell into a comfortable silence as Diago noted landmarks. Thus far, he'd been extremely lucky in being able to follow the plan to the letter. But one never knew when circumstances might call upon him to improvise. He hoped Rousseau's Néphilim would get him home, but he didn't intend to count on them.

The ghost-music faded from his consciousness, conspicuous in its absence. "Does anyone still hear the music?"

She shook her head. "Those who could hear it said that it stopped a few weeks ago."

Because it found me, Diago thought, and the idea felt so right, he didn't discount it. Just as he had attempted to hunt the composer, so had the musician cast a wide net, searching for the one nefil who might respond to the music's siren call—*and that nefil is me.*

This wasn't some random anomaly, then. The missing Stradivarius coupled with the presence of the brooch seemed to confirm his suspicion that he was the target. Now he just needed to find a way to turn the tables on his hunter. The secret lay in connecting the brooch with the music, and the answer to that mystery lay with the Grier brothers. Of that Diago was certain.

They rounded a curve and the Rhine lay before them—the waves bristling and blue in the late afternoon light. The water was, Diago suddenly realized, the same color as Lorelei's eyes.

She steered the car down a little used road and the river dipped momentarily out of sight. At the bottom of a hill, the Rhine came back into view.

Stopping at the end of the road, Lorelei cut the engine and got out. "Now we walk."

With his bag in tow, he followed her into the brush. The winding deer path led them to a marshy cove, where the waves lapped against the shore.

While they waited for the sun to go down, Diago found a rock that was reasonably flat. He hummed a tune, the vibrations of his song burning green and black in the air. Shaping a sigil, he used the stone's coarse grains to reshape the rock's natural outline. Soon he had smoothed a bench that would easily seat them both.

Lorelei watched him. "I've never seen a nefil who could do that before."

"You've not known many daimons."

"But you're angel, too. That's what they say."

"Sometimes the things they say are true." He settled comfortably on the rock. "There is enough room for both of us."

"No. I have no one to impress tomorrow, so I can get as dirty as I like." She took off her shoes and left them on the bank, immersing her heels into the river. A few heartbeats passed in silence, and then she asked, "Is your wife sweet-voiced and kind?"

Diago considered lying, or simply saying yes, but something in her question provoked him. He recalled Miquel's kiss at the train station. *How does it feel not to hide?* "He's my husband," he said before he could change his mind. "And his voice is strong, a baritone. Miquel has much heart and sings what we call cante jondo, or deep song."

No sooner had the words left his mouth than a rush of freedom sent his pulse hammering, and he suddenly understood Miquel's need to push societal boundaries. He watched her face carefully, waiting for her reaction as she absorbed his statement.

Her lips parted, and he fully expected her to laugh, or to call him a marica, or whatever might be the current French slur for a fairy. Instead her mouth opened in a slow smile. "How delicious. Is he dark like you, this husband?"

"He is Gitano, so he is darker."

"And his eyes?"

"They are the color of a starless night, and they are as deep as the sky."

She made a low sound in the back of her throat, not quite a hum, not quite a word. "Maybe someday we can all meet and get to know one another's songs intimately."

"Miguel doesn't have sex with women."

"Only men?"

Diago nodded.

"What about you?"

He shrugged. "I have loved both men and women."

"And now you are true to Miquel."

"Yes." *But not always.* Without thinking, Diago reached once into his pocket to touch the brooch. Rather than guilt, he encountered only curiosity. *What happened with the owner of this love token is in the past. Miquel is my present and my future.*

Lorelei turned back to the river and gazed at the water. "How very sweet," she said, sounding as wistful as the waves kissing the shore. "Unfortunately my sisters, who remain in the Rhine, won't care about your husband."

"Are they rogues?"

"Deadly rogues, even to a nefil such as yourself." She scanned the river and kept her voice low. "If they sense your presence, they will try to sing you into their arms."

"Can I help you somehow? Perhaps by rowing?"

She shook her head. "I'll get us across swiftly, because I know how to navigate the river. You would be in the way. All

I need for you to do is remain still and quiet. Don't answer their song. If they pull you under, I will try to save you, but they are strong, and I am only one. Do you understand?"

Her message was clear. If the Rhinemaidens took him, he was on his own. "I do."

[11]

SANTUARI, SPAIN

Guillermo lined up the three drawings on a corkboard: Jordi's composite, Bernardo's rough illustration of the brooch, and the sketch of his nightmare. He dragged two chairs in front of the arrangement just as his wards chimed.

Ysabel, still dressed in her funeral clothes, entered the office.

Guillermo turned so that his body blocked the images on the board. He wasn't quite done protecting her from the adult world of Los Nefilim. *Baby steps . . . for both of us.* Besides, the less she knew about Diago's situation, the less she would inadvertently give away to Rafael. "So what did you find out?"

"Everyone was there, Papá." She sounded disappointed.

He gave her a couple of beats, and when she didn't continue, he decided to prompt her. "Let me ask you this: When we sang our glyph to honor our fallen comrades, did everyone join their auras with our song?"

She frowned at him as if he'd asked her to decipher the ligatures of a complicated glyph. A greater length of time elapsed before she admitted, "I don't know. I was so busy looking to see if everyone was there, I didn't pay attention to their songs." She thought about her answer for a moment and then flushed pink. "You're teaching me something, aren't you?"

Guillermo nodded. "You have to be aware of your surroundings on multiple levels. It's the hardest skill you'll have to develop, but it'll save your life." *And your foray into spycraft won't proceed until you've proven to me that you can watch your back in a crowd.*

"I'm sorry, Papá. I let you down."

"Don't be sorry. You learn more by making mistakes than you do through success." *As long as those mistakes don't kill you.*

"Do you know who didn't add their auras to our song?"

"I do." In fact, Sofia Corvo already had the pair under surveillance. If either of them were reporting to Jordi, Guillermo would soon know.

Eager now, Ysa leaned forward. "Will you tell me who they are?"

"No. That information is on a need-to-know basis." When she started to protest, he raised his finger. "And you don't need to know."

The sigils alerted them to someone approaching the office. Miquel entered and then paused with his hand on the doorknob. "Am I interrupting?"

"No." Guillermo gestured for him to come in. "Ysa was just heading downstairs to find Rafael. Weren't you, sweetheart?"

"Yes, Papá." She started to leave and then hesitated. "We will talk later?"

"Later." Guillermo pointed to the door. "You're dismissed."

Miquel held out his hand to her as she passed him. "What is this? No hello? No good-bye?"

She gave his palm a light punch. "Hello, Uncle Miquel. You will teach me that new guitar riff tomorrow?"

"Absolutely."

She turned back to Guillermo. "I will do better for you next time, Papá."

"You did fine." *You stayed out of harm's way.*

"Good night." She opened the door and then disappeared down the stairs.

"Good night, my little star," he murmured to the empty landing. "She frightens me," he confessed to Miquel.

Taken off guard by the statement, Miquel glanced at the door. "Who? Ysa?"

"She has to learn to temper her greed for power; otherwise, it'll be her downfall just as it was Jordi's." *And mine*, he thought as he moved away from the corkboard. "I worry that she is growing too fast."

Miquel shrugged. "I don't know. I believe Diago has swerved in the opposite direction and is too overprotective of Rafael."

"It's a difficult balance to strike," Guillermo conceded as he straddled his chair and crossed his arms over the back.

Miquel wandered over to the board. He hesitated in front of the nightmare sketch. "That dream you dreamed," he whispered. "It's not a prophecy, is it?"

"Usually prophecies come in the form of symbols. That"—he pointed at Diago's image—"might be my own fear talking." *He's worried and that meeting with Christina did nothing to allay his fears.* He motioned for Miquel to sit. "Speaking of Rafael, how is he doing . . . you know, with the funeral and Diago's absence?"

Miquel dragged his gaze from the drawing and found his cigarettes. "We talked this morning, and he seems okay. He's too much like Diago sometimes—he holds his darker emotions close. Although he is excited about spending the evening here. He brought his map with him."

"Oh? What kind of map?"

"He drew a picture of Diago on a train, and Eva cut it out for him. Every day, he moves the train up the map into France. He doesn't know it but Eva is teaching him geography."

"That's cute." Guillermo chuckled and produced his lighter. Flicking the lid, his demeanor grew serious once more as his gaze returned to the drawings.

The wards around the stairs chimed again and Suero entered.

Cheeks flushed from the climb, he carried a file along with his pad and pen. "There isn't a lot, but Bernardo and I did find some information."

Guillermo nodded to him. "Good. We'll start with you."

Suero took his place at the conference table and opened his file. "In eleven hundred and forty-five, the nefilim were too few to command an entire country. The Inner Guards worked more like crusaders, guarding the Thrones' territories at the angels' bidding. There was a Sir George recorded as king of the Western Inner Guard after the Carolingian War. Sir George carried the blessing of the Thrones and was anointed with the ring you now wear." Suero flicked a worried glance in Guillermo's direction.

The blessing of the Thrones. Guillermo clicked his lighter open and shut. The golden signet and its deep red stone caught the light. The band was thick and the sigils cut deep. *Everyone covets the power of the Thrones; very few can endure the obligations of the role.* The responsibility for the lives under him was a heavy burden, and today, he buried two in his care, having failed that duty. Outwardly, he showed no emotion, but inside, the thought of his failure pierced him.

But this is my destiny, and I will not run from it.

He said to Suero, "Jordi and I have battled for the kingship of our nefilim since our firstborn lives. You're not going to shock me."

Clearing his throat, Suero continued, "Sir George and his nefilim were sent to oversee the angels' interests during the transition period after the Treaty of Verdun. Rogue angels were a problem during those years."

"Those are the details we need," Guillermo whispered. He shifted his attention to Bernardo's depiction of the brooch, glaring at it as if he could somehow wrest the answer from the angel's lips. A memory teetered on the edge of his consciousness, ready to roll straight into his brain, but he couldn't seem to nudge it in the right direction.

Something about the angel . . .

Definitely a Messenger and not a Throne or Principality, whose physical appearances all differed dramatically.

Miquel's cigarette burned low. He crushed it in the ashtray. "The angel."

"What about him?"

"We're looking for a link between Jordi and Diago." He pointed at Bernardo's sketch. "Who is the angel? An adviser?"

Guillermo frowned at the sketch. "Suero?"

"The records didn't indicate an angelic adviser was ever given to Sir George."

"Now isn't that interesting." He made a mental note to check with Juanita as he thumbed the lid of his lighter. "Bernardo told me the brooches were made as love tokens. Sir George wore one, Diago the other."

"Not Diago," Miquel murmured. "Yago. His name in that life was Yago. I was Michel and you were Guillaume. Yago found us in Verdun after the war. I remember now. Rumors of a rogue angel led us to George's estate, and we followed them, because we needed a way to bring down George and return you to power."

"Good, good, your account matches Bernardo's." Guillermo recounted what the priest had told him.

Miquel straightened. "Bernardo, then Bernard, couldn't get close enough to prove the angel existed. Which is why Yago offered to help us."

Guillermo stroked the lighter's warm metal. "It was his way of reaching over the incarnations to undo the harm we did to one another in our firstborn lives." He focused on the composite of Jordi's face. "We had to be careful, because George's castle wasn't large. It began as a simple house built on the eastern side of a lake."

As he spoke, the office receded and Guillermo recalled the necessary details of the last time he saw Yago alive.

Throughout the years George added to the original building until the main house looms over the two-story structures that comprise the northern, southern, and western sides of the courtyard. The northeastern and southwestern corners have towers of equal height, and there George's banners snap in the wind. A moat is the castle's only fortification. More isn't needed. The angels and the daimons have engineered a period of peace, and they abide by the treaties still freshly carved in their hearts.

Guillaume observes the castle grounds from the crossroad and marks each building's location in his mind. Later, he will sketch the layout from memory.

He camps in the hills and waits until he sees George ride out on a hunt without Yago at his side. Wearing a heavy cowl, Guillaume poses as a traveler whose horse needs a shoe. While he waits, Bernard sends his stableboy to bring Yago to the stables on some pretext.

Keeping to the shadows, Guillaume watches for any evidence of the angel. The rogue remains out of sight.

The stableboy emerges from a side door with Yago on his heels. They cross the courtyard and soon reach the barn.

Yago walks past Guillaume without a glance and directs his question to Bernard. "What's the matter?"

"It's your mare. She's not eating." Bernard heats the shoe for Guillaume's horse in the fire and gestures for the stableboy to attend the bellows. "Take a look at her and let me know if she's getting colicky."

Guillaume notes the brooch Yago wears over his heart. It seems he has made some friends.

Yago goes to the stall that holds his mare. He murmurs to the animal, soothing her with his voice.

Bernard bellows out a hearty drinking song. He keeps the rhythm by pounding on the shoe.

Guillaume wanders away from the forge. His horse is stabled adjacent to Yago's mare. When the stableboy is distracted by Bernard, Guillaume eases into the stall, speaking in whispers to his mount. He sings a glyph for silence over the door. Through the slats, he sees Yago has placed a similar sigil on his stall.

Yago runs his palm across the mare's chest. His lips barely move as he speaks. "Christ, but your audacity is astounding. If George finds you here, he will burn you alive for the joy of hearing you scream."

"Relax. George will hunt until he kills something, and I've chased most of the game deep into the forest." Guillaume strokes his horse's coat and then murmurs sweetly, "Speaking of my brother, are you sleeping with him yet?"

Yago gives him a vicious side-eye through the slats. "He doesn't remember me from our previous incarnations if that's what you want to know."

"Michel sends his love."

The malice leaves Yago's glare at the mention of Michel. "Carry mine back to him."

"I will. Now tell me what you've found so I can get out of here."

"Bernard is right. There is a rogue Messenger here. He calls himself Frauja. He shows himself to George and to me. No one else."

Guillaume is relieved. Now Yago can leave George's castle. "Don't endanger yourself anymore. Come back to Verdun."

"Do you want to be like your brother, wearing a paper crown, or would you prefer to hold the secret of the Key?"

Guillaume's heart stammers. "What are you saying?"

"Frauja has promised to teach us."

"The angels say nefilim's voices cannot replicate the Key?"

"That was the point I made, but Frauja proved me wrong.

He guided us through the initial chords and I saw into another realm, Guillaume, I *felt* it. It seemed like a mirror of this mortal realm, but *different*."

Guillaume's breath feels tight in his chest. "Different how?"

"The sky was still blue, the grass green, but the colors were more vibrant, more *alive*. This"—he gestures to the air to indicate the mortal realm—"feels like an illusion, surreal." Yago moves closer, his voice dipping low beneath Bernard's song. "Whatever else Frauja has done, he has given me a beginning." He leans against the boards that separate the stalls, his dark green eyes sparkling with excitement. "Do you know what this means? If we can control the pathways between the realms, we can affect the outcome of battles, or hide within the creases of time, or even create new worlds where there is no war."

Outside the stall, Bernard's hammer rings against the shoe. The blows emulate the steady tick of time. The temptation to ask Yago to stay is heavy. Were Guillaume the one taking the chance, he might go forward, but he doesn't want to risk Yago's life. They have come so far from the disaster of their firstborn lives when Solomon's greed for power destroyed Asaph and himself.

"Take the beginning," Guillaume whispers. "You can compose the rest later. We'll let the rogue answer to the Thrones. Keep your eye on the goal: we have enough evidence against George. The Thrones will give me the blessing of the signet."

"What if the Thrones find Frauja has done nothing wrong? He will leave and make his proposal to another nefil, one who won't have your best interests at heart."

The temptation returned. *He has Satan's silver tongue. He*

knows just want I want and how to dangle the prize before me. "No, it's too dangerous. Come away in the morning."

But he doesn't count on Yago's obstinance.

"I'm staying. This is my choice. I'll decide the risks I'm willing to take. If I can solve the mystery of Frauja's intentions and get the Key, no one will ever again question either my loyalty to the angels, or your rights as king."

Although Yago's whisper is barely audible, Guillaume hears his determination loud and clear. Yago intends to overcome the traitorous reputation he earned in his firstborn life when he was Asaph. Nothing will stand in his way.

Guillaume considers the plan. He doesn't like it, but he sees no way to quickly dissuade his friend. "Three weeks. If you're not back to us in three weeks, we will come for you."

A faint smile touches Yago's lips. "Watch for me," he whispers, and then he is gone.

Gone from me forever in that incarnation, Guillermo thought as the memory faded. He quickly related the events to Miquel and Suero. "That answers the portion of Christina's reading where she spoke of rushes on the floor, a red cote, and the banner."

"But the dark sounds Christina mentioned . . ." Miquel crushed one cigarette and lit another. "What do those mean?"

Guillermo pointed at the map on the wall. "That goes back to our black pin. Let's stick with what we know—Jordi is after Diago."

"Why? Revenge?"

"Jordi wants the same thing I want—the Key. And the one person who holds the secret to that song is Diago." As he spoke, he realized he should be excited. After all, isn't that what he'd wanted throughout this incarnation? To initiate the memories that would lead Diago to the Key?

Yet instead of excitement, he felt nothing but dread, because now he recalled the ending of that failed adventure. "I remember now. I was uncomfortable with Yago's plan from the beginning. You don't know how many times in those three weeks I almost went back, but I was determined to show him that I trusted his judgment. I didn't listen to my instincts, and though I regained my sovereignty over the Inner Guard, it came at the cost of Yago's life. Frauja killed him. I remember Yago dying in my arms."

Miquel glared at Jordi's picture.

He remembers, too. Guillermo turned to Suero. "Do you know if Diago has reached Strasbourg?"

Suero nodded. "My French contact said he and Lorelei left the train station this afternoon."

Too late to stop him. The only other course of action was to send backup. "I need someone I can move in a hurry to go after him. Who do we have?"

Miquel tapped one finger against the back of his chair. "Our nefilim in other countries are in deep cover. I can't pull them without jeopardizing entire operations."

He gave Guillermo such a look of naked hope that Guillermo knew all he had to do was speak the word and Miquel would call one of them in. *But I can't speak that word . . . not for Diago, not for anyone.* They had too much at risk.

When Guillermo didn't answer him, Miquel went on, "Sofia asked for more people to hunt Muñoz, so I gave them to her. Until tonight he was the priority. I've got Bernardo and Carme working on wards and they've each got five nefilim under them. Before Lucia turned traitor, I might have recommended eight to ten more, but they're closely associated with either her or Muñoz. Until they've been cleared, we can't send them."

Guillermo listened with a frown. Usually in a situation where they suspected a rogue angel, he would call Queen Jaeger and ask her for help. But this wasn't a normal situation. Given Rousseau's espionage and the fact that he'd slipped Diago into Germany under Jaeger's radar, calling Die Nephilim's queen was out of the question. "What else?"

"Juanita could take out a rogue angel."

Oh, yes, she could, but sending her meant leaving Santuari at risk, not to mention Ysabel. Guillermo refused to leave his daughter unprotected. *Because it's only a matter of time before Jordi sees Ysa as a threat.* Knowing that Diago would approve of his decision to protect Ysa's life over his didn't lessen Guillermo's guilt. "If Jordi has found some way to free Frauja, they might attack Santuari, so I need Juanita here."

A muscle ticked along Miquel's jawline. "I'll go after him, then. You can afford to lose me."

Guillermo shook his head. "Bravery and love are mighty weapons, Miquel, but they don't stand a chance against the power of an angel. No."

This is mine to do. Diago had no one outside of Los Nefilim to watch his back. *And he has watched mine all these centuries.* The problem was that Diago was a soldier within the Guard, and Guillermo wouldn't go after one of the others. *I need a reason—one that no one can refute.*

Fortunately, the answer to this one was easy. He pocketed his lighter. "Ilsa Jaeger has had every opportunity to inspect the wards in that region, but she hasn't. Our Treaty of Versailles doesn't give Rousseau the right to enter Jaeger's territories; however, with the information we have gathered, I can justify a clandestine review. If I get there and find evidence of Frauja's presence, I am entitled to summon the judgment of the Thrones on him. This I must do to fulfill my oath to protect the mortal realm."

In spite of his protest, a measure of hope returned to Miquel's face. "You're needed here."

"You can take care of Los Nefilim for three days. Tell them I've gone north to see Rousseau on a matter."

"But Jaeger . . . she will kill you if she catches you in her territories."

"She will not dare. My status is my protection. If I die in Germany, Jaeger has to explain what happened to the Thrones, and they will hear the lies in her voice. Then they will destroy her and Die Nephilim."

Suero cleared his throat. "In spite of the Thrones, kings and queens of the Inner Guards don't always follow protocol."

"Thank you for that history lesson." Guillermo tossed a glare over his shoulder and Suero blushed scarlet. "I know Jaeger. She will make me miserable for a period of time, but she won't risk killing me. We'll do it like this: I'll let you know when I cross the border. If you don't hear from me within forty-eight hours, Juanita will summon the Thrones."

Miquel considered the plan. "What if she uses you as a hostage to make demands on Los Nefilim?"

"I would hope that you would be smart enough to free me before you had to concede to any such demands."

Lifting his hand in surrender, Miquel capitulated, but Guillermo didn't miss the relief in his friend's eyes. *He won't admit it, but he's terrified for Diago.*

"How are you getting into Germany?" Miquel asked.

"By stealth. I don't want to test any of these theories if I can avoid it." *Or risk my own life needlessly. Diago isn't the only one with a child depending on his guidance.* Los Nefilim needed him; Ysabel needed him more. *Especially with my brother hovering over us like the shadow of death.* "My goal is to get in and out before Jaeger knows I'm there. If things get messy, then my story to Jaeger is simply this: we had intelligence about a rogue angel and conferred with Sabine Rousseau. We agreed that discretion was necessary until we established the facts. Rather than report the disturbance directly to the Thrones, I offered to serve as intermediary so we could determine the truth of the allegations."

Miquel looked suitably impressed. "Did Diago teach you to lie like that?"

"Yes."

"We're still sticking our necks out here."

"That's what happens when you're on the verge of war. The stakes keep rising." Guillermo paced around the table and placed his hand on Suero's shoulder. "Have Alfonso fill my Suiza with petrol. She's fast enough to beat any train."

[12]

THE RHINE

Diago and Lorelei had the cover of a moonless night, but she showed no inclination to begin their journey until midnight, when she gestured for him to follow her. Silently, they uncovered her boat. Diago helped her push it into the water.

Lorelei rowed with long easy strokes, knowing when to pull hard and when to drift; she guided the boat as if she swam beneath. They were over halfway across when he heard the first siren's song: a deep haunting sound, like the wind in pain, crying, crying . . .

Lorelei hissed through her teeth.

Another voice joined the first and they harmonized: "Come down, come down, come down into the river, into my arms so sweet . . ."

He felt their song touch his will, but the effort was as tentative as a tug from Rafael on his sleeve. *They think I am a mortal. They're not trying very hard.*

Before the sirens could strengthen their song, however, Diago felt another assault on the back of his mind, and it kept him focused. The violin screeched in raw discordant notes.

Someone dropped it. His heart stuttered at the thought. *Fine. Drop it, destroy it.* He didn't care as long as the hateful thing finally ceased its hold on his mind.

In the ensuing silence, something bumped against the side of the boat. He tried to convince himself it was flotsam. Then the sirens' song came again, louder, more intense. He recalled the angel Candela and the golden snake she'd used to enchant him. *I will give you a song . . .*

He resisted the urge to lash out at either the Rhinemaidens or the ghost-music from the violin. Even a sigil of protection could work against him by alerting the Rhinemaidens to his supernatural nature. On land, he might fight them and win. On the river, he would be helpless as the water filled his lungs.

Under normal circumstances, his voice was his life, but silence was his best weapon now. Lorelei was his protection. He had to trust in her.

"Almost there." Lorelei's mutter caused him to open eyes he hadn't realized he'd closed.

No lights burned on the opposite shore. They might as well be floating into an abyss.

He needed something to occupy his mind, something to drive the Rhinemaidens' insistent song from his thoughts. Shutting his eyes again, he counted backward: *five hundred, four hundred and ninety-nine, four hundred and ninety-eight . . .*

The first Rhinemaiden whispered, "Come into my arms and I will sing you a song."

. . . four hundred and ninety-seven, four hundred and ninety-six . . .

The squawk of the violin struck his consciousness. Diago envisioned a hand grasping the neck. Long tapered fingers—*lovely hands*—took their position on the strings—*white so white, could a mortal be so white?*

He forgot to count. Lethargy suffused his limbs. It would be easy to slide beneath the waves and sleep . . .

"In my arms," sang the second maiden. Cold fingers caressed the back of his hand.

Then came the attack and punch against the strings—*three quick jabs of the bow: strike, strike, strike*—and then a pull, slurring to become the malignant leitmotif Diago now called his own. The violence of the music wrenched him from the somnolence induced by the Rhinemaidens' song. Arpeggios reverberated blue and deep like the waves sloshing against the side of the boat.

The tempo picked up speed, the beats coming harder, faster, like the slap of fins *(oars)* on the water. The wind touched his face, and the promise of a melody was whispered to his mind.

Return to me, and I will give you a song, wept the violin with long, sweeping strokes that floated over the night deeply, sadly, moving into a dirge. The notes faded, softer and softer, shifting into a tremolo so that the bow quivered over the strings until the water drowned the last of the chords, and five heartbeats passed with nothing but the splash of oars to fill the quiet . . .

Then the bow resumed its attack and punch against the strings *(strike, strike, strike)* and the boat hit the opposite shore, and the night came down, and the world went black, and silence descended quick and hard, like the stillness that follows the falling of a bomb.

Diago jerked awake.

Lorelei sat across from him, her hair plastered to her cheeks with sweat. "Don't move," she whispered.

Something splashed behind him. River water showered his back and hair. He didn't turn.

Minutes passed. The Rhinemaidens remained silent. Then came the chirrup of a cricket. A frog answered. The night sounds resumed around them, a clicking whirring chorus of normalcy.

Lorelei's arms trembled from her exertion. "We can go now."

He followed her gaze. A few errant waves testified to their passage; otherwise, the current flowed unbroken until a figure surfaced in the center of the river. It could have been a shapely thigh or hip, or perhaps a smooth branch rolling before being pulled under by the current. Without the light of the moon, it was impossible to tell.

Behind him, Lorelei whispered more urgently, "Let's go before they come back."

He helped her drag the boat free of the current. She motioned for him to wait, and then she disappeared in the darkness. While she was gone, he retrieved his bag and set it on a rock.

Whatever he might think of Durbach, someone in that house had just used the violin to save his life. Another moment beneath the sirens' song and he might have slipped bonelessly into the water to be carried below the waves.

Or did he misinterpret their motives? He recalled the savage strikes of the bow against the strings. *Did they save me for the sake of love . . . or revenge?*

He still hadn't found an answer by the time Lorelei returned with a tarp. Diago helped her cover the boat. Once they were done, she took the lead. A kilometer later and on higher ground, they reached an old barn. Beneath an overhang was a newer model Citroën—this one a four-door.

"I'll leave you in the morning." She passed him the keys and then got into the back, closing the door quietly.

Pocketing the keys, he took off his boots and climbed into the front. "Should we keep a watch?"

"We own the property from here to the river. Rousseau has some of our people patrolling to make sure no one steals the car. We're safe here tonight."

"We're never safe," he whispered.

If she heard him, she made no sign. She gave a mighty yawn and stretched out on a blanket someone had already spread over the backseat.

As Lorelei's breathing slowed, the violin began to play again, tugging at Diago's will like a playful child. *Return to me.*

Diago gritted his teeth against the urge to turn the key in the ignition and start the car. He stared at his reflection in the windshield and whispered, "Lorelei?"

"Hmmm?"

"Do you remember your past lives?"

"Sometimes . . . in my dreams."

He fished the brooch from his pocket and ran his thumb over the darkened emerald. "I used to say the past is dead and that we should leave it in its grave. But now I don't know if that was wise at all."

"We can't run from our past, nor can we allow it to consume our present. Make peace with it, Diago." She turned her back to him, the leather creaking beneath her. "Make peace with it and go to sleep."

He wished he could, but rather than sleep, all that came to him was a melody, crying like the wind in pain.

1
September
1932

watch for me

[13]

AVIGNON, FRANCE
13 RUE MUGUET

It was after midnight when Jordi left the train station. He called Nico to let him know he'd arrived, and then he managed to find a cab. Tossing his bag in the backseat, he climbed inside and said, "Université d'Avignon."

It was a common destination, not one that would be remembered. As the driver pulled away from the curb, a light drizzle misted the air.

Jordi sniffled and withdrew his handkerchief. He wiped his nose. A few drops of blood spattered the cotton. As soon as he finished this job, he would cut back on his cocaine intake and give his body time to heal. Moderation and good management were the keys to utilizing the drugs properly. Unfortunately, circumstances dictated he remain alert, so cutting back wasn't an option right now.

Soon, though. Soon.

The French territories under the control of Sabine Rousseau and the members of her Inner Guard weren't quite as dangerous to him as Guillermo's Spanish holdings, primarily because Rousseau's Guard had taken enormous casualties during the Great War. Her numbers were fewer, so she used her nefilim more judiciously. As long as Jordi kept a low profile and everything in Nico's name, he evaded her scrutiny.

Sniffing again, he daubed his nose and then returned the handkerchief to his pocket. As he did, the brooch reminded him of its presence by pricking his finger. Jordi withdrew the pin and rubbed the pad of his thumb over the angel's face.

The driver turned on the radio. Jack Hylton's orchestra rolled through the ever cheerful "Happy Days Are Here Again."

Happy days were indeed coming his way. Jordi's trip to Spain had been fruitful in many ways.

The taxi's wipers slushed back and forth in a hypnotic beat that ran counterpoint to Hylton's jazzy bounce. As the singers rolled into the refrain, the music grew distant. A thin wave of static seeped in beneath the radio's signal.

From the radio's speakers, a chorus of voices murmured, "*Stein, strick, gras, grün.*"

The driver made no sign he heard the strange words, nor did he adjust the dial. He tapped his fingers on the steering wheel and hummed along with the song.

He can't hear the static or the voices. Jordi clutched the brooch and listened.

The voices continued, "Do you remember, George?"

Yes, of course he remembered. He almost answered aloud. A discreet glance at the burly driver told him that would be a bad idea. If the driver suspected Jordi was crazy, he'd put him out, and midnight cabs were hard to find. This wasn't Barcelona, where Jordi could strong-arm the mortals undetected. Avignon was his home, and a low profile kept him and his Nico safe.

Watching the dark streets, he turned his thoughts to the words *stein*, *strick*, *gras*, and *grün*. The letters *S.S.G.G.* were engraved on the Germanic nefilim's daggers and stood for "stone, string, grass, green." The word *stone* represented the jewels that corresponded with the color of the nefilim's songs; the string their ties of loyalty to the angels; the grass represented the physical plane they guarded; and green symbolized the color of the lights defining the border realms.

A dream clung to the corners of Jordi's mind. The angel on his brooch smiled and moved his lips in time with the murmuring voices.

"Remember . . ."

George walks to the courtyard gate, his soldiers standing at attention. He recognizes the ceremonial dagger—*stein, strick, gras, grün*—holding the parchment to the post, because he carries an identical one on his hip. He rips the parchment from the blade. Guillaume has summoned him to vehmgericht, the secret trial by which the nefilim rooted out traitors to the angel-born.

George's bowels loosen with fear as he reads his brother's accusations. Guillaume claims Frauja is a rogue angel, who is wanted by the Thrones for war crimes committed during the Carolingian War. He accuses George of aiding the enemy. If the Thrones find George guilty, they will force him to abdicate.

The page shakes in his hand. His fingers tighten around

the hilt of the dagger and he jerks it from the post. He's been betrayed by someone in his ranks. *But who?*

The ring of the blacksmith's hammer causes him to turn. The blacksmith, Bernard. A relative newcomer, he had only been at the castle for a year. He made the brooches and obviously recognized the significance of the angel.

Is the smith a spy? Both possible and probable, George decides. Bernard saw anyone who came or went through the castle gates. In spite of his size, he remained circumspect about his presence, watching—always watching.

What has our friend Bernard seen?

It wouldn't hurt to arrest him. Question him. If the blacksmith is innocent, then all will be well for him. *But if he is guilty, I will make an example of him before the others.*

George gestures to one of his guards. When the man draws close, George tells him, "Arrest Bernard. Take him to the cellars and silence him behind your strongest wards. I will question him later."

The guard bows and goes to gather enough nefilim to execute the task. George feels better and more in control. Unlike Guillaume, George has an angel on his side. He'll first root out the traitor and then the information to destroy Guillaume's credibility with the Thrones.

A man in black strides across the courtyard. It is Yago.

George wonders briefly if Yago might be the spy, but immediately discounts the idea. Yago hasn't left the castle grounds since his arrival, and except for a few random instances, he is rarely out of either George's or Frauja's sight. His heart is in his compositions, nothing else.

No, it can't be Yago. He calms at the sight of the other

nefil. Yago has the cunning George requires to outsmart Guillaume. Yago will know what song to sing.

"*Yago* turned on you," whispered the voices through the radio. "He said he would join his song with yours. When the crucial moment came, he forswore himself."

"No." Jordi breathed the word through parted lips. *He said he loved me.*

The driver's gaze flicked to the rearview mirror. "Monsieur?"

Jordi ignored him. Gripping the pin until the metal edges bit into his flesh, he closed his eyes and tried to delve deeper into the memory. Sweat shimmered across his brow. *What happened next? What did Yago do?*

Not what he did. What he *didn't* do.

He was supposed to help us and for some reason, he turned on us. Jordi sat straighter in the seat as the recollection settled in his mind. Bernard *was* a traitor, but so was Yago.

Diago.

Suddenly the note that accompanied the brooch made sense. *We will judge the traitor in vehmgericht.*

He was going to Durbach to judge the traitor Diago.

"Monsieur?" A note of exasperation touched the driver's voice. "We have arrived." A fact the driver seemed very relieved to announce.

Jordi opened his eyes and blinked. They were at the corner of rue Louis Pasteur and rue de Rascas.

"Are you all right, Monsieur?"

"Yes," Jordi whispered. "I'm fine. It's been a long journey." *And I have miles and miles to go.*

A quick glance at the meter told him his fare. He shoved the brooch back into his pocket and withdrew the francs. Dragging his bag behind him, he escaped the driver's bored concern.

Chill air smacked his cheeks and drove his somnolence away as he followed the rue Rascas in the dark. Reaching into his pocket, he cupped the brooch. Now everything made sense. This was why Diago was with Guillermo and Miquel in this incarnation.

He was never loyal to me.

"Son of a bitch," he muttered. "I'd almost trusted him a second time." Had it not been for the brooches and the memories, he would have.

Jordi drew the brooch from his pocket and kissed the angel's face. Frauja had saved him from making a grave error.

But did I make a mistake in giving Diago the other brooch? Under the lingering influence of the opium dream in Barcelona, it had seemed like a good idea at the time.

Jordi's pace faltered. "Shit," he muttered to the falling rain.

Diago would divine the emerald—only a fool wouldn't, and he would remember . . . *what?*

Christ, but why didn't Frauja come to me? Why send brooches and that cryptic note? The answer was obvious. *Because he can't. He's locked away and the only thing that can release him is . . . the Key.*

The realization jolted Jordi to a halt. Frauja had taught Yago the Key. *He tried to teach both of us, but it was Yago who best understood the complex arrangement.*

"And it is Diago who must remember that song in this incarnation so he can use it to free Frauja." Whether he damn well wanted to or not.

Jordi exhaled, relief flooding his body with warmth. He started walking again. Sooner or later, he would have given Diago the brooch in order to trigger his memories, so if he did err, it was a minor issue. He couldn't worry about it now.

Looking up, he realized he had arrived at his destination. Inside, Nico's rooms were warm, and a kettle whistled cheerfully from the kitchen. The coatrack already contained a fedora and a jacket, both of which belonged to Nico.

Jordi almost forgot the lateness of the hour. He closed the door and shook the rain from his garments. "Have I told you lately how much I appreciate you?"

"Not nearly enough." Nico smiled as he went to the stove and removed the kettle. "Who else would make you midnight dinners?"

Like Diago, Nico possessed a slight build and moved with a dancer's grace. A full century younger than Jordi, Nico was Michelangelo's David with black hair that hung in a tousled mess over his pale forehead. The shadow of a beard darkened his jaw. He wore a robe and pajama bottoms, nothing else.

He assessed Jordi with eyes as gray and somber as his song. "Are you well?"

Jordi had no doubt that his bloodshot eyes stared from a face too pale. "I'm fine."

Nico didn't argue, though it was clear from his frown that he considered Jordi's condition anything but fine. Nonetheless, he tactfully changed the subject. "Did you get the package I sent to Barcelona?"

"Yes, everything arrived safely. Were you able to arrange my car?"

Nico nodded. He made the tea and brought the meal to

the table. "Stay long enough to eat something. You've grown too thin again."

Jordi tossed his bag to the couch and joined his lover. The sight of the food ignited his hunger. A manila envelope beside his plate kindled his curiosity.

He sat and opened the folder, which was thin, but he hadn't expected much. "What did you find?"

"Not a lot," Nico admitted as he took the chair across from Jordi. "After I got your telegram, I contacted a friend in Berlin. Fortunately, the Griers were in the public eye, so he put together the story and gave me some dates. Since it was in a major paper, the university librarian was able to make copies from their microfilm records."

Jordi stopped eating and met Nico's gaze. "Let me say again how much I appreciate you."

"You can show me later," Nico said with the hint of a smile. He reached over and tapped the folder. "It seems that Karin Grier, the mother of the boys and Joachim's wife, suffered an aneurysm in nineteen twenty-eight. When she fell, she struck her head against a wall in the ballroom at Karinhall."

A grainy newspaper shot of the family showed Joachim and the two sons standing around Karin's chair with the stiff formality of knights guarding their queen. A hint of amusement glittered in Karin's eyes as if someone would soon reveal a joke.

Jordi chewed his food while turning the pages. "That's a very sad story."

"Sadder still, the eldest son was accused of murdering her. It seems they were arguing when Karin suffered her *an-*

eurysm. The crack in the ballroom mirror indicated that her head hit the wall with quite a bit of force."

"I bet that played well on the society pages."

"Be glad that it did." Nico indicated the article on top of the pile. "They found Karl innocent based on Rudolf's testimony."

The clipping showed Karl on the courthouse steps with Joachim beside him. Both father and son stood in poses of righteous vindication. The younger son, Rudolf, had sidled apart from them and stared into the distance.

"That"—Jordi tapped Rudolf's miserable expression—"is the face of a liar." His money was on Karl as Karin's murderer with Rudolf pressured into establishing an alibi.

The comment elicited a small shrug from Nico as he lit a cigarette. "After the sensational trial, the father sold their Berlin house and returned to Karinhall along with both of the boys. Publicly, Joachim supported his son, but those who attended the séances said they felt a great tension between Joachim and Karl."

"Séances?"

Exhaling twin streams of smoke through his nostrils, Nico nodded. "Joachim wanted to make contact with Karin to know the truth behind her death. The only spirit he ever summoned was the specter of bankruptcy."

"When did he die?"

"Earlier this year. Heart attack."

Jordi closed the file. *Heart attack, my ass*. A boy who cracks his mother's skull against a wall isn't going to patiently wait for his father to die a natural death.

Nico continued, "Karl has taken over the estate, which is

in considerable debt. My Berlin source mentioned that Karl meets regularly with an attorney in Offenburg. He's trying to forestall foreclosure by his creditors."

"Anything else?"

"I'm afraid not." Nico finished his cigarette. "Stay the night. You need some rest."

That he did. He hadn't slept in more than catnaps since Monday. The meal left him feeling drowsy, and the rain continued to fall. In the warmth of the apartment, he considered the proposal, but the urgency he felt in Barcelona returned. *Especially now that I know I'm on the trail of a traitor.*

On edge now, he pushed away from the table. "I can't."

"Would you like for me to come with you?"

"No. I'm going to take a shower and change. Then I'll go." He felt Nico's gaze on his back as he went to his bag and retrieved his cocaine.

"I'm worried about you," Nico said.

The cocaine turned to fire in Jordi's sinuses, and his words came out sharper than he intended. "I'm fine."

"I didn't say you weren't. I just said I'm worried." Nico lit another cigarette. "I wish you would trust me."

Jordi took off his shirt and compared Nico to Diago. The two shared similar personalities. *But there is a fire within Diago—something wild and dirty and sweet—that my Nico lacks.* Nico was safe. He grounded Jordi. *He's what I need. Diago is dangerous and that is what I crave.*

"Jordi?"

"What? Do you think I have a lover stashed in Durbach?"

Usually the accusation won Jordi a scoff or a smile. Tonight, Nico didn't take the bait. He glared at Jordi's attempt at humor. "This trip is all very sudden and disconcerting."

The cocaine sharpened Jordi's anger. He didn't like Nico's tone. "This is what we must do to remain ahead of my brother."

"I understand that. But you're pushing yourself hard." Nico's cloaked reference to the cocaine didn't go unnoticed by Jordi. "It could affect your judgment in adverse ways."

Wadding his undershirt into a ball, Jordi threw it at the couch and whirled on Nico. "Why are you trying to pick a fight with me?"

"You once told me that you valued my insight. Was that flattery? Or did you mean it?"

"I don't say things I don't mean." Jordi kicked off his shoes and took off his pants.

"Then listen to me." Nico lowered his voice until he was barely audible. "Word on the streets is that members of Los Nefilim are hunting Salvador Muñoz. Further word states that Guillermo knows you're involved in the murder of three of his nefilim, because you left a calling card stuffed in the larynx of one of the corpses."

"How did you find out about that?" Jordi asked.

"I heard it through one phone call. The dead travel fast, my love. The nefilim faster. What the hell were you thinking?"

A blast of rage filled Jordi's chest. "Why are you questioning my judgment?"

Nico flinched but didn't back down. "Benito called to check in. He made it to Lisbon. When I asked him why he was in Portugal, he told me about Salvador and the jacinth."

"Good." Jordi calmed at the news. Benito was one of the spies Jordi had planted in Santuari. It was sheer luck that he'd been on assignment in Galicia when Lucia was captured.

"No word on the other two in Santuari?"

"Not yet, no."

"You can relax. Everything is going according to plan. I needed to distract Guillermo to give my people time to leave the country. The jacinth was all I had at my disposal. I'd hoped that he would chase me and leave Salvador alone. Unfortunately, my brother's web is large."

Jordi folded his trousers, running the crease between thumb and forefinger, and offered Nico a smile. "Besides, I've been watching Guillermo from the shadows for almost a century now, biding the moments while gathering my forces. We are as ready as we will ever be, Nico. It's time to bring this fight into the light."

Nico winced and turned his gaze to the ashtray. Only then did Jordi realize how full it was. *He's smoking more because he's concerned.*

Jordi went to his bag and retrieved a file. "I didn't just go to Spain to harass my brother. The Sanjurjada is over."

"I don't know what that means."

"That's what the Spanish called General Sanjurjo's coup against the Republic—it just means the Sanjurjo affair." Jordi sat beside Nico and opened the file to reveal a neatly typewritten report and several photographs. "All that matters to us is that the Spanish courts found Sanjurjo guilty of treason."

Nico shrugged. "So they'll execute him."

"No. He's a decorated general, a hero, awarded the Legion of Honor for his part in the Rif War." Jordi took one of Nico's cigarettes and lit it. "As such, President Azaña commuted the sentence to life imprisonment. Sanjurjo is going to the penitentiary at Dueso. I've got two nefilim who have offered to work there as guards, and a third, who is going in as a prisoner."

"You're going to help Sanjurjo escape?"

Jordi shook his head. "That would draw too much attention to him and to us. I've got another person in Madrid, who is very close to a politician by the name of Alejandro Lerroux." Jordi sifted through the photographs until he found the face of a distinguished-looking man with white hair and a thick mustache. "Lerroux has a history of corruption and scandals."

"He can be bought."

Jordi winked.

Nico smiled suddenly. "I love intrigues. I think I see where this is going. You intend to have your person persuade Lerroux to free Sanjurjo, because that will put Sanjurjo in your debt."

"Brilliant! Then we whisk Sanjurjo to . . ." He brushed his fingers over Nico's hair. *I miss watching him sleep.* "Where? Where would you like to live next?"

"Someplace warm."

"We whisk Sanjurjo to Portugal and gather our forces to restage the coup, but this time, we plan carefully to ensure its success."

"So Sanjurjo will help us win?"

"Maybe. Frankly, I'm not as enthralled with him as the mortal generals are. They want to install him as president, but I don't like him. He's rash, undisciplined, too convinced of his own invulnerability. The only reason Sanjurjo is valuable to me is because he is my link to another mortal general"—Jordi tapped the photograph of a smug-looking man with a toothbrush mustache—"Francisco Franco. He is cautious and brutal—two qualities that will serve us well against Guillermo. However, Franco won't move against Sanjurjo, so we suffer the peacock while we groom the lion."

"And why would Franco join forces with us?"

"We have the money along with the German and Italian connections they need to acquire more planes and ammunition. In return, the rebels will destroy the Republic's forces and their equipment. Then we use the mortals to smash Guillermo and his nefilim."

Nico studied the photographs. "How long will it take?"

"Five mortal years, maybe six. Time is nothing to us. This will be mere days to the nefilim." Jordi cupped Nico's chin and gently forced him to meet his gaze. "We're going to have such a beautiful war. Are you still with me, Nico?"

"Always."

"I know you're worried about the drugs," he whispered in Nico's ear. "You think they're affecting my judgment. They aren't." But that was a lie. Were it not for the opium, he might not have given Diago the other brooch as quickly as he did. Still, Nico didn't need to know that. "As soon as I've finished this task I'll stop. I promise."

Nico nodded, but his gaze slid away.

He doesn't believe me. "I will," Jordi insisted. "For you and for no other reason."

"You swear it?"

"I swear it." Jordi kissed him gently before he stood and then went to the bathroom. Closing the door, he took a fast shower. By the time he emerged and dressed, Nico had cleared the table.

Jordi grabbed his bag and met his lover at the door, where Nico gave him a set of car keys.

"It's the white Monastella Cabriolet on the corner. I tried to find you something with style."

Jordi brushed his fingers over Nico's throat. "Watch for me."

[14]

THE FRENCH COUNTRYSIDE
BETWEEN MONTPELLIER AND NÎMES

Guillermo chased the night through the rain. During the day, he'd pushed the Hispano-Suiza H6C to speeds over a hundred and sixty, blowing through the Spanish and French countryside. The car was a bullet and Guillermo's pride.

Night had slowed him and the rain more so. Somewhere between Montpellier and Nîmes, the steady beat of the Suiza's wipers lulled him. Sleep threatened to take him. He sipped coffee from his open thermos and cranked the radio's dial through the static until he found a late-night station playing Duke Ellington's "Mood Indigo."

"Now that's better," Guillermo muttered as he capped the thermos and set it within easy reach.

Ellington's work was little known and hard to find in Europe. Guillermo had never heard of the American until Diago recently brought him to the nefilim's attention. Of course it had been Diago—he was always chasing new sounds.

Guillermo settled himself in to listen. The tires of his car hissed beneath the beat. A muted trombone moaned through the top of its register. Behind it came a clarinet low and sweet. The trumpet played the middle tones of the piece, inverting the registers listeners were used to hearing and creating the auditory illusion of a fourth instrument.

A sax, Guillermo thought drowsily as he hummed along. *It sounds like a sax*.

The music leaking from the radio groaned and twisted, becoming sharper, more intense. The speakers crackled. An unpleasant buzz drowned the music. The sound resonated through Guillermo's eardrums, vibrating across his sinuses like a razor.

Suddenly wide awake, he slowed the car. Beneath the hum of the engine, he heard hushed voices. They murmured in a dozen different tongues—*German, French, English, Spanish, Russian*—in a babble.

The only constant was the static, corralling the voices and nudging the syllables together. Like a master puppeteer, the razor sound threaded its way through the other voices until it was finally able to form words.

"You're already too late," they said in unison, a hellish chorus held together with the band saw voice.

Chills rose across Guillermo's arms. He gripped the steering wheel until his hands ached. *I'm not dreaming. This is real.* He reached down and shut off the radio.

The speech oozed from the speakers uninterrupted. "You murdered Yago with your greed, your lust for power. Now Diago will die for a song."

Coils of oily black liquid seeped from the dial and dripped to the floorboard. Something cold brushed Guillermo's ankle before it slithered beneath the pedals.

The engine suddenly roared and the Suiza shot forward. White lines rushed beneath the fenders. The road beyond the reach of his headlights became the open mouth of an abyss.

The speedometer edged over sixty, then seventy kilometers per hour—far too fast for the weather and the road. Guillermo lifted his foot from the accelerator.

The dial edged over a hundred.

"Die," whispered the voices.

Guillermo jammed his left foot on the brake. The pedal hit the floor. No resistance. The brakes were gone.

"No. No," he muttered through gritted teeth. His life would end one day. "Not like this." He fought to bring the car under control.

"No, no," the chorus mimicked him. "It ends like this. Die."

"Fuck you." Slamming the clutch to the floor, Guillermo knocked the gearshift to neutral. In defiance, the speedometer drifted over one hundred and ten.

The radio popped and spit sparks into the floor. The acrid smell of burnt wires filled the car.

A wide puddle loomed ahead. No avoiding it. Guillermo held the steering wheel with his left hand and reached over the dash. He traced a sigil of protection on the misty windshield and charged it with the vibrations of his song. Fiery shades of orange and red spread across the glass, seeped down the dash, and turned the interior into a blaze of light.

The dead radio crunched back to life in another burst of static. Timpani played the opening of Siegfried's funeral march.

The car hit the puddle. The front end slewed left. Instinct took over.

The music soared. The world spun. It seemed like hours.

It was less than a minute. Guillermo turned into the skid, wrenching the wheel left, then right as he fought to correct the car's trajectory. With every spin, the blaze of his sigil flamed brighter, making the car seem as if it was on fire. On the radio, Valhalla burned.

Guillermo's foot found the brake again and this time it responded. He pumped the pedal. The tires grabbed the road. The car skidded to the right. The passenger side struck a hedge. Leaves showered the air in his wake, and with a thump, the slide finally came to an end.

The engine died. The radio gasped in short bursts of static reminiscent of dying flames before it fell silent. The only sound was Guillermo's ragged breathing. He clutched the steering wheel as the fires from his sigil faded into the night.

Through the open window came the sound of rain and the tick of the cooling engine. Guillermo took the keys from the ignition, grabbed his torch, and got out to inspect the damage. He walked around the car until his knees stopped shaking and his step was firm once more.

Opening the hood, he moved the light over the motor. Remnants of his sigil sparked and popped around the cylinders. It was impossible for him to see whether his wards had killed . . . *What? What the hell was that thing?* After centuries of fighting both fallen angels and daimons, he'd never encountered anything quite like this.

Back in the car, he restored order. The thermos and bag had fallen to the floorboard. He rooted in his case until he found a flask of orujo. Two hefty swallows of the liquor quieted the last of his nerves.

That was luck. Another hour on the road, and his reflexes would have been too slow. He lit a cigar, drawing the nicotine deep into his lungs. Glaring at the radio, he tried to resurrect the creature's voice, but it was the accusation that returned to rattle him.

Your greed, your lust for power. It drives you now . . .

Was that why he'd allowed Yago to convince him to wait three weeks? Had his reluctance been because he wanted—no, hoped—that Yago would be successful?

"Maybe," he conceded. "But that's the past, and there is nothing I can do to change it." The present was his to control, and he damn well intended to avoid the mistakes he made as Guillaume.

But I've just made one by underestimating my adversary. He needed to understand how the attack happened and who, or what, initiated it. He quickly eliminated Jordi. His brother couldn't have engineered an assault like that with a legion of nefilim.

"Frauja?" Guillermo whispered the angel's name with a nervous glance at the radio. Of the two, the angel remained the most logical choice. Angels commanded the principle of fire and could channel their voices into radio waves.

Fine—but we locked Frauja away in another realm. That I do *remember.* The sigils binding that realm should have the same effect on the angel's magic as if he was imprisoned behind a soundproof wall.

Somehow he has managed to get through.

Guillermo needed to talk to Juanita.

Turning the key, he pumped the gas. The Suiza resisted, but he coaxed the vehicle back to life.

The radio's light remained out. *Take no chances.* He warded the radio and dash with protective sigils. Then, just to be safe, he did the same with the accelerator, brakes, and clutch.

He put the car in gear only to have the back tires spin. "Shit and bitter shit." Clamping the cigar between his teeth, he rocked the car between reverse and first gear until the vehicle gained purchase.

Back on the road, he remained especially attentive as to how the Suiza handled until he was certain no internal damage was done. Picking up speed again, he watched for the lights of Nîmes.

He had to make a phone call.

It was close to dawn when Guillermo finally found a service station. He parked beside the pumps. The attendant sauntered out of the building with a yawn.

"Do you have a public phone?" Guillermo asked.

"Inside." He nodded to the station office.

"Good. Fill it up and check the lines. I skidded in the rain, and I want to make sure nothing is damaged."

The man nodded and went to work.

Guillermo entered the station. An announcer's voice rolled through the radio on the counter. Assured that the station's mechanic was out of sight, Guillermo eased around the counter, switched the radio off, and then placed a protective ward over the speakers.

With that threat nullified, he turned to the public phone, which was in a narrow closet against the opposite wall. He squeezed his bulk inside and dialed the operator.

Juanita answered and accepted the charges.

Guillermo didn't waste time with pleasantries. "Help

me, my angel." Conscious of the operator on the line, he switched to Old Castilian—a medieval form of Spanish that bore the same relationship to modern Spanish as Old English did to English—and recounted the accident. "In my last incarnation with Diago, we shut Frauja away in another realm. I am certain of it. So help me understand how he can send his voice into my radio."

Juanita was silent for a moment. Then she said, "If the resonances from the Great War damaged a glyph in the area, as we suspect they did, then he might have garnered enough of an opening to transmit his voice into the mortal realm. From what you described, he is not using sound waves, because they wouldn't carry over such a great distance. The only way he could project an attack into France is by using radio waves. And this angel, who calls himself Frauja, is likely one of the Firstborn, so light would be his natural state of being."

"Yes, but conducting his voice over such a distance to direct it at me . . ."

"You don't understand, Guillermo. He's not using his voice. He designed an angelic glyph using electromagnetic waves, which he then channeled across mortal frequencies. He couldn't do that without help."

The mortals. That would explain the Griers and their involvement. Guillermo held the suspicion close. He didn't want to interrupt his wife's train of thought.

Juanita continued, "For angels to throw a spell of that magnitude across such a vast space is like shooting into the dark, hoping you hit the right target. That's why we rarely utilize mortal electronics—it's an imprecise technique that is more often a waste of energy."

"Then how did he make it work?"

"He must have something connected to you. Otherwise he is simply broadcasting to every radio tuned to that frequency."

An idea occurred to him. "Could he be using the Stradivarius?"

She made a sound of assent. "It would explain how he channeled the sigil directly at you. The violin belongs to Diago, and it carries a portion of his aura and his song. You've performed with Diago while he played the Stradivarius, so a measure of your aura would be entwined with his on the instrument."

"Okay," Guillermo muttered and shifted his position in the booth, "this is bad."

"Anything Frauja does on this realm will be intermittent," she tried to reassure him. "If I was in his place, my focus would be on shattering the damaged wards."

"So the odds of him striking Santuari?"

"Are slim. I've already begun to design sigils that will protect us. Now that I have a better idea of how he is working, I can strengthen them even further."

Guillermo exhaled with relief. That was one less thing to worry about. "Have you managed to find anything about this angel?"

"Nothing. The name is a generic word for god. It's a common alias used by several Firstborn angels."

Guillermo rubbed his eyes. *Shit and bitter shit again.* That was the second time she'd referenced Frauja as one of the Firstborn, who were the oldest and most dangerous Messengers. "Okay, okay. None of this is good. Any word from Diago?" Guillermo glanced over his shoulder.

Outside the attendant popped the hood.

Juanita said, "He met his friend. We're guessing they have crossed over by now."

And shit again. It's definitely too late to stop him. "How about our lost servant?" *My good lost servant Salvador Muñoz.*

"Still missing."

The attendant lifted his torch and shined the beam down into the engine. His body tensed.

"I've got to go," Guillermo whispered. "Kiss Ysa for me."

"I will, my love," said Juanita.

"Watch for me." Guillermo hung up and went outside. Although the day had brightened somewhat with the coming morning, pockets of shadows retained the night.

The attendant remained poised at the fender, playing his light over the engine.

"Is something wrong?" Guillermo asked as he neared.

The man gestured with the beam. "I don't know. Something down there is glowing. I'm worried you might have an overheated rod."

Guillermo took the attendant's light and shined it in the vicinity of the accelerator. A tentacle, wrapped in one of Guillermo's dying sigils, jabbed the air weakly.

The attendant said, "Can you keep an eye on it while I get my creeper? I want to slide under and take a look."

"Sure." As soon as the attendant disappeared into the garage, Guillermo leaned over the engine. He traced a curve, three sharp lines, and joined them with a ligature. He charged the ward with a soft growl. A thread of gold from his ring entwined with his song. He cast the glyph at the tentacle.

The new ward flashed once when it touched the creature. Ichor fell to the pavement beneath the car, curling in on itself before dissipating in a hiss of steam as Guillermo's sigils burned it. *That*, he hoped, *is the last of it*.

The attendant returned with the board under his arm. He reclaimed his light and dropped the creeper with a rattle of wheels. "It'll just take a second."

Guillermo nodded and stepped back.

Within minutes, the attendant rolled from beneath the car. "Must have been a trick of the light. You've got some dirt where you dug ground, but nothing appears to be broken or hot."

Guillermo thanked the man and paid him.

Behind the wheel again, he drove north and he drove hard.

[15]

GERMANY

A soft click undercut the cacophony of gunfire in Diago's nightmare. It sounded like the bolt of a rifle drawn back to insert a round into the chamber. His eyes snapped open, but he didn't move. *If someone has the drop on us, we're dead already.*

Everything was quiet. A moment passed and then two. No other noise accompanied the click that had awakened him.

His position limited his range of vision. Ignoring the protest of his sore muscles, he sat up and looked over the seat to see that Lorelei was gone.

A note rested on the folded blanket. He snagged the paper, which consisted of a few lines in her graceful hand.

> When you get to the road, turn left. I will see you on the other side. Watch for me.—L

He slouched in the seat with relief. *I heard the car door closing.*

From the corner of his eye, he glimpsed the brooch on the floorboard. Snatching it up, he caught the distant sound of drums *(bombs).*

Then the last vestiges of the nightmare receded into his subconscious. *But they're becoming more intense again.* A sense of gloom washed over him. He pocketed the piece and checked his watch, which had stopped, because he'd forgotten to wind it.

"This day isn't starting well," he muttered as he rubbed his eyes. They felt swollen and full of sand. *I need coffee and food, and I'll get neither of those things here.*

He tucked Lorelei's note in the pocket of his bag before he retrieved his shoes and socks and put them on. The boots remained beside the car where he'd left them the previous night. After stowing his bag and the Wellingtons in the trunk, he started the car and drove into the field.

Sunlight washed over a narrow path through the weeds, where the Citroën's tires had obviously bent the grass on the drive to the barn. Diago followed the trail to the road.

By the time he reached Kehl, he'd gotten a good feel for the bulky vehicle. He located the Angel's Nest but avoided the inn. If the German nephilim found him in their territories, he didn't want his steps traced back to any of Rousseau's establishments.

Instead, he chose a busy café and parked the car. No one gave him a second glance as he slipped into the lavatory. After a brief toilet, old habits from his days as a rogue took over, and he found a table at the back of the room.

At this hour, the patrons were mostly businessmen and a few women, all grabbing a bite before heading to work. A radio played folk music in the background.

As he set his watch, Diago realized it was early enough that he should be in Durbach by noon. If everything went well with the Grier brothers, he would have time to search for Guillermo's anomaly.

They'd planned for him to stay in Germany, at the most, forty-eight hours. If he managed to procure the violin today, that left him tomorrow to investigate the disturbance in the Black Forest. Not even Carme could argue against Diago's value to Los Nefilim if he cracked the mystery signified by the black pin. The idea lifted his spirits.

While he ate, he studied his map, noting alternative routes between Durbach and Kehl in case events went bad. Feeling somewhat fortified by the coffee and meal, he folded his map and went to the counter to pay.

On the radio, the lament of Johannes Brahms's "In the Still of the Night" played like some dark premonition. The café's door opened and two men wearing Sturmabteilung uniforms entered the restaurant.

Brownshirts. The fact that members of the Nazi Party's paramilitary wing wore their uniforms openly in the town disturbed Diago. The waitress's warm greeting did even less to reassure him. *It seems I've stepped into a snake's nest.*

A mirror behind the counter allowed him to surreptitiously measure the duo. The shorter, dark-haired man was mortal. His companion was a large nefil with white-blond hair and eyes the color of a mountain lake.

The nefil's cheek was pitted with shrapnel scars, which disappeared beneath his collar. On his right hand, he wore a heavy ring inscribed with sigils of power and an angel's tear of blue and ivory in the setting.

Noting the ring's dominant glyph, Diago realized the nefil

was one of Ilsa Jaeger's Nephilim. If he read the insignia on the nefil's collar correctly, he wore the rank of sturmführer—the equivalent of a second lieutenant.

No need to wonder about Jaeger's political affiliations, then. If she had seeded him into the Brownshirts as a spy, like Guillermo kept Bernardo in the church, the nefil wouldn't be openly wearing her glyphs.

That was the kind of detail Guillermo would be most interested in knowing. *As long as I can get out of here without being discovered.* It was a trick he intended to perform without magic.

Mercifully, the waitress was so taken with the blond nefil she made short work of settling Diago's bill before grabbing her pad and hurrying to the men's table.

Good, now to make for the door. Diago pulled on his gloves—both to cover Prieto's tear and to disguise his maimed right hand. Men with nine fingers were remembered. Knowing that, he always chose his clothing with care, and today, the habit served him well. His black gloves blended with the dark fabric of his coat so that anyone who glanced his way wouldn't immediately notice his missing pinkie.

If the lieutenant glimpsed the fire of the nefilim in Diago's eyes, then he would demand to know what brought Diago onto German soil. *And that will lead to questions I don't want to answer.*

He took his sunglasses from his breast pocket and slipped them on. As he stepped casually past the Brownshirts' table, he lifted his hat to shield his face. Just beyond them, he settled the fedora on his head and tugged the brim over his eyes. Each movement was perfectly natural and precisely timed.

He had almost reached the door when a hard hand landed on his shoulder. "Do I know you?" It was the lieutenant.

I didn't even see him rise. Diago tried to ignore the hammering of his heart. *Christ, what have I done to give myself away? Had they detected the slightest Spanish accent beneath my German?*

No, that couldn't be it. He mastered languages the way nefilim mastered songs, and he'd worked hard to make sure his German was flawless. Maybe that was the problem, maybe it was too flawless.

Too late to do anything about it now. He turned and faced the nefil. Relying on the sunglasses to obscure his eyes, he pretended to study the other man's face and then shook his head. "No, I don't think we've met."

"You're familiar to me. Something in the way you move." He edged closer.

That means he saw me from a distance. Diago relaxed somewhat. *Probably from a trench during the war.*

The nefilim had been like wraiths, flitting through the smoke on one deadly errand after another. Those quick movements distinguished them from the lumbering mortals.

Diago jerked himself from the memory. "I must apologize"—he glanced at the nefil's insignia again—"Sturmführer . . . ?"

"Heines."

The mortal Brownshirt rose and maneuvered behind Diago.

"Sturmführer Heines, but you've mistaken me for someone else. If you'll excuse me, I have an appointment in Frankfurt and I am already behind schedule." He turned to find the mortal blocking his path.

The man leered at him. "Are you a movie star, you wear your sunglasses indoors?"

"Doctor's orders." Diago offered the man a smile, glad the dark lenses hid his murderous glare. "I'm sensitive to sunlight."

"I think you're lying," said the mortal.

A hard note edged into Diago's voice. "You can think what you please."

Heines tapped Diago on the shoulder. "Do you have papers?"

Diago turned back to the deadlier of the two threats. As he did, he scanned the faces of the other diners. Most made no secret they were watching to see what Diago would do next. Nor did anyone seem motivated to intervene on his behalf.

He considered Heines's request. Legally, he didn't have to give the lieutenant the time of day, but to refuse might invite a visit by the local police. *And I can't rely on Guillermo's money and influence to bail me out of here.*

Diago reached into his coat with his left hand. He carried two sets of papers, and he was careful to give Heines the set with his German alias.

Heines scanned the documents and his frown deepened. "Herr Jacob Schwarz?"

"That is me."

Heines gave Diago a long suspicious look before asking, "What business do you have in Frankfurt?"

"I am an appraiser."

"What do you appraise?"

"Things of value." Diago held out his hand for his papers.

One of the diners snickered.

Heines's lip curled.

The other Brownshirt wasn't amused. "He's a slippery little Jew, isn't he?"

"I'm Catholic," Diago said. Not that he was, but it was his usual cover and matched his papers.

Heines sounded amused as he returned the documents to Diago. "Tell me, Herr *Schwarz*, do you believe in angels?"

He is toying with me, hoping I'll give myself away. Diago scoffed. "I believe I have to go." He nodded to both of them. "Gentlemen."

Heines followed him onto the street. The mortal remained in the café.

Of course, because Heines doesn't want a mortal to witness any altercation between us. Diago forced himself to maintain an unhurried pace. He reached his car and turned to face the nefil. "Is something wrong, Sturmführer Heines?"

The lieutenant drew close. His gaze flickered to the car's German plates and then back to Diago. "You're familiar to me, and I *will* place you."

If I'm lucky, not until I'm long gone from here. Diago got inside the car.

Before he could close the door, Heines grabbed the frame and leaned down, his gaze sweeping the interior and lingering on the blanket in the backseat. "This is your last chance. Who are you and why are you in Germany?" He punctuated each question with a tap of his finger on the vehicle's roof.

He's tracing a sigil. Diago made no sign that he noticed the nefil's spell. "My name is Jacob Schwarz. I am an appraiser on my way to Frankfurt to value a violin. That is all, sir. I bid you a good day." Diago tugged on the door handle, hoping Heines would get the hint.

The lieutenant smirked and slapped the roof with his palm before he stood back. "Fine. Have a pleasant trip . . . Herr Schwarz."

Diago yanked the door shut and started the car. As he pulled onto the street, he noticed the colors of Heines's song following his vehicle.

It was a tracking sigil. Although he'd expected no less, rage flooded his chest.

"Damn it!" He shoved the gearshift to second.

A quick glance to the rearview mirror assured him that Heines remained on the sidewalk. Blue sound waves spooled from his palm up and over the rear window to the roof of Diago's car.

The Brownshirt was clever: to counter the spell meant revealing his true nature as a nefil. *I've got to transfer it to a different vehicle.*

He started toward Frankfurt, sure that Heines and his mortal would eventually follow. He just hoped he could do this quick enough. Looking for a neighborhood where he could work undisturbed, he kept his eyes peeled for an opportunity. On the outskirts of town, he finally found an empty shed on the back of an industrial lot.

Highly conscious of the time, he pulled the car beneath the shelter and parked. He looked hard behind him, expecting the other nefil to show up any second. When no other car arrived, he took in his surroundings. From the next block came the sound of heavy machinery.

Perfect. The noise would mask Diago's song from other nefilim.

Sliding across the bench seat, he exited via the passenger door. Across the roof, the glyph crackled and writhed like an octopus.

"Goddamn it!" He smacked the hood with frustration as he circled the car. This was going to cost him time. *Just deal with it.*

He forced himself to calm. This was a problem that required finesse, not brute force.

The ward didn't appear to be a complex spell, but that made the lines no less potent. Strengthened by the magic of Heines's angel's tear, the threads glowed with malevolence. Were it not for his own signet with Prieto's tear, Diago would have no way to disable the ward.

Miquel will be so pleased when he finds out how his gift saved the day, Diago thought as he removed his gloves. *There will be no living with him.*

Resigned to his task, he nudged the outer band of the glyph with his fingernail. The ward's tentacles swirled and chittered in soft C notes.

Outside the shed, life moved on with a steady rhythm. Diago let the beats soothe his rattled nerves. He needed to work with care. An error on his part might trigger the equivalent of a tripwire, which could entail anything from maiming to death.

Minding the colors of Heines's ward, Diago sang a counternote and edged a thin spiral of his aura beneath the veins of light. Strands of silver from Prieto's tear joined the deep green and black of Diago's magic.

Working slowly, he manipulated the threads of his aura

until they came between a strand of indigo and ivory. The silver of Prieto's tear gently loosened the hold of Heines's glyph from the car's roof.

Diago chose the next thread and repeated the process. It was like defusing a bomb with a hair-trigger mechanism. The going was tedious, but Diago memorized each note within the sigil and eventually managed to work the tracking sigil almost free.

He checked his watch. Nine o'clock. The job had taken far longer than he liked, but Heines seemed to be taking his time beginning his hunt. *He probably can't slip away from his mortal without arousing his suspicion. Besides, why hurry, when he can stalk me at his leisure?*

But he wouldn't wait too long, of that Diago was certain. Removing his handkerchief, he wiped the sweat from his face and got back inside his vehicle. *Now to find another car to place it on.*

He took the road to Frankfurt. At least this way if Heines caught up to him, his alibi was intact.

An hour and a half later, he found a vehicle that matched his at a roadside inn. Parking beside the other Citroën, he got out and sang a sharp note as he swiped his hand beneath Heines's ward. Then he tossed the sigil onto the other car's roof, waiting to make sure it adhered to the metal.

Without missing a beat, he returned to his car and traced sigils on each of the windows to tint them with a smoky haze. The glyphs would lie dormant unless he charged them with his song. Then anyone looking into the car would simply see his silhouette.

Behind the wheel again, he continued toward Frankfurt for several more kilometers. He didn't want to return the way he had come. The chances were too great that he might pass Heines on the way back to Kehl.

A low constant fear clung to his throat until he found a turnoff leading to a back road going south. The winding route took him longer, and twice he got lost, but with fewer cars on the road, he could easily ascertain that no one followed him. It was almost five by the time he finally entered Durbach.

When he turned onto the mountain road leading into the Black Forest, he opened his window and let the sigils fly to the cold wind. A chill ran through him. He hoped it wasn't a premonition.

The sky turned leaden as Diago neared his destination. The forest thickened along the roadside and created a tunnel of greenery. Shadows clung to the trunks and obscured the ditches. The Black Forest earned its name with its dense pines, heavy with age.

According to Suero's instructions, Diago should be close to the estate. He slowed until he glimpsed the pale tongue of a driveway protruding between a pair of stone pillars. Pulling off the road, he shut off the engine and removed his sunglasses.

The house wasn't visible from where he sat. The usual forest rhythms were strangely absent—no birds chirruped, no rodents scurried beneath the undergrowth. *Like last night when the Rhinemaidens sang.*

The neglected gates and rutted drive didn't fit the image Diago had of the tuxedoed concertmaster. The property seemed derelict, possibly abandoned.

Maybe it's not the right place. Diago left the car. *Or it's a trap*. He thought of Guillermo's Talavera tiles. The pine needles on the drive could easily hide sigils that would activate if anyone drove over them.

He wondered briefly if his run-in with Heines had simply left him paranoid. Then again, a little paranoia had saved his life more than once. *Better to be safe*.

With a stick, he drew a sigil in the dirt. Humming a tune, he channeled the vibrations of his aura into his ward. The lines flamed in hues that were more black than green and took the shape and weight of his car. He sent the phantom automobile through the gates with a gesture while he watched for the warning flash of any active sigils.

Nothing happened. Diago allowed the glyph to fade and the decoy car disappeared. Keeping the stick in his hand, he walked to the pillars, the foundations of which were constructed with old stones. There had once been a wall here, but not within the last century.

Or maybe more, Diago thought as he moved the ivy aside. A metal plaque, with KARINHALL spelled in Gothic lettering, was centered on the pillar.

"This is definitely it," he muttered as he dropped the stick. Returning to the car, he got in and guided it onto the rutted drive. Foliage closed in on both sides, brushing the doors and occasionally slapping the windshield.

Then the trees fell back and the road widened as the manse came into view. Diago pulled into the yard, parking near an empty garage with open doors. He shut off the engine, hoping the brothers were home.

The house seemed normal enough, if a bit neglected. Three stories tall, the rectangular building had been constructed in the classicist style and boasted pediments on the rooflines of the left and right wings. Embedded in the center of the triangle on the left was the letter *k* and on the right was the letter *j* in the same Gothic script as on the gate.

Karin and Joachim. How deeply they must have loved each other.

Fleurs-de-lis were set at each corner of the windows. Grecian columns held up the balcony that sat above the porch. Cornices were decorated with angels' faces, cherubs with pudgy hands and open mouths, like no angel Diago had ever seen.

In better days, it might have been an imposing structure, but the seeds of rot had taken hold. The fleurs-de-lis had shed petals, and streaks of black stained the columns. On the balcony, missing balustrades gave the railing a snaggle-toothed grin. Paint peeled from the wooden trim, and the friezes were chipped and broken, leaving the angels with jagged lips and broken smiles.

Diago left the car and walked across the weedy yard. The front door had no knocker or bell, so he raised his hand and gave the wood three sharp raps. A minute passed and then two. He knocked again. From the other side he finally heard footsteps moving rapidly in his direction. Locks clicked and the door opened a crack, emitting the odor of cabbage and onions.

From somewhere within the house, someone played a piano. The light notes of a waltz drifted onto the porch, the music at odds with the dark suspicious eye squinting at him through the slim opening.

"Ja?" It was a woman's voice.

"Good afternoon, I am Diago Alvarez, and I'm here—"

"Not buying." The door slammed shut.

Diago blinked. How many salesmen wandered into this desolate area? He knocked, and when the door creaked open again, he said, "I'm here to see Herr Karl Grier about a violin."

The eye stared at him.

"A Stradivarius." He withdrew the letter of introduction Guillermo had given him. "I'm here on behalf of Don Guillermo Ramírez de Luna of Spain." He pushed the envelope toward the crack, hoping that Guillermo's name might trigger a response.

"Not buying," enunciated the woman very slowly, as if speaking to an idiot. "Leave."

And then he placed the accent. The woman wasn't German, she was Czechoslovakian.

He switched to Czech. "I'm not selling anything, madam. Herr Grier is expecting me. I'm here to evaluate the Stradivarius for Don Guillermo of Spain."

She snatched the letter from his hand as if he intended to grab her and yank her onto the porch. The door slammed in his face. Three minutes passed before she returned and swung the door wide.

An imposing woman with rough red hands filled the doorway. She wore a faded housedress and a kerchief over her hair. Woolen stockings sagged around her ankles and the left one disappeared into her sturdy black shoe. Diago guessed her age to be thirty but wouldn't have been surprised to find her younger. The story of a hard life was written on every line of her face, which didn't look on him any more kindly even though she now knew he was expected.

"Come this way, Herr . . ."

"Alvarez," he said.

She gestured for him to enter the house.

Diago removed his hat and stepped inside. The grand entryway revealed the home's faded opulence. A marble staircase dominated the main hall, the stone still polished to a high sheen. In contrast, dark wainscoting met sagging wallpaper to lead the eye upward, where tobacco smoke and water stains discolored the ceiling.

A large hall tree, which would have been more at home in a medieval castle, squatted to one side of the entry. The mirror, mottled with age, formed the chair's back and was surrounded by angels. It took Diago merely a glance to see they were falling.

He took his time removing his gloves as he ran a practiced eye over the shadows that gathered in the corners. No dark sounds seemed to be immediately evident, indicating no violent deaths had recently occurred inside the house, which lent credence to the story that Karin Grier's death was an accident.

The housekeeper cleared her throat and held out her hands. Pushing his gloves into the coat's pockets, he allowed her to take his jacket and hat. As she hung them on the tree, he noticed a flash of crimson by her foot. Reaching down, he rescued a silk scarf from the floor. The initials HL were embroidered on the scarf's tail.

Diago recognized the garment immediately. It had belonged to a rogue who called himself Harvey Lucas—a British nefil with a jovial voice and a brash song. They had met during the Great War, and when Diago had admired the scarf, Harvey had sworn he'd never willingly part with it. If

Diago remembered correctly, it had been a gift from a mortal paramour.

A hole on the opposite end further confirmed Diago's suspicions. *It was caused by a shell fragment.* He'd been in the trench beside Harvey when it happened. Another spot was frayed, and Diago recalled the scarf had caught on barbed wire during a different battle. *Had the ghostly music drawn the Brit here, too?*

"This is incredible," he said as he offered the scarf to the housekeeper. "I know a man who owns a scarf just like this. His name is Harvey Lucas."

Her mouth twitched at the name.

She knows something. "I haven't seen Harvey in years. Is he here?"

"No," she snapped as she grabbed the scarf. "There is no one here by that name." She draped it over one of the wooden hooks near his hat. "This way," she said as she began walking again.

Harvey Lucas had once crawled under machine gun fire to retrieve that scarf when it caught on a strand of barbed wire. He wouldn't have casually left it behind as he walked out the door.

The housekeeper paused when she realized Diago wasn't behind her. "This way," she said more firmly.

With an uneasy glance at the scarf, Diago followed her down the corridor. She led him to a music room cluttered with furniture. Photographs of Joachim during his days as concertmaster were intermingled with family portraits.

An exceptionally pale young man with hoarfrost hair and eyes the color of ice sat at a grand piano. When Diago entered the room, he glanced up and smiled.

The letter rested unopened on the top board. Nonetheless, the youth offered his hand without rising, and said, "Buenos tarde, Señor Alvarez. Bienvenido."

Diago went to him and shook his hand. "Mucho gusto, Señor Grier."

"How is my pronunciation?" he asked eagerly. "I've been practicing ever since I found out you were coming."

"You speak Spanish very well." *And I'm a good liar*, he thought as the youth blushed with pleasure.

The young man held on to Diago's hand just a moment too long and then said in German, "Thank you. Unfortunately, I've exhausted my entire vocabulary with the greeting." He gave Diago a beat to appreciate the joke before he rushed on, his words tumbling over one another. "I'm Rudi, by the way. Karl isn't here right now; he had several matters to attend in Offenburg today. Frau Weber was just making tea. It should be ready soon." Without taking his gaze from Diago, he spoke to the housekeeper. "We'll take our afternoon tea in here today."

Frau Weber nodded and left the room.

"Please, have a seat." Rudi waited until Diago was comfortable. Then he ripped a jazzy tune from the keyboard. "Do you play, Herr Alvarez?"

"I do."

A quick glance to Diago's hands prompted him to ask, "With nine fingers?"

"I've learned to improvise," Diago said, noting that Rudi's gaze lingered on the signet with Prieto's tear.

"Are you good?" Rudi switched to another waltz.

"Some people think so." *He's moving from one piece*

to the next in order to showcase his skill. Although Rudi clearly understood style and form, he played without feeling, and the lack of emotion rendered the recital flat.

Frau Weber chose that moment to return with the tea. She placed the tray on a low table and scuttled out as quickly as she had appeared. Diago noted there was only one cup.

"You must excuse her," Rudi said. "She doesn't speak much German. I think that is one of the reasons Karl keeps her. She can't blab the family business all over the town."

"Is your family often the topic of local gossip?"

"We have money and they resent us. Of course they're going to scandalize us. In their eyes, it brings us down to their level." The notes slowed and became cloudy like the sky before they morphed back into the waltz.

Nodding toward the tray, Rudi said, "Help yourself, Herr Alvarez. We don't stand on ceremony here."

The single cup seemed odd. Rudi had distinctly used the plural when he mentioned they would take their tea in the music room. Had Frau Weber misunderstood? Diago thought of Harvey's scarf hiding beneath the hall tree.

Something wasn't right about this pair of mortals. *Could Harvey still be alive and trapped somewhere in the house?*

It was time to test Rudi's knowledge on the subject. "I noticed a lovely red scarf in the hall. A friend of mine by the name of Harvey Lucas owns an identical garment. I'm curious if you know him."

Rudi's fingers slowed over the keys. "No, I don't recall ever meeting anyone by that name."

"Oh, you would remember Harvey. He is a large Brit. A regular pugilist. His nose has been broken several times and sits a bit crooked on his face. But for all of his size and bluster, he handles his violin with the delicacy of a virtuoso. He has a beautiful old piece that he made himself."

In the increasing gloom, the circles beneath Rudi's eyes grew deeper. An unpleasant tone seeped into his voice, almost a buzz, like hornets, agitated by a threat. "I said I don't know him."

His body language contradicted the denial. *He and Frau Weber have seen Harvey and they're hiding it.*

On the other side of a pair of glass doors, the foliage swayed over the terrace's broken stones. A creeping sense of unease settled around Diago's heart. He glanced at the lone teacup and decided he wasn't thirsty.

The shadow fell from Rudi's face and the timbre of his voice returned to normal. "We'll soon have a storm." He used the piano to mimic the patter of falling rain. The notes segued into the opening of Franz Schubert's "Erlkönig"—the story of the elf king seducing a young boy from his father's arms.

As if on cue, the front door opened and shut. A deeper more resonant voice spoke with Frau Weber. Their brief conversation was muted and spoken in murmurs.

Rudi gave Diago a dazzling smile that didn't hide the fear in his eyes. "That must be Karl. Now you get to meet the boring brother." He stood and went into the hall.

The reaction to his brother's arrival was interesting. *What is he afraid of?*

Rudi called out, "We're in here, Karl."

"I noticed the car outside," said Karl as his footsteps preceded him down the corridor. "Do we have company?"

"Herr Alvarez has arrived from Spain." Rudi glanced back into the room as if to ascertain Diago was, in fact, still there.

Karl stepped past his brother and his smile froze at the sight of Diago.

Clearly, I'm not what he expected. Of course, to be fair, Diago had envisioned Karl in a Sturmabteilung uniform, proudly displaying a Nazi armband. Instead, he wore a conservative suit that seemed a little large on him. Judging from the cut and style of the lapels, Diago went so far as to guess that it was one of his father's old suits.

With dark blond hair and a ruddier complexion, the young man was his father's image right down to Joachim's sublime smile. Nothing sinister marked his features, but then again monsters generally moved through the world unobtrusively, camouflaged by banality until their deeds manifested in the form of dead bodies or broken souls.

Rudi, taking a great deal of delight over Karl's shock, turned to Diago. "Herr Alvarez, may I present my brother, Herr Karl Grier."

Offering his hand as he stood, Diago greeted Karl. "Herr Grier, I'm pleased to meet you."

"Welcome, sir." He made short work of his greeting and had barely grasped Diago's hand before he released him. As he continued to the sideboard, he brushed his palm against his pants leg as if wiping something filthy from his skin.

It was a subtle gesture, not one that was meant to be noticed. Diago forced himself to remain impassive to the slight. There was a time for confrontation, and there was a time for diplomacy. Right now, he was here on Guillermo's behalf and the violin was the priority. His job was to play the courtier and ignore indignities, and that's what he would do. Unless they became insufferable.

And then . . . we shall see.

Karl spoke over his shoulder. "I had no idea that Don Guillermo was sending a Jew."

"I'm not Jewish," Diago said for the second time that day. The disavowal was an odd refrain, one he wasn't used to giving. *And it's a song that I'm growing tired of singing.* In spite of his ire, he kept his tone civil, but barely. "Besides, I don't see how that makes any difference. We're here to do business, not worship together."

"I was speaking in terms of ethnicity." When Diago didn't dignify the statement with a response, Karl raised an eyebrow as he lifted a decanter from the sideboard. "A Moor, then."

Christ. When Guillermo said Karl was obsessed with genealogies, I thought it was just his own. "Moor is a medieval word, which has no ethnological value whatsoever. My father is a Spaniard. His lineage can be traced back to the Berber tribes of Morocco."

"And your mother?"

Was an angel. "Was from Catalonia, where people are descendants of the Visigoths. You might be familiar with them since they were one of the ancient Germanic tribes."

The color rose to Karl's cheeks. "You misunderstand me, Herr Alvarez. I am not prejudiced against dark-skinned people."

There was no misunderstanding. *Still, here is a chance I dare not lose.* Karl was taken aback and probably wanted Diago out of the house, and that suited Diago's needs just fine. *I can return after dark and search for Harvey.*

He allowed his irritation to seep into his voice. "Your actions indicate otherwise, sir, so let me be clear: I am here to assess the value of a Stradivarius on behalf of Don Guillermo Ramírez. If you will kindly bring out the violin, I will do my job and vacate your premises so you need not be offended by my presence."

Rudi became very still.

Karl reevaluated Diago with a critical eye. Clearly such a curt response to his behavior was unanticipated. He seemed unsure how to proceed. He opted for civility. "We seem to have gotten off to a bad start, Herr Alvarez. I can assure you that I did not mean to offend you by my line of questioning, but you are a stranger here, and we are somewhat isolated. I must be certain you aren't a charlatan."

That he automatically equated Jews with charlatans wasn't lost on Diago. *Let it go. He's searching for a way to save face and I need to give it to him until that violin is in my possession.* Diago gestured toward the piano. "I have a letter of introduction from Don Guillermo if that would put you at ease."

"He does!" Rudi burst into motion and hurried to snatch up the envelope. "I forgot all about it." After he delivered it to Karl, he returned to Diago's side.

Karl made a great show of examining the note. When he looked up again, his lip twitched, this time with a smile, although there wasn't a trace of humor in the mortal's eyes. "My apologies, Herr Alvarez. You are who you say you are. Please, let us begin again." Karl raised the decanter and poured the amber liquid into a glass. "Have a drink with me."

The apology was superficial at best, but Diago pretended

to be mollified. He stepped forward and accepted the proffered glass. "Thank you."

Rudi's relieved sigh was audible in the hush.

Diago lifted his glass to Karl, but he didn't drink. "Perhaps now we can discuss our business."

Karl poured a drink for himself. He didn't offer his brother one. "Please forgive me, but today has been nothing but endless meetings and business. Perhaps we can relax this evening and attend to the terms and conditions of the Stradivarius in the morning. You must stay the night."

"I would hate to impose on you."

"Please, it's the least I can do after our rough beginning."

Rudi hovered nearby. "It's really no imposition, either. When Don Guillermo confirmed you were coming, Frau Weber prepared the guest room."

"Besides, there is the storm"—Karl gestured to the window, where the first drops of falling rain struck the patio—"and these mountain roads can be treacherous at night. We won't take no for an answer."

Diago feigned hesitation for merely a moment. Staying on the premises kept him off the roads, where he might accidentally run into Heines or other members of Die Nephilim. *Besides, between sleeping rough last night and disabling Heines's glyph this morning, I'm exhausted.* "If you insist."

"Excellent." Karl placed his drink on the sideboard.

Untouched. Not a sip.

Rudi gestured to the door. "Let me show you to your room, Herr Alvarez."

They're herding me. More, it's not the first time they've done this. Now that he thought of it, everything between the brothers had the aura of a performance. Had they played a version of this scene before? With Harvey Lucas perhaps?

Entirely possible. Harvey was a rogue. Once lured here, with nothing but wilderness between the manse and the next town, it would be tempting to stay the night.

After all, what harm could come from a pair of mortals?

Diago paused as if a thought suddenly occurred to him. "May I use your phone to call Don Guillermo? I promised I would contact him once I arrived. It will be a collect call without any charges to you."

The brothers grew still. It was Karl who apologized. "Unfortunately, our phone is not working. It was another of the matters I had to attend today. Tomorrow, I'll take you to my solicitor's office in Offenburg, and you may place your call there."

"I see." *Was that what they told Harvey?* "Well then"—Diago bowed his head to Karl—"I am at your mercy for the evening."

And tomorrow suddenly seems very far away.

[16]

As Diago passed the hall tree on the way to retrieve his bag, he noticed Harvey's scarf seemed to have disappeared. Had either Frau Weber or Karl removed it?

It was possible, but with Rudi by his side, he couldn't pause to look. The rain started to pick up, so Diago hurried to his car, grabbed his bag, and returned to the house, where Rudi waited by the front door.

"Oh, you made it just in time." The youth shut the door before turning toward the stairs.

Diago hesitated by the hall tree, allowing Rudi to draw ahead of him. He shifted his coat aside and slipped the papers for his German alias into his bag. With Heines on the hunt for Jacob Schwarz, that pseudonym was dead to him now. He glanced at the floor in case the scarf had merely slipped again. It had definitely disappeared. Nor did he see any other evidence of Harvey's presence. *What happened to you, my old friend?*

Rudi paused by the banister. "Is something wrong?"

There is a lot wrong here. "No, nothing at all," Diago lied easily as he caught up to the youth and followed him to the second-floor landing.

Rudi indicated the wall plate beside the stairs. "The switch," he said as he pushed the button. Harsh yellow light washed over the threadbare carpet lining the floor.

Just ahead, the stairs ascended upward toward the third floor. Darkness engulfed the upper risers, but the lack of dust testified to their use.

Rudi went to the stairs and pulled a pair of pocket doors shut. He locked them and dropped the key into his pocket, treating Diago to a cat smile. "My apologies. We use that floor for storage nowadays, and the climb can be dangerous. Wouldn't want you to hurt yourself should you get turned around in the dark." He turned left and continued down the hall.

Diago hesitated by the pocket doors. Nothing but a cold draft seeped through the sash.

Another wing stretched to the right of the stairs, but the corridor had an abandoned feeling to it. The four doors—two on each side of the hall—were shut.

Rudi, who apparently hadn't noticed that Diago remained on the landing, continued down the left wing. "Karl's room is there." He pointed to the first door on the left. "I'm beside him. There is a lavatory at the end of the hall." He nodded toward the dark bathroom.

Diago caught up to the youth just before he turned to the door on the right, which he opened. "And here you are, directly across from me."

It was a spacious room; most likely at one time it had

served as the master bedroom. A settee and chairs gathered around the cold hearth, which was stacked with firewood. A large double-door armoire dominated the opposite wall. The bed commanded the center of the room and could have easily accommodated all three of them. The mahogany frame was carved with angels, like the hall tree below. They swarmed around the posts, openmouthed and crying.

The engravings disquieted Diago.

"Interesting, isn't it?" Rudi whispered, his voice right beside Diago's ear. "They look frightened as they fall."

The wind chose that moment to scream through the eaves. Beneath the long howl, Diago heard the faintest murmur of voices, like the sound of a crowd all speaking at once, but from across a great distance *(chasm)*.

Again, he looked for evidence of dark sounds but saw nothing out of the ordinary. *Because the voices are from my nightmares, they're in my head.* A shiver glided down the back of his neck.

The rain pelted the room's windows, hesitantly at first, and then picking up speed with the storm. The icy downpour brought the night prematurely into the room.

Rudi's nearness was disconcerting.

Diago moved away from him and went to the bed. "The workmanship is marvelous." He ran his thumb down an angel's wing. The clawed talons were stretched just over another angel's arm.

"I thought you might appreciate it," Rudi said.

Diago caught another cat smile on the youth's face before his host turned his back. "Please make yourself at home. Dinner will be served in an hour." Then he closed the door.

Loosening his tie, Diago removed it and tossed it to the

settee. He walked around the room, giving it a closer inspection.

Overhead, a series of large rust-colored blemishes, similar to the ones downstairs, streaked the ceiling just above the bed's headboard. It appeared as if a water pipe had ruptured, leaving stains and damaged plaster as a testament to the leak.

The armoire was locked and the key was gone, which seemed rather odd. He checked around the base but the key hadn't fallen, nor was it in either of the bedside tables or on the mantel. *Why place a guest in a room with no way to hang their clothing?*

It was a mystery that could wait until after dinner. For now, he needed to make the best use of his time while the brothers were downstairs.

At least, he hoped they were still downstairs. Unbuttoning his shirt, he stripped to his undershirt, and then stepped into the corridor. The brothers' bedroom doors remained shut and no light shined beneath the thresholds.

Rudi must have returned to the music room, because the languid notes of another waltz drifted up the stairs.

The lavatory was only a few steps away so Diago slipped inside. Someone, probably Frau Weber, had left him a washcloth and towel. He turned the hot water valve and, after a moment of chugging, the pipes ejected a steady flow of deliciously hot water. Leaving the door open so he could watch the hall, he completed his toilet and considered his next move.

He doubted he would be alone on this floor again, and a cursory search might reveal more information about the whereabouts of the violin, or Harvey. It was an opportunity he couldn't afford to waste.

Moving stealthily, he padded over to Rudi's room. The brass knob turned easily and the hinges gave a soft creak as the door opened. The room seemed innocuous enough: a bed, an armoire, and chairs. Each thing had a place and was immaculately arranged.

Diago thought back to his son's room, which was a clutter-filled testimony to the things that interested Rafael: pictures, his fútbol, the stuffed horse on his bed. Even Diago's and Miquel's bedroom held books and trinkets.

Yet not a single memento, photograph, or book testified to Rudi's interests. Diago had seen hotel rooms with more personality. *But people, like songs, are layered. Maybe Rudi keeps his interests beneath the surface.*

He checked the armoire. No sign of the violin or its case, and other than Rudi's neatly folded clothes, no personal effects.

A radio squatted on the night table beside a glass of water. Inside the drawer was an expensive woman's compact. From the popular art deco design on the cover, Diago guessed it probably belonged to Karin Grier.

Curious, Diago opened it. The cracked mirror fractured his face. Although it had been wiped completely clean, the light scent of facial powder still clung to the metal interior.

So he was close to his mother and must still grieve her passing. That information might prove useful later. Diago returned the compact to the drawer, careful to place it in the same position as he had found it.

The bed was old-fashioned and high. Diago knelt and lifted the bedspread. Not even a dust bunny marred the clean floor. As he rose, he noted the corner of a page protruding between the mattress and the box spring. Lifting the edge of the mattress, he found two well-worn copies of *Die Filmwoche*, a popular movie magazine. Both issues had pictures of the handsome German actor Conrad Veidt on the covers.

Diago flipped through the magazines. *Why is he hiding them?*

And then he saw the black hearts, which had been meticulously drawn beside each publicity shot of Veidt. In one place, Rudi had been bold enough to write "Rudi loves all things Conrad" in the margin. It was an ambiguous statement that could refer to Veidt's films or to the actor himself.

But it was the hearts that clued Diago to Rudi's desires. The youth was in love—a very dangerous love that carried a prison sentence in Germany of six months to five years if he was caught.

Rudi obviously knew the consequences of his behavior. Karl either lived in denial of Rudi's sexuality, or he openly disdained it, otherwise Rudi wouldn't go to such lengths to hide the magazines. *But he's chafing at those restraints. Writing his desires is a way of articulating them.*

Downstairs, Karl's voice rose over the strains of the waltz Rudi played. The music ceased.

What now? Diago returned the magazines to Rudi's hiding place and retreated to the hallway. Easing the door shut, he winced when the hinges squeaked.

Crossing the hall to his room, he watched the stairwell, ready to slip inside if anyone appeared.

Karl grew louder, more strident. Although his words were muffled by the distance, his anger was not. When he finished his diatribe, Rudi launched into the prologue of Wagner's *Götterdämmerung*. From the way he hit the keys, Diago suspected Rudi nursed a fury of his own.

Apparently, the previous musical selection had been too passive for Karl's taste. Diago waited in front of his door for a full minute. No one came upstairs.

How much longer do I have before I've pushed my luck too far? Karl's door tugged at his curiosity. If information was to be had, it would be in the dominant sibling's possession.

Diago didn't give himself time to waver. He crossed the corridor and entered Karl's room.

Whereas Rudi hid his deepest desires, Karl showed no such inhibitions. The books stacked throughout the room encompassed subjects from the higher maths and physics to topics more in line with what Diago expected from Karl. A copy of *Theozoology* rested next to Hitler's autobiography, *Mein Kampf*. Issues of *Ostara*, another of Lanz's occult publications, were stacked next to *Die Chiromantie*, a magazine dedicated to the Association of Palmists in Germany.

Intrigued as to what fascinated Karl about palmistry, Diago had only to glance at the cover to recognize the name, Ernst Issberner-Haldane, a noted member of Ordo Novi Templi. Open next to a pad of paper on the desk was a copy of *Ariosophische Bibliothek*, in which Haldane had an essay discussing one of Lanz's theories.

Karl had jotted notes on the pad in the obvious attempt to prove a point. An envelope protruded from beneath the blotter.

Diago glanced at the door before he eased the envelope free. Inside was a typewritten letter bearing the Ordo Novi Templi letterhead. Karl's application to join the organization as a full member had been rejected. Someone—presumably Karl—had scratched out the author's signature with such vehemence that the pen had torn the paper. Fortunately, the name was also typewritten beneath the letterhead: Ernst Issberner-Haldane.

Apparently, Karl wasn't pleased with the development or Herr Haldane. *He'll be even less pleased if he catches me snooping in his room.* Diago returned the letter to the blotter.

A battered cigar box perched on one corner of the desk. Diago lifted the lid to find an odd assortment of colorful wires, alligator leads, and diodes.

What are you doing, Karl? Diago scanned the room, but he saw nothing else related to the strange collection of electronic parts. Another mystery, although given Karl's other interests, this one seemed almost benign.

Downstairs, Rudi played as if he would never tire. *But he will and when he does, he may wander back up here, which means I must move fast.*

A quick check for the violin and then I'm done. As he had in Rudi's room, he looked beneath the bed, but the space was free of clutter.

That left the armoire. Diago opened the doors. A gas mask swung from the hook. Light from the hallway flickered in the celluloid eyes, and for just a moment, Diago imagined he saw battlefield flames reflected in those lenses. The distant sound of drums *(bombs)* echoed in the back of his mind.

Behind the mask was the armoire's mirror, a plate of glass that reflected not the room, or Diago's startled face, but a cloud of swirling colors mottled with cancerous shades of gray and black. Diago recognized these hues. The dark sounds of the dead.

He'd seen them in France. A flashback returned him to the Great War: *helpless under the Germans' fire, he'd squatted in that trench, clenching a piece of wood between his teeth as the cacophony of bombs bent reality, pushing the waves of time like taffy until the threads between the worlds parted, and he saw into another realm, one made murderous by angels gorging on those dark sounds made by the dead.*

The memory was so intense, Diago thought he felt the floor vibrate beneath his feet. An icy sweat broke over his body.

The piano stopped.

Diago blinked. A single drop of sweat trickled down his cheek.

When he looked again, the gas mask was just a mask. The edges of the mirror reflected the room behind him. Mouth dry, he glanced down, almost afraid to see what other horrors the armoire might hold. On the floor were Joachim's field pack, ammo pouches, and bread bag.

I had a flashback, Diago reasoned as he wiped the sweat from his face. *That was all. I saw the gas mask and it revived the nightmare that's been plaguing me. I haven't slept, my mind is wandering, and if I don't pull myself together, one of the brothers will find me here.*

Down below, Rudi didn't resume playing.

What if he's coming up the stairs right now? The thought was enough to startle Diago into action. He closed the armoire's doors and retreated to the hall, easing Karl's door shut behind him.

Returning to the lavatory, he splashed his face with cold water until the gloom of that battle left the corners of his mind. If he kept slipping into waking dreams, he would slip into a fatal error.

I've got to pull myself together. He dried his face and gazed longingly down the hall to the rooms in the other wing. Did one of those closed doors hide a clue to Harvey's disappearance, or the violin?

Frau Weber called out to Rudi.

"I'm going to my room for a few minutes," Rudi answered. It sounded like the youth was already halfway up the staircase.

Diago swore under his breath. The rooms on the other side would have to wait. With no desire to see either of the brothers, he returned to his bedroom and shut the door.

Grabbing a fresh shirt from his bag, he put it on and chose a tie. Moments later, Rudi turned on his radio. The dial squawked through the frequencies until Rudi found a jazz station.

Oh, I bet Karl loves *that*, Diago thought as he knotted his tie. *Probably as much as he loves Jews and homosexuals.*

He wandered to the window and pushed the drapes aside. Cold hard rain pelted the house in time with the drummer's beat.

Leaning his forehead against the cool glass, he absently withdrew the brooch from his pocket and ran his thumb over the emerald. He closed his eyes and let his thoughts drift as he hummed along with the tune.

Across the hall, static seeped into the radio signal and garbled the music. An unpleasant buzz infiltrated the station's frequency.

Diago fell silent, listening.

A voice—that was a chorus of voices—snaked into his room on the back of the song and whispered one word, "Vehmgericht."

Vehmgericht. It was a word from another incarnation, another time. But the sound of it triggered the memory he had on the train—of standing before a window in his last incarnation while sigils crackled and died on the walls . . .

Diago's heart suddenly constricted in his chest. The pain magnified until it became an agony, but it wasn't a heart attack, it didn't feel like a heart attack, no it felt like his heart burned . . . on fire . . . he was unable to breathe . . .

Across the hall, Rudi snapped off the radio, abruptly ending the song.

The brooch slipped free of Diago's palm and clattered to the floor. Air rushed into his lungs.

"What the hell was that?" he whispered. *The anomaly? Was Guillermo's black pin in the Grier house?*

The voice definitely wasn't angelic, nor was it daimonic.

Yet it feels familiar. Unnerved, Diago skirted the brooch on the floor and walked the perimeter of the room, searching for what, he did not know.

He tried the armoire again: locked.

Under the bed: nothing.

Outside the window: the storm.

Nothing seemed out of place. He knelt and retrieved the pin, rubbing his palm over the discolored silver. The angel's smile seemed to have broadened.

"Don't be ridiculous," he muttered. He'd simply rubbed more of the tarnish away.

Someone knocked on his door.

Diago jumped at the sound. *Steady.*

"Herr Alvarez?" It was Rudi. "Dinner is ready."

"Just a moment." Diago pocketed the brooch. Grabbing his jacket, he put it on and wished for a mirror. He would just have to hope he was presentable.

When he stepped into the hall, he noticed that Rudi had

changed into more formal attire for dinner. He'd also taken the time to oil his hair into a fashionable style.

Before Diago could stop him, Rudi reached out to straighten Diago's tie. "There." He brushed a piece of lint from Diago's shoulder. "That's better."

"Thank you. I couldn't open the armoire. The key seems to be missing."

A cloud passed over the youth's features, but the scowl was there and gone before Diago could be sure whether the frown was directed at him or the inconvenience of a missing key.

Rudi finally whispered, "Be glad."

Before Diago could question the odd answer, the youth smiled his cat smile and led the way downstairs.

[17]

The dining room, like the rest of the house, had seen better days yet somehow managed to retain its former glory. A great mirror in a gilded frame hung over the fireplace's ornate mantel. The oak table was made to seat twenty but was only set for three. A sideboard with a small array of steaming dishes occupied one wall.

Karl stood by the chair at the head of the table, leaving no doubt as to how he perceived his status within the home. "Herr Alvarez, I hope you found your accommodations to your taste."

Diago hadn't found anything in this house to his taste, so he opted for diplomacy with a compliment. "You have a very lovely home, Herr Grier."

"It is our pride." Karl gestured to the sideboard. "I'm afraid Frau Weber leaves us each day at six so we must serve ourselves. Please help yourself."

"Thank you." Diago took a plate and examined the dishes

suspiciously. He hadn't forgotten Harvey Lucas's missing scarf. Turning to Rudi, he asked, "What do you suggest?"

Flushing with the pleasure of being acknowledged, Rudi lifted the lid of the silver tureen. "I'm having the potato and bean casserole. Frau Weber makes the best I've ever eaten."

Diago followed his lead and portioned a small amount to his plate. He didn't intend to touch a bite.

Rudi filled his plate and took the seat across from Diago.

Karl returned to the head of the table and continued the conversation. "Did you know there used to be a castle here?"

The image of soldiers loading bodies into a cart sprang back into Diago's mind unbidden. "Indeed?"

"In the twelfth century, as a matter of fact."

The twelfth century. The approximate date matched the soldiers' armor that he'd envisioned on the train. *And the workmanship on the brooch.* He resisted the urge to reach into his pocket and touch the pin.

Diago picked up his fork. "That's very interesting."

That was all the encouragement Karl needed to continue. "We were clearing an area for a garden when I came across a set of foundation stones. Being something of an amateur archaeologist, I began to excavate. Thus far, I've uncovered the outline of what appears to be a chapel."

Diago recalled a red-haired king walking toward a chapel. *He holds a dagger in one hand and a piece of parchment in the other. He's angry—I can tell by the flush of his cheeks. His aura snaps around him in red-gold sparks as he speaks to a soldier and nods at the smithy. My name is Yago, and later I learn that Bernard has been arrested. His detention terrifies me.*

The scene disappeared from his mind almost as soon as

it arrived, but not the knowledge that Yago's fear stemmed from the fact that he was spying on that red-haired king. *And Bernard was my contact.*

Vehmgericht. That ugly word rolled back into his brain. His heart fluttered in his chest.

Diago tried to hide his sudden unease behind a smile. "You must tell me about your findings."

Enthused by Diago's interest, Karl continued, "I have it on good authority that Karinhall was built on sacred ground. Local legend has it that a Wotanist priest-king by the name of Sir George Abellio ruled this area in the twelfth century. His rule ended in eleven hundred and forty-five. The church denounced him as a heretic, claiming he was a member of the Antichrist's army. They murdered him and razed his castle to the ground."

Diago barely heard him, because now he recalled Sir George and Guillermo's brother, Jordi, were the same. His mind raced with the implications of this revelation. *Was it Jordi who bumped into me and deposited the brooch in my pocket in Barcelona? If so, is he using the Griers to further his own agenda?*

No. That didn't fit Jordi's methodology—he didn't trust mortals and never worked with them. Something else was going on here, something deeper.

But what?

Karl carried on the conversation as if Diago hung on his every word. "Sir George is something of a legend here in Durbach—a King Arthur archetype. It is said that he will one day return to reclaim his place as sovereign." A fanatical gleam touched the young man's eyes as his voice rose in pitch. "Then he will lead us in a righteous war to cleanse the world of its corruption."

Diago stirred the tines of his fork through his food. "That's . . . um . . . quite a story."

"It gets more ridiculous by the telling," Rudi said as he tore his bread with slightly more force than necessary.

Karl reined in his enthusiasm for the subject. "As I said, it's merely a legend."

It was obvious to Diago that Karl had learned to test other people's reception to his apocalyptic theories before holding forth too deeply on the subject. Even so, no amount of circumspection could hide Karl's desire for Lanz's mythological battle, which would bring about the racist utopia he so desperately craved.

That had to be why he had commandeered his father's war gear. *Except the guns*, Diago suddenly realized. *Where are Joachim's guns?*

An uneasy silence fell over the table. Diago took a sip of his water, wishing it was coffee. *Strong and black enough to wipe this fatigue from my brain.* He needed Karl to keep talking, because if Jordi *was* somehow involved with these mortals, Diago needed to know how and why. *Mollify him.*

Diago cleared his throat. "I must say, most legends are rooted in truth. Have you located any artifacts?" *Brooches engraved with Messenger angels, perhaps?*

"Not yet, but since it is just me and my crude implements, the work is slow."

Rudi curled his lip. "When he's not sitting in the yard, digging like a farmer, he's in the basement of the town hall."

Karl's jaw tightened in anger, but he didn't retort. Instead, he gestured at Diago's right hand with his knife. "Now that I've told you about my house, you must tell me about that magnificent piece on your finger. What is the story behind it?"

Diago glanced down at his ring and shrugged. "It was a gift from a friend."

"I've never seen a stone quite like it. If you don't mind my asking, what is it?"

"It's rare," Diago hedged, trying to think of an appropriate name for it. *Why lie?* "I believe the common name is an angel's tear."

Rudi pushed his food around on his plate and flicked a coy glance to Diago. "Don't tears come from the heart?"

Karl ignored his brother. "Do they all have the same coloration?"

"No, they come in a variety of hues. The name seems to have more to do with the hardness of the gemstone. A friend once told me the angel's tear is equal to the diamond on the Mohs' scale."

Rudi sipped from his water glass. "Do you think angels have hard hearts, Herr Alvarez?"

Karl glared at Rudi before addressing Diago with another question. "And the symbols engraved in the band?" he asked. "What do they mean?"

"I don't know," Diago lied. "As I said, the ring was a gift from a dear friend. He only told me about the stone. I'm afraid that's all the information at my disposal."

"That's interesting, because the symbols are identical to the ones on the violin."

Christ, why didn't I think of that? Because they weren't identical, at least not to Diago or to any other nefil. Each sigil was as unique as the nefil who created it, but to the mortal eye, they could seem similar. It was the kind of detail that he had never failed to obscure when he lived among the mortals. Santuari had made him lazy. *Make the best of it.* "Perhaps we could compare them after dinner."

A smile turned the corner of Karl's mouth. "You don't believe me?"

In spite of his best efforts, Diago's rancor crept into his voice. "I don't doubt you. I am curious why the whereabouts of the violin are such a mystery."

Karl shrugged. "It's a valuable piece."

"Priceless," Rudi muttered as he toyed with his food and stared at Diago.

Karl leaned forward. "You must understand that my pursuit of archaeological details about the house has led me to other ancient texts. For example, those symbols"—he pointed to the band of Diago's ring—"are used by nefilim to work their spells of intent."

How in the hell had Karl discovered that?

"Spells?" Diago choked on the word. He couldn't be seen taking this kind of talk seriously. *And I have to do it without insulting him.* He treated Karl to an incredulous smile and raised his eyebrows. "By nefilim? I thought they were biblical giants, not witches."

"That is what they have led the mortals to believe. You see, the nefilim controlled the narrative by writing mortal histories. They inserted falsehoods into the myths of ancient beings to disguise their presence among the mortals. Nefilim are actually hybrids, who are the children of angels and mortals."

Karl was dangerously close to the truth. Nor was it lost on Diago that he used the word *mortals* in the same context as the nefilim.

Because he thinks he's one of us.

Diago peered more closely at the brothers. *Could that be true?* Rudi met Diago's gaze boldly and it was there that Diago caught the lamplight reflecting in his pupils, giving them the faintest shimmer of luminosity.

Amazing—they are *the progeny of lesser nefilim, probably thirteenth or fourteenth generation and definitely angel-born.* Far enough removed from their ancestor to have strong psychic abilities for mortals, but according to the nefilim's laws of consanguinity, the brothers would be considered mortal.

Rudi caught the intensity of Diago's gaze and winked at him. Suddenly Diago put the coy cat smiles with the wink and realized Rudi's intentions weren't nefarious, but *amorous.*

Christ, I've been so busy looking for undercurrents, the waves just rolled over my head. He's flirting with me.

Diago could just imagine what Karl would think of such a tryst, not to mention the police. *Or worse, a judge.*

He was almost grateful when Karl redirected his attention back to the subject of nefilim. "I seem to have shocked you."

Christ, between Rudi's flirtations and Karl's sanctimonious blathering, the two of them could keep anyone off balance. Diago returned his attention to Karl. "That's quite a theory."

Karl took a bite of food and smiled. "Rest assured, Herr Alvarez, it's more than a theory. It's a fact. Nefilim are real and they walk among us."

"Really? How do you differentiate them from mortals? Do they have wings? Do they soar through the air and work miracles? Are they more beautiful perhaps?"

"No. Their appearance is like you or me; although I believe the nefilim tend to be more charismatic, sexual even."

"Sexual?"

"Sensuous," whispered Rudi.

Karl scowled at his brother.

Rudi's smile withered under his brother's glare. He bowed his head and nudged his food with his fork.

Diago turned back to Karl. "And is personal magnetism their only supernatural trait?"

With Rudi properly subdued and sidelined, Karl chuckled and ate as if he had not a care in the world. "It's in their eyes and in their voices." He tapped his throat for emphasis. "They recognize one another by the way their eyes either reflect light or swallow darkness. And when they sing, they can discern the colors of one another's songs."

Karl knew far too much. *But does he know everything?* Diago's bemused expression felt like a grimace. *Nothing to do now but see this charade to its finish.* "There is color in song?"

"Sound waves displace air and produce vibrations, which are invisible to the mortal eye but apparent to the nefilim. It's a form of chromesthesia, and they use this ability to twist these vibrations into sigils. When the glyphs are in their proper form, the nefilim charge them with the power of their voices to give them a signature that enables them to project their intent onto the ward, which, in turn, is directed toward a unique magical purpose."

Diago's mouth dropped open. *Christ, he understands it perfectly.* Immediately on the heels of that thought came another: *and I can't let him know that.* Closing his mouth, he projected a note of suspicion into his voice. "Sigils, you say?"

"Wards, glyphs that are symbols of intent. Like the ones on your ring."

"I see," Diago said, feigning curiosity and surprise as he looked at the ring. "And what do they do with these symbols of intent, invoke magical acts?"

Karl brightened as if he had enlightened a particularly difficult student. "Precisely! They use them to make their desires manifest."

Placing his napkin on the table, Diago said, "That is . . . um . . . an interesting hypothesis, Herr Grier."

"It's not a theory. I've seen them."

Who could Karl have possibly seen? Jordi?

No. Jordi might use the mortals to further his own means, but he would never reveal his true nature to them.

Harvey Lucas, perhaps? He *had* been in this house. Diago was certain of that fact, just as he was certain Harvey, like Jordi, would never reveal himself to mortals.

Diago cleared his throat. "You've *seen* nefilim?"

"Let's drop this farce, shall we?" Karl nodded at Diago's ring. "No one but a nefil would wear such a symbol so openly."

Diago pointed to himself. "And you think I'm a—"

"You're one of the dark races, so my guess is that your power isn't very great."

Diago laughed at him, which wasn't hard, given the absurdity of Karl's comments. "Surely you can't be serious."

Rudi burst into laughter, too, thoroughly enjoying his brother's humiliation.

As their mirth dissipated, Diago noticed that Karl's lip twitched in what was becoming a familiar tic. *He's angry.*

Nonetheless, Karl remained resolute in his claims and managed to shift into a conspiratorial tone. "I understand your need for discretion, Herr Alvarez, but I would wager the Stradivarius that both you and Don Guillermo are actually nefilim. I would even hazard a guess that it was he who gave you that ring."

"Why, you are positively psychic."

Rudi's sharp glance told Diago that the youth had detected his sarcasm.

The derision was lost on Karl, however, who waved the compliment aside with his fork. "I am merely in touch with my true nature, Herr Alvarez. I am knowledgeable about the world around us, both the seen and the unseen."

"This is all quite . . . disconcerting and amazing." Diago briefly considered killing the brothers, but that would be messy and bring mortal authorities to the scene. *Not to mention members of Die Nephilim.* The last thing he needed right now was another meeting with Sturmführer Heines and his Brownshirt goons, who would probably drag him before Queen Jaeger, which would be precisely the kind of incident that would bleed across the border into Rousseau's territories.

I've got to prove to Guillermo that I can work within the confines of Los Nefilim. He needed to find another way to silence Karl.

With a much gentler laugh, Diago wagged a finger at the mortal and said, "I see where this is going. You think that legends of nefilim and angels and mystical glyphs will exaggerate the value of the violin to Don Guillermo."

Karl's smile slipped. "What are you implying?"

"I'm not implying anything, Herr Grier. If you've changed your mind about selling the violin, I understand. As Rudi said, the Stradivarius is a priceless instrument, which I am sure has great sentimental value to you."

Rudi's shrill laugh startled them. "He could not care less. He hated Father."

Karl's face turned a dangerous shade of red. He made a visible struggle to master his rage. "Shut up, Rudi," he snapped before turning back to Diago. "I'm not trying to influence the value of the violin. And I certainly haven't changed my mind about selling it. But you have to understand there is much more at stake here than mere money."

Rudi sneered. "He wants you to take him to this mystical Don Guillermo and present him as a neophyte. He thinks we're nefilim. He's swallowed the bunk of that ridiculous Ordo Novi Templi, the New Templars, they call themselves, but they've rejected him. Now he's looking for a new group of fanatics to follow."

Karl dismissed his brother's criticism. "You don't know anything about what I'm trying to do."

"I saw the rejection letter you received yesterday."

Karl hit the table with his fist. The table settings jumped, as did Diago.

Rudi flinched as if Karl had struck him.

Because he probably has. It was the kind of reflex commonly seen in abused children, one that Diago knew well from his own experiences. *One that Miquel helped me overcome.*

Nor was he naive enough to think that Karl initiated the abuse. He had probably learned it from their father or mother, whichever one ruled with the heaviest hand.

Rudi glared back at Karl in open rebellion.

He is balking at Karl's tyranny. The argument was merely one small sign. The possession of the magazine with tiny black hearts beside the actor's picture was another;

openly flirting with a man at dinner constituted a third. *How far will Karl let him go?*

Karl slowly unclenched his fist.

Because striking your sibling in front of guests is so gauche.

Karl cleared his throat and made an effort to modulate his voice. "I'm sure Herr Alvarez is not interested in Ordo Novi Templi. He and I have a much more ancient affiliation."

Rudi threw his napkin into his plate. "Christ, I wish you could hear yourself."

Obviously not caring about appearances any longer, Karl rose and struck his brother hard enough to knock him from his chair. The violence began and ended so quickly, Diago had little time to react. He shot to his feet, prepared to intervene while recalling a similar incident—*in my last incarnation*—when George stood in the castle's main hall, the dagger and summons in his hands. *His rage billows around him like a cloak. I try to calm him with a touch, and he spins, striking out with his fist, knocking me to the floor.*

It was a lifetime ago. It felt like yesterday.

Rudi's perfectly sculpted hair fell across his brow in an oily mess. He daubed his bloodied mouth and lowered his head to hide his tears.

Karl ran his hand over his chest and smoothed his rumpled shirt. "Now look at what you've made me do. Get out. Go to bed."

Rudi's lip trembled. It was clear he wanted to deliver a verbal slap of his own, some harsh riposte that would save his damaged dignity.

Diago went to the youth and offered his hand. "Are you all right?"

Averting his gaze, Rudi rose and fled from the room without looking back. Diago easily imagined his humiliation.

An uncomfortable silence remained in Rudi's wake.

Karl moved first. He righted Rudi's chair and took his seat again. "I apologize for my brother's conduct. Rudi is emotionally ill. I didn't want to tell you because I was afraid you wouldn't come."

Twice Karl had sent Rudi to escort Diago to and from his room—not the kind of responsibility given to someone who was emotionally ill. Then a thought dawned on him: *Or does Karl believe Rudi is emotionally ill because he is homosexual?* That type of bourgeoisie mentality would fit. With enough money and influence, Spanish nobility had entered their young men into asylums on the pretext of insanity when their only crime involved loving another man.

Diago, who thought himself quite numb to those atrocities, found himself beginning to feel a measure of empathy for Rudi.

Be careful. He recalled Rudi's response to his earlier questions about Harvey. *Until I can ascertain differently, he might very well have murdered, or participated in the murder of, Harvey Lucas. No matter what, this is not a house of innocence. And it's clearly a place accustomed to violence.*

"Please, Herr Alvarez, sit."

Diago glanced at the door again.

"Please," Karl said again, gesturing to Diago's empty chair.

Diago wanted nothing more than to be done with Karl so he could flee the mortal's presence. *But I have a job to do and part of that job is listening.*

With a resigned sigh, he returned to his seat, but he didn't place his napkin on his lap; he was done with any pretense of eating.

Karl watched him carefully, evaluating Diago's every move. "Thank you," he said after Diago sat. "Rudi's doctor and I thought we had his medication regulated. He was very attached to our mother. When she died, he began to rebel in various ways, pushing against the rules that were in place to protect him. Father managed him much better than I do." He took a cigarette from his pocket and lit it. "I see you're married. Do you and your wife have a family?"

"I have a son."

"How old?"

"Seven."

"And his mother?"

"She is dead."

"I'm sure he still longs for her."

"Every day."

"Then you see how hard it is."

No, he didn't. The differences between Rafael's and Rudi's ages were ten years and a great deal of maturity. Still, he let the comment go with a nod.

Karl exhaled a cloud of blue smoke over the table. "Rudi is a talented musician, and though it vexes me to say this, I feel his power is greater than mine."

Although Diago had made no move to speak, Karl lifted his hand as if to ward off protests to the contrary. "I think that getting a message to Don Guillermo and his nefilim will help Rudi more than all the medications in the world. He has this incredible talent and power that he simply doesn't know how to channel. I need your help."

Stunned by the mortal's audacity, as well as his callous willingness to use his brother to further his own agenda, Diago wasn't sure what to say. *They're not my responsibility. I need the violin and then I must escape their madness so I can report to Guillermo.* At this point, his best course of action was to play along with Karl's conceits. "I will speak to Don Guillermo on your behalf."

Karl crushed his cigarette in his plate. "Thank you."

"But two things must happen first: I must see the violin, and I must have a phone."

"Tomorrow. You may examine the violin, and then we will go into Offenburg."

Unless I find that violin tonight. Diago rose. "I hope you will excuse me, then. It's been a rather long day."

"Of course." Karl stood and bowed.

Diago made it to the door before Karl spoke.

"Oh, and Herr Alvarez—one more thing."

Diago paused, one hand on the doorframe.

"The house is old. You might hear noises in the night. Think nothing of them. Just don't leave your room to investigate. You might be hurt, stumbling around in the dark."

[18]

Diago left the dining room and wandered into the corridor, where yellow light glowed from the second-story landing. He gave the staircase a longing glance, wanting to do nothing more than to retreat to his room and fall into the bed. But if he did, he wouldn't awaken until morning, thereby losing any opportunity to search for the violin.

I can sleep when this is over. He turned away from the temptation.

The clink of china drifted down the hall as Karl cleared the table. Hoping Rudi was upstairs in his room, Diago decided to explore the lower level. *If there is a phone to be found, it will be somewhere down here.*

He paused by the music room, and after a moment's hesitation, ducked inside. His daimonic lineage gave him superior night vision, so he didn't bother with the lights.

Moving like a wraith, he retraced his path through the

cluttered furniture. Rudi said Karl hated their father, but the photographs indicated nothing but familial harmony.

A snapshot—a freeze in time. Anyone can feign joy for a moment. Diago turned in a slow circle. Nothing seemed out of the ordinary.

He left the room and continued to a set of closed pocket doors. Pushing one door aside, he gave himself just enough room to slip through. It was a parlor.

Even in the dim light, Diago could see how the elegant furnishings showed their age. An afghan disguised the threadbare condition of the couch, and the furniture was arranged to mask the frayed areas of the carpet.

Diago circled the room, searching for a phone. All he found were pictures of Karl.

On the mantel there was a photo of Karl posing with the body of a slain hart, his gun proudly clasped in his hands, and beside it was another with him standing over a bear, and yet another with a different hart . . . Karl apparently liked killing things.

Continuing his circuit, Diago found a framed photo in the back of the room. In it, Karl worked at a table with two refined gentlemen, one on either side of him, watching his movements with interest.

Diago recognized the mortals. The man on the left was Herbert Reichstein, a known publisher of German occult publications, and on the right was Ernst Issberner-Haldane—author of the renowned rejection letter on Karl's desk. Both were known members of the Nazi Party.

And so is our friend Sturmführer Heines. Were they all somehow connected? He examined the photo more closely, wondering how deeply members of Die Nephilim were involved with these mortals and their occult activities. That was a question Guillermo's spies would need to answer.

Returning his attention to the photograph, Diago noticed that Karl held a pen and was obviously in the process of drawing a sigil. On its face, the act was harmless. The mortal couldn't possibly bring the glyph to life since he lacked the nefilim's fire in his voice.

Still, this isn't some mortal parody of an angelic glyph. Karl had drawn an actual ward.

Turning the picture upside down, Diago peered at the sigil beneath Karl's pen. The camera had captured three loops and eight . . . maybe nine . . . lines over the rune Fehu.

Diago considered the meaning behind the rune. It signified freedom.

But freedom from what? he wondered. The angle of the camera obscured the rest of the sigil, so Diago couldn't get a clear idea of what Karl was trying to achieve, other than to impress Reichstein and Haldane with his arcane knowledge.

Startled by the sound of footsteps, Diago almost dropped the picture. The pace was clipped and nothing like Rudi's soft tread. *Karl.*

Diago's heartbeat picked up speed. He hadn't pulled the doors completely shut. *Shit.*

The footsteps stopped outside the parlor doors. Karl grasped the handles and closed the doors. Then his footsteps receded.

Diago waited for a slow count of sixty and then went to the pocket doors. When he heard no hint of movement from the other side, he slipped back into the hallway.

The corridor was empty. He had no idea where Karl had gone. Directly opposite was another set of doors. Like the parlor, the room was unlocked. It was a library.

Diago stepped inside and shut the door behind him. Outside the storm lashed the house. The rain changed to sleet.

A couch and three Georgian library chairs were placed around an imposing coffee table fashioned from the same period. A dry bar stood in one corner. Squatting before a pair of tall windows was a desk with a phone perched on one corner.

Dare I hope the brothers are lying and it works? He dared. Turning to the door, he traced a sigil of silence over the panels. With the power of his voice, he charged the glyph to life in shades of black and jade. The spell allowed sound to enter the library, but if Karl was still out there, he would hear nothing.

When Diago finished, he went to the desk and picked up the handset. A dial tone met his ear. He dialed the operator.

When she came on the line, he said, "I need to make a collect call." He gave her Guillermo's number. Within seconds he heard the phone ringing in Santuari.

"Ramírez residence."

A flush of relief went through him at the sound of Miquel's voice and left him weak. Moving around the desk, he sank into the chair, barely able to wait for the operator to establish that Miquel would accept the charges before he spoke.

Miquel must have felt the same way, because he cut the operator off before she could finish. "I'll accept the charges." She rang off and Miquel said, "Where are you?"

"I'm at the Grier house. I haven't seen the Stradivarius yet. Karl is cagey about the whereabouts and the younger brother probably doesn't know. There is some kind of anomaly here."

"Diago—"

"Listen to me, Miquel. I don't know how long I have before I'm discovered. Karl unearthed a set of foundation stones on the property from the twelfth century. As he told me about this, I recovered memories of a previous incarnation with a Sir George Abellio."

A thin buzz interrupted the line.

Miquel must have heard it, too, because he asked, "Are you still there?"

"Yes."

"Good. Listen to me. We know about . . ." The buzz grew louder, masking Miquel's words.

Know about what? Jordi? It was possible they were remembering, too. If that was the case, then Guillermo knew about Jordi and could take precautions.

The receiver crackled in Diago's ear. Maybe Karl hadn't lied about the phones after all. "Miquel? I didn't hear you." *Christ, not now, please, there is so much he must know.* He gripped the receiver so hard his hand ached. "Please, operator, the connection is deteriorating."

She didn't return to the line. Diago waited but the connection didn't clear. *Damn it.* "Miquel, I can't hear you. I can only hope you can hear me. I'm going to get the violin and get out of here as soon as I can."

"No . . ." The whine butchered Miquel's response into random words. ". . . the violin, you've got to get . . . Diago?" Then the buzz became a roar.

Diago winced. When the noise abated somewhat, he said, "I'll call you tomorrow with a full report."

Miquel's voice came through clearly once more—"Get . . ."—the buzz saw whine intensified again.

"Give my love to Rafael." Whether Miquel heard him or not, he didn't know. "I love you."

Miquel didn't answer.

Instead, the static growled through the earpiece. Diago thought he detected voices beneath the hum—a multitude of people speaking in a strident racket of different languages and dialects.

There couldn't be that many voices, not even on a party line. *It's an auditory hallucination.* He hung up.

Outside, the rain came down and the night wore on.

[19]

SANTUARI, SPAIN

Miquel sat behind Guillermo's desk and pressed the receiver against his ear. "No. Forget the violin. You've got to get out of there. Diago? Get out of that house tonight."

A loud hiss crackled across the line before it rose in pitch and squealed, like a radio dial crashing through the frequencies. The receiver suddenly went dead.

"Diago?" He'd lost the connection, and he still had no idea if his husband had heard him. "Christ. Come on. Diago, are you there?"

A low murmur was his answer. *Maybe I haven't lost him after all.* "Diago, please."

The murmur rose to a clamor, and several voices suddenly spoke at once. "Michel?"

The hair on Miquel's arms rose. "That's not my name," he said.

"But it was," murmured the macabre chorus. "In that incarnation, you were Michel, and Yago betrayed you. Do you remember? You rode into the courtyard at Guillaume's side. Yago stood with George and Frauja—he sang with them against you."

Miquel shook his head. *No. That is a lie.*

But it wasn't.

The moment was a snapshot in his brain. He remembered looking up and seeing Yago at the window, using the lyra's bow to punch the strings—*quick jabs: strike, strike, strike*—then what?

Then my horse panicked, turning in a tight circle. Miquel tried to reconcile Yago's betrayal with the man he loved in this incarnation. He closed his eyes and whispered, "Diago, can you hear me?"

The murmuring voices continued, "Yago made no move to save you. Do you know why? Because he doesn't love you. He never loved you. He is here with us now."

The dial tone suddenly buzzed in Miquel's ear. He stood perfectly still, waiting for his heart to stop beating so fast—*it's too fast, everything is happening too fast and I can't control it, not from Santuari.*

Miquel suddenly understood Guillermo's desperate need to go after Diago. He wished he could hand the reins over to another nefil and fly after both of them, but that was wishful thinking. Guillermo was right: love was a powerful force, but it wouldn't save him against creatures like Frauja.

"Miquel?"

Startled, he dropped the handset. It thumped on a stack of files and landed on its side.

Juanita stood in the doorway. "I didn't mean to startle you." She came to the desk and placed the handset on the cradle. "Who was that?"

"It was Diago. At first. He tried to call, but we had . . ." *What? What the hell caused interference like that?* He swallowed hard and started again. "On the phone, just now, I heard Diago's voice. He was trying to brief me on what he'd found when the line erupted with interference, and then voices. It began as a hissing sound and then turned into a Greek chorus. Is this what Guillermo heard on the radio?"

Her frown did nothing to reassure him. "It's similar. The difference is that Frauja used the phone lines from the Grier house to get into ours."

"Can he do that?"

"The phones were warded. He shouldn't have gotten through." She paused and considered the handset. "Unless the old sigils trapping Frauja are more damaged than we thought. Somehow he must have tapped into the Griers' wiring. Try calling back."

Miquel dialed the Griers' number. The steady pulse of a busy signal was all they heard.

Juanita traced a new glyph over the transmitter and hummed an ethereal note. The bright lines wiggled into the handset and then disappeared. "That should prevent him from getting through again."

Should. Miquel scowled and sat in Guillermo's chair. "Should" wasn't nearly good enough to set his mind at ease, but he didn't question Juanita's judgment. Instead he occupied himself with shuffling the stacks of folders until he found his cigarettes.

Juanita took the seat across from him. "You mentioned the voices spoke to you. What did they say?"

Times like these, he wished he had his husband's penchant for brusque retorts. *But that's not my way. Besides, the more she knows, the better she'll be able to diagnose the problem.*

He sighed and said, "They called me Michel. That was my name in my last incarnation. They said Yago betrayed me and Guillaume—that he sang with our enemies."

"Do you believe that?"

He lit his cigarette and avoided her gaze. "The voices didn't lie. I remember that day."

"And you believe Yago betrayed you and Guillaume?"

Miquel took a fraction too long to respond. "I don't know what to think."

"Miquel. Really? Do you think Diago betrayed you?"

He exhaled a cloud of smoke and rubbed his eyes. "You don't understand."

She leaned forward and rapped the desk with her knuckles. "I understand better than you think. Those voices you heard colored Yago's participation to fit a certain narrative, and now your imagination and doubts are doing the rest."

"It's not that *I* doubt him. I'm worried about what the others will think if they hear of this." Or was that a convenient lie he told himself?

Juanita settled back in her seat and considered him with her cool gaze. "So that explains his behavior."

"Who?"

"Diago."

"What are you getting at?"

"Diago went for centuries in this incarnation without using his natural abilities. I suspect that had more to do with appeasing you than any excuse he tells me or himself. If he denied his song, then neither angels nor daimons could accuse him of treachery, and that made you happy, not him."

Miquel scoffed at her. "Do you really think I have that kind of power over him?"

"Have you ever seen his face when you speak harshly to him?"

Miquel's incredulous smile faded. Against his will, he recalled Diago's hurt when he'd accused him of deliberately not working on the Key. *He was exhausted and afraid and I berated him like he was a child.* Nor was that the only incident during their long relationship.

"You're right," he whispered. "Jesus. I've treated him badly. I owe him an apology."

"You're missing the point. You're also endangering yourself and Diago. Frauja couldn't have exacerbated your insecurities unless that anxiety was already seeded in your heart."

Miquel's gut clenched as if she'd punched him. *Because she did, only instead of using her fist, she hit me with the truth.* For one fleeting moment, he had believed that Yago betrayed him, and if Yago betrayed him, wouldn't Diago eventually do the same?

But he wouldn't. Not Diago. "How could I think such a thing about someone I love?"

"This is why the angels are forbidden to instigate the nefilim's memories. It's too easy to manipulate vague impressions into facts." Her smile grew gentle now that she saw he understood her concerns. "Besides, Diago has hurt you in the past. He is no saint, but he is not half the sinner some of our nefilim believe him to be."

Miquel sighed. "I am so afraid . . . no, that's wrong." He met her gaze. "I'm terrified for him. Especially with this business with Lucia and Muñoz. Do you know what it will do to him if he's accused?"

"You're not the guardian of his virtue. You have to learn to step back. Give him the freedom to make mistakes. Otherwise, you force him to adhere to impossible standards of conduct, and when he becomes stressed, he backs away from you, from us."

In the past, they had parted ways when Diago needed space to breathe. *And that is what he always called it: space to breathe. Only now there is Rafael to consider, and as a member of Los Nefilim, Diago can't simply walk away.* "Okay. I see what you're saying. I'll back off."

"Good."

The sigils chimed, indicating that someone was on their way up the stairs. Miquel went into the conference room and Juanita followed him.

Sofia Corvo entered the room. Like Juanita, she favored loose trousers and soft-soled shoes, and there any resemblances ended. Where Juanita healed, Sofia killed and she enjoyed her work. Her chestnut curls escaped her bun and clung to her pale forehead, framing a face that projected the cunning of a cat.

"Please tell me you have good news," Miquel said as he circled the table.

"We found Muñoz."

Finally, he had a situation within the realm of his control. "Great work, Sofia. Thank you. Is he at the finca yet?"

Her scowl told Miquel he wasn't going to like the next part. "He had cyanide."

"Oh fuck."

"And a ticket to Lisbon in his pocket."

"Who does he know in Portugal?" Miquel went to the wall map, but instead of Lisbon, his eyes kept following the lines north to Durbach. "Sofia, do you have counterparts in the Portuguese Inner Guard who might be helpful?"

She shook her head. "The Portuguese Inner Guard keep stalling me when I ask for information. They know something, but they're not willing to share."

"Do they say why?"

"General Sanjurjo's attempted coup spooked them. Since mortal events often mirror ours, they fear the Spanish Inner Guard will soon be challenged from within its ranks. They want to maintain neutrality until they're sure Sanjurjo's rebellion is an isolated incident constrained to mortal affairs."

"Do they want to remain neutral, or pick up the pieces and broaden their territories if the Spanish Guard falls?" He turned and pinned her with his gaze. She didn't answer. She didn't need to. "I want to know the names of every nefil in Los Nefilim who has had contact with our Portuguese friends, and then find any correlations in their activities. Start with military records, the church, bank accounts. This might be a time to follow the money."

"Is that all?"

"For now." Miquel nodded. It was a slim lead, but he'd take anything he could get. "Thank you, Sofia."

Sofia nodded and left them.

The door had barely closed when the staccato beats of the teletype startled them.

"Christ. What now?" Miquel went to the machine. His blood turned to ice as he read the type: *He doesn't love you, he never loved you. He is here with us now . . . here with us now . . . here with us . . . with u—*

Miquel reached down to unplug the machine. Juanita grabbed his wrist. She motioned for him to stand back. When he was nearly at the door, she placed her palms on the clacking machine and closed her eyes.

Thin lines of electricity popped around her fingertips to encompass her arms. Her mortal body fell away and she stood before the machine in her angelic form. Three sets of wings spread wide and almost touched the ceiling. Midnight fire coiled around the otherworldly orbs that were her eyes.

She gave a sharp cry and shaped a sigil over the teletype. A surge of power flowed from her hands to envelope the metal casing with indigo flames.

The flash was so bright, Miquel covered his eyes. When he looked again, Juanita's fire shot downward, through the wiring and into the electrical socket. The house lights flickered from the surge.

A loud bang erupted from the Creed Model 7 followed by the acidic smoke of burning wires. As the house lights brightened, the blue flames receded. Juanita's mortal form coalesced around her again.

Miquel hurried to the machine and ripped the casing open. He jerked the roll of paper out to prevent it from catching fire.

"Jesus Christ, what the hell did you do?" He went to the window and threw it open.

"I gave him a taste of his own medicine." She stepped back and folded her arms as she frowned at the machine. "I wonder what's happening in Durbach right now."

[20]

KARINHALL

Diago stared at the telephone. Hesitantly, he lifted the receiver to his ear again. Not even a dial tone hummed through the earpiece. He hung up. *I'll call them tomorrow from the Angel's Nest.*

The silencing glyph still burned bright over the door. *Take advantage of it.* Opening one of the desk's drawers, he searched through the receipts and papers, looking for any connection between Karl, Jordi, or Heines.

The checkbook indicated the house was running in the red. No surprise there.

A quick search through another file labeled "Correspondence" produced no evidence that Karl was in touch with any nefilim Diago knew. All he discovered were several terse notes between Karl and Haldane, and these outlined a relationship fraught with disagreement and discord. Nor did he find any indication that Karl knew that Sir George Abellio had reincarnated as Jordi Abelló.

On a more mundane level, a letter from Karl's solicitor

suggested having someone test Karinhall's wiring, because the house seemed to use an abnormal amount of electricity.

I'm hitting dead ends. With nothing else of interest coming to light, Diago returned the documents to the drawer. He looked around the room. Rotating bookcases were the stuff of films, and although he checked any and all cabinets that might conceal a violin, his search turned up empty. As he eased the last drawer shut, he noticed the edges of his sigil were beginning to fray. *Time to go.*

At the threshold, he paused and listened. Cracking the door, he saw no one, so he stepped quickly into the corridor. The lights flickered. An electrical whine hummed through the house, sounding almost like a thing in pain.

Diago looked up at the light over the entryway. *A power surge and a strong one at that.* Karl's solicitor was right in suggesting an electrician should check the wiring.

The hall tree's mirror flashed, almost as if someone had fired a flashbulb directly at the glass. The glimmer of a shadow passed across the surface. A closer examination revealed only his reflection.

Jesus, I'm spooking myself. He backed away and went upstairs.

He still hadn't investigated the rooms in the wing to the right of the stairs. *Do I dare risk it?*

To his left, Karl's door was shut, and the light was off. Diago assumed he was still occupied somewhere downstairs.

Light spilled from Rudi's open door.

Rudi's voice floated into the hall. "I miss you so terribly."

A search of the other wing would have to wait.

"Please come out. Just for a moment. Please?" He sounded

lost, like a child. "Stop being angry. This is the last time I'll help Karl. I promise."

Now he had Diago's undivided attention. *Help Karl do what?*

Another pause. "I know I promised before, but this is different. I really mean it this time. He said that if I help him, he'll let you go and stop the voices in my head."

Is the boy actually psychotic? It was possible, yet something about the diagnosis left Diago troubled. *The explanation is too pat, too easy . . . too . . . what?* he mused as he reached into his pocket and touched the brooch.

Too mortal.

And didn't Juanita warn me against relying on mortal remedies?

Psychosis was a mortal diagnosis, and the situation in this house was definitely supernatural. Possession, on the other hand . . .

The brothers were descendants of lesser nefilim, and as such, both Karl and Rudi would have been ripe for possession during their prepubescent years. The chemical imbalances in their brains opened channels that either an angel or a daimon might exploit. Once the malignancy gained a grip, it would hold on until the boys aged enough to reclaim their minds.

Rudi was seventeen, so the spirit's hold on him was probably fading. *But it still retains some power.* He recalled the unpleasant buzz in Rudi's voice when he denied knowing Harvey.

Diago made a slight noise to alert Rudi to his presence and paused at the youth's door. "Hello."

Rudi wiped his eyes. "Hi."

"I don't mean to intrude. I just wanted to see if you're okay."

"I'm fine." The flirtatious youth from the dinner table was gone. "And I'm not insane," he whispered.

"I know," Diago said.

Rudi sniffled and faced the wall for a moment, struggling to master his emotions. When he turned again, he attempted to resurrect his former jocularity. "Did you finally get tired of Karl's ridiculous posturing?"

"Your brother has some interesting ideas."

"That's putting it mildly." Rudi held the compact and turned it over in his hands. When he noticed Diago watching him, he explained, "It was Mother's."

"I see."

"It's all I have of her now."

"I'm very sorry."

"Do you believe in hell, Herr Alvarez?"

Diago thought of the Great War and the no-man's-land at the front. "Yes, though I often believe it is a place of our own making."

The youth's eyes shined. "If we make our own hell, can we unmake it?"

He feels guilt about something, and if he feels guilt, he has a conscience. Whatever this spirit manipulated him into doing, Rudi wasn't a willing participant.

Diago realized the youth was waiting for an answer. "I think . . . no, I *believe* these . . . hells . . . become a part of us, but they don't have to be the only part. If we examine how we have wronged others and accept responsibility for those actions, then we can work toward repairing the damage. It's not the same as unmaking it, but it's better than allowing it to consume us."

"But hell can also be a place."

Diago thought of the western front. "Sometimes."

Rudi was very still and quiet for a moment, and then he said, "You know, my mother wanted to sell Karinhall. She claimed that something evil walked in this house—that it was a little piece of hell."

If he had any doubt about the anomaly being inside the house, he lost it now. The boys most likely inherited their angelic nature from Karin Grier, and as a female descendant of the nefilim, her power would have eclipsed that of her sons. "Were you angry at her for wanting to sell the house?"

"No, not me. But Karl was furious."

Diago recalled the information from Guillermo's files. "Is that why the constables accused him of killing your mother?"

"It was Father. He was in such a state of grief when he found her . . . both of us were." His voice trailed off and he was silent for a moment, consumed by memories Diago couldn't see. "Anyway, Father made all sorts of wild accusations. When he blamed Karl for Mother's death, a constable heard him, and events spiraled from there.

"Once Father regained his senses, he was mortified and did everything he could to ensure Karl's exoneration. Of course, Berlin's society pages delivered the scandal to the masses, and the locals in Durbach embellished even the most insane rumors. Karl has never forgiven them. That's why he travels to Offenburg to conduct his business." Rudi shrugged and touched the corner of his swollen lip. "The end."

"The end," Diago murmured.

Rudi rose and came to the door. "I must apologize, Herr

Alvarez. I'm not feeling well all of a sudden. I hope you won't think me rude if I retire."

"Of course not." Diago bowed his head. "I wish you a good night."

"Good night, Herr Alvarez."

Before Diago reached his room, he heard Rudi's door snick shut behind him. He paused, noticing that Rudi's shadow remained beneath the threshold. *He's waiting to hear my door shut.*

Was it so he could continue his one-sided conversation, or did the brothers have a more perverse reason for retiring so early? Karl's warning not to wander the halls after dark was still fresh in Diago's mind. Was the caveat meant to keep him in his room, or to incite his curiosity?

Only one way to find out. Diago shut his door and locked it.

He fashioned a sigil of protection over the lock and charged it with his voice. Feeling somewhat safer, he removed his tie and shirt, and then drew one of Miquel's favorite sweaters from his bag, inhaling his husband's scent as he pulled the garment over his head.

Christ but I miss him and Rafael. He envisioned them back in Santuari, going through their evening rituals. He wished he was home, preparing to sleep in his own bed with Miquel sprawled next to him and Rafael across the hall, telling Ghost about his day.

Rudi's radio burst into life, jerking Diago from his pleasant reverie. The static hissed until the dial found the ninth movement of Berlioz's *Requiem*. A tenor, singing the "Sanctus," was echoed by other voices. The chorus sounded odd, nothing like the cohesive performances Diago had heard in the past.

The radio signal is probably picking up interference from other stations, he mused before turning his attention back to the business at hand.

Rolling the sweater's too long sleeves over his wrists, he planned his next move. Once the brothers were asleep, he intended to slip into the other wing and have a look inside those rooms. If he managed that without waking either of them, then he would break the lock on the pocket doors and inspect the third floor.

And the minute I find the violin, I'll get out of here. He packed his bag and set it beside the door. As he did, he found his eye drawn back to the armoire.

"It's time to see what they're hiding under my nose," he whispered.

[21]

Diago examined the armoire's lock. Something appeared to be jammed in the keyhole. He tested the doors, but they still didn't give. *Fine. A sigil then.*

He formed a glyph over the metal plate.

Across the corridor, static growled as *Requiem* came to an end. Rudi must have fiddled with the dial, because the radio squalled and then homed in on a new station's signal. The announcer introduced the Royal Albert Hall Orchestra's recording of Tchaikovsky's *1812 Overture.*

The violas and cellos moaned through the opening hymn, soft and plaintive as a prayer. Diago waited for the brass to enter the piece, so the horns would cover the sound of his song. When the music segued to the underlying melody of "La Marseillaise," he gave a sharp cry. The colors of his aura charged the ward and shattered the lock.

The doors popped open. Diago caught them before they could swing back and hit the wall.

A full-length mirror covered the inside of the right-hand door. The glass was mottled and black in places. He barely made out his reflection. *Was this why Rudi told me to be glad the armoire didn't open?*

He shrugged off the idea and turned to examine the cluttered contents. A man's brightly embroidered jacket with a satin lining hung on a rack. Judging from the pictures he'd seen of the family, the coat wouldn't fit the Grier men, nor could he imagine any of them wearing anything so flashy. The style was more in keeping with the taste of a rogue Diago had once known by the name of Rainier Laurent.

Diago lifted the jacket and checked the pockets. They were empty. Something within the fabric crinkled, though. Curious, he ripped the seam, and there, in the lining, he found a set of identity papers for Pierre Laurent, one of Rainier's many aliases.

"Rainier?" He glanced at the armoire.

A muffled moan seemed to come from the other side of the mirror. Diago's flesh horripilated at the sound. *What the hell?*

Outside, the wind howled. The house creaked and groaned.

"Christ," he murmured. No one moaned behind the mirror—it was only the house, shuddering beneath the storm. "I'm spooking myself again."

He turned back to the armoire just as a woman's blue cloche hat fell from the top shelf. Diago dropped Rainier's coat in time to catch the hat. The bow was torn and hung askew from its ribbon. Inside, bits of bone and brown hair were stuck to the name written in black marker on the lining.

Laura Howe.

Diago touched the rust-colored bloodstains. The bone shards were thin—*like someone shattered her skull.*

He had known her, too. She used to sing in the Parisian cafés, her voice full like the summer sun. He'd once played his violin in the park while she turned her freckled face toward the sky.

And someone murdered her here. With a sinking heart, Diago removed the armoire's clothing piece by piece. He found identity papers, jewelry, and coins sewn into hemlines. More ominously, he found bullet holes and bloodstains on the clothing that soon lay piled beside him.

The cabinet seemed bottomless.

He opened a drawer. A flash of red caught his eye. He hoped he was wrong. He knew he wasn't. It was Harvey's scarf.

"No," he whispered, clenching the silk in his hands. Had Frau Weber returned it to the armoire while Diago was engaged with Karl and Rudi in the music room? Probably.

Anger threaded through his veins . . . and fear. How many nefilim had died in this charnel house?

On the other side of the hall, cannon fire erupted during the finale of Tchaikovsky's *Overture*. Diago's head snapped up at the sound. *That isn't right. Cannons weren't used in that recording.*

The distinctive thunder of a howitzer overrode the cannon fire. It came from his right. *From behind the mirror.*

Sweat slicked Diago's palms as he forced himself to look.

Fog undulated over the glass and formed around the splotches to spread . . .

Not fog . . . , Diago thought.

Dark sounds. Hundreds, maybe thousands, of dark sounds, coalescing and congealing on the other side of the mirror in shades of purple and black and gray. Thin cracks wormed between the lines and stretched across the mirror. Ichor seeped from the crevices.

A palm smacked the glass.

Diago jumped backward. Harvey's scarf slipped from his hands and fluttered to his feet.

The owner of the hand swiped at the colors. The dark sounds smeared but never really parted. Even so, Diago made out the broken nose that sat crooked on Harvey Lucas's face.

With his own breath loud in his ears, Diago stared in disbelief. "Harvey?"

Harvey's mouth moved soundlessly but Diago could read his lips. *Copped it, mate, I've copped it.*

It was a phrase Diago knew well from the war, one that echoed through the trenches after a shelling. For the mortals, it meant they'd caught a shell; for the nefilim it signified they'd been hit by a killing glyph. The result was all the same—it was a mortal wound.

"Harvey, no . . ." He stepped forward, ready to give his old friend whatever comfort he could.

Harvey shook his head and signed for Diago to stay back. With great effort, he forced his finger through the colors of the dark sounds, tracing his warning in large sloping numbers and letters: 0 HOUR AT 0300 DON'T TOUCH MIRROR OR UR NAPOO SOULEA.

Harvey's eyes went wide. Something yanked him away from the glass. The bruised colors flowed over the spot and dissolved the words.

"Harvey!" Diago shouted. He started forward and caught himself before he rapped his palm against the mirror. DON'T TOUCH MIRROR OR UR NAPOO.

Curling his fingers into a fist, he backed away from the armoire and quickly deciphered Harvey's message. The first two parts were easy.

Zero hour at 0300. Whatever attack was coming would happen at three. *Napoo* was trench jargon for "finished." *Don't touch the mirror or you're finished.*

Which meant the strike would probably originate from that tainted glass. Now Rudi's response to Diago's comment about the locked armoire made perfect sense. *Be glad.*

"The bastard knew this was going to happen." Diago grabbed an armchair and dragged it to the armoire. He slammed the doors shut and shoved the chair against them.

As he backed away from the closet, he considered the last word: *SOULEA.* It made no sense. He didn't believe it was a part of the war lexicon from any of the combatants.

All I know is that something grabbed Harvey. Some *thing* big enough to wrench the huge nefil backward like he was a rag doll.

The anomaly. *It has to be.* The entity was trapped and attempting to free itself.

And the Grier brothers are helping it. But how? Diago looked at the clothing and personal effects spread across the floor. The answer was obvious. "They're feeding it nefilim."

And if I don't get out of here, I'm next.

He went to the door and grabbed his bag. The doorknob refused to budge.

Standing back, he formed a sigil to break the lock. This time he didn't wait for the cover of music. No sooner had he finished the last line did he snap his song at the ward. Shades of black and green enveloped the plate, swirling over the metal. The glyph's tongue flicked into the keyhole.

Without warning, a brilliant flash of light shot from the lock and blinded Diago. Somehow his song had turned against him. He dropped his bag and formed a protective ward, but he was too late.

The white light struck him, the blow landing like an electric shock, knocking him off his feet, and the floor rushed up, and the night came down, and the world went black, and silence descended quick and hard . . . like the stillness that follows the falling of a bomb.

Diago dreamed of digging. They were in a field. Maybe it was at the Somme, maybe Dammstrasse—he couldn't remember where, because the relentless bombing made everyplace the same. In need of a trench, his company dug into the mud.

They were two meters deep when Diago's shovel went through a man's stomach. It was a grave from earlier in the war. The uniforms were French. The bodies were putrid and had begun to liquefy; their flesh was the color and texture of Camembert cheese—yellow and soft, dissolving beneath the rain.

Someone shouted, "Incoming!"

Then came the distinct riffle in the air that preceded a shell.

They didn't try to pinpoint the threat. Their bodies were conditioned to respond to the noise.

Automatically, they threw themselves into the grave. The ground shook. A plume of mud showered them, miring the living to the dead.

A heartbeat passed and then two. They rose and began to dig again.

Dark sounds erupted around them. Diago saw them as purplish clouds, black like flies, rising over the landscape. They seeped into his ears and crawled into his mouth . . . and still he burrowed through the dead until . . .

A ferocious crash thundered through the room. Diago's eyes snapped open. His clothes were clammy against his flesh. Bile rose to the back of his throat. His head pounded and his vision blurred. He rolled to his knees. The dream clung to him like a caul.

I'm in Durbach. In Karinhall. Wake up, wake up, wake up!

His gaze swept over the face of his watch.

0300.

Zero hour.

That did it. He finally sloughed his way free of the nightmare.

The armoire's doors burst open, flinging the chair across the room. It shattered against the wall.

Static hissed from Rudi's radio.

The lamp dimmed and brightened.

Diago scrambled to his feet.

Overhead, a hairline crack zigzagged through the plaster and stopped when it met the wall over the bed's headboard. The rust-colored blotches throbbed in shades of crimson and black.

Those aren't stains from a leak, Diago suddenly realized. *It's a sigil.*

He whirled to face the armoire's mirror. "Who are you?" *What are you?*

Four loud knocks struck the walls in rapid succession. The wallpaper rippled as if something moved beneath it. The bulge was too thin to be a mouse or rat. More like a fingernail, tracing a line to a certain point.

Another undulation swelled over the headboard. This one was thicker. Diago designed a sharp-edged sigil and sang it to life. The white fire of Prieto's magic joined with his. He shaped the glyph with a sinister edge and threw it at the wall.

The ward stabbed the bulge. A scream, high and thin, pierced the night. The paper darkened around the tear. The same oily black substance that had oozed from the mirror dripped to the wainscoting. A hard shudder heaved beneath the paper. Then the bulge disappeared.

Trusting neither the armoire nor its tainted mirror at his back, Diago moved toward the center of the room, closer to the hearth.

The lamp's bulb burst in a shower of sparks. With the storm outside clouding the bare fingernail of a new moon, the complete darkness hampered even his superior night vision. He summoned a sigil for fire and tossed it toward the fireplace. The dry wood caught and flames blazed to life.

Across the hall, the radio sputtered through the frequencies and then landed on a choral arrangement. The violin's half-familiar melody knocked against the back of Diago's brain, worming its way toward his tongue. The desire to join the strange chorus grew until it became an unbearable need.

The chorus sang through Rudi's radio. "I remember when you were Yago."

Diago reached into his pocket and withdrew the brooch. The memory of that incarnation came flooding back. Bernard and George and the chapel were just the beginning.

Or maybe closer to the end. "And you are Frauja," he said. *Or are you?* Frauja was an angel, but this creature's voice was muddied by a thousand voices, constructed with the dark sounds of violent deaths. How could they be the same?

SOULEA.

Diago finally comprehended the mystery behind Harvey's warning. *Soul-eater. Harvey tried to write soul-eater, because this* is *Frauja. He has absorbed the auras of both the daimon- and the angel-born; their voices augment his, but they have also become a part of him. And it is the songs of the daimon-born that have masked his angelic nature.*

That likewise explained the unholy chorus. Frauja's true angelic voice was lost to him now. *He can only speak through the dead.*

This was Durbach's anomaly.

And he will be my death if I don't move with care. "Frauja." Diago gripped the brooch tightly. "I remember you."

"You asked for my song and I sang you my beginning: how the Firstborn angels lost our rebellion and how we were banished from that dimension."

"You told me that many tried to return," Diago whispered. "But their songs were turned against them and they died, flaming like stars as they fell."

"Yes," hissed the chorus. "So we fled until we discovered the earthly realm. Here we found the mortals and conquered the daimons to establish our rule. Remember me."

"I remember you loved me," Diago blurted. "Amor vincit omnia—that is what you said to me on our first night together . . . love conquers all."

As soon as the words left his mouth, he knew they were a lie. What they had experienced in that incarnation, it wasn't love. Call it infatuation, a burning need to possess another, or even simply lust, but it was not love.

Still . . . if Frauja recalls it as such, I might be able to win his trust. All he needed to do was buy time. If zero hour was at three, then the attack probably ended at dawn. He glanced at his watch. It had stopped.

Static growled through the radio.

From anger or because Frauja wants to hear more? After another moment of silence slipped past, Diago took a chance it was the latter. "I remember your eyes . . . they are the color of tourmaline threaded with ribbons of gold, and they become a brilliant green when you wear your mortal form. Your body is perfection."

"I am burned and scarred from the war," snarled the chorus.

You're also vain. Diago trapped the retort behind his teeth. "Only on your left side. You think those old wounds mar your beauty, but they don't. They lend you character and grace."

Mollified, the chorus murmured, "Liar." But they gave the insult a note of affection.

Diago glanced toward the window. Would the dawn ever come? "I remember we would walk in the night with the stars raining over us."

"Why did you betray me?" asked the chorus.

Diago's heart stammered. He fought to keep his fear out of his voice. "I didn't."

"Liar." This time the slur carried the angel's acrimony. "You sang against me and locked me in this prison realm."

Diago ran his thumb over the brooch's emerald. The setting pricked his finger. Blood stained the angel's mouth.

He stared at it dumbly. *Christ, think, say something, any-*

thing! "It was George," he said. "He was jealous of us. He locked you away and killed me."

Frauja didn't reply. The silence stretched between them.

Does he believe me? Afraid of the answer, Diago didn't dare ask.

The armoire's door widened until the splotchy mirror reflected the outline of Diago's body.

"Come to me, Yago," sang the angel with his dark sounds. "Come to me now and I will believe you. I will offer you forgiveness and forget the past. There will be no vehmgericht if you give yourself to me tonight."

Harvey's warning came roaring back into Diago's mind: *DON'T TOUCH MIRROR OR UR NAPOO.*

If he stepped through that mirror, Frauja would never let him leave. *And I will never see my son again, or Miquel, never hold them or feel their love.*

"No," he whispered. "No," he repeated, louder. "What we had is no more. I cannot go back into the past."

The angel on the brooch opened its mouth, screeching like a violin in pain—in his mind Diago heard the bow punch the strings (quick jabs: strike, strike, strike)—and the cacophony of bombs whistled with a thunderous clamor, like the percussion of a thousand drums, the beats coalescing into the steady pulse of timpani playing a funeral march, a dirge that sounded like nefilim crying, crying, crying as they sang . . .

Harvey's cheek suddenly smashed against the glass.

Diago instinctively reached out for his friend.

Harvey tried to shake his head, but a massive hand that could only belong to Frauja pinioned his face against the mirror.

Diago stepped forward. "There has to be a way, Harvey!"

Harvey's mouth said, "Help me." The sound of his voice came not from the armoire but through Rudi's radio.

Because it isn't Harvey speaking. Frauja is manipulating him like a puppet.

As if to confirm Diago's suspicions, Harvey traced a new warning, *DON'T.*

Frauja's fingers squeezed the dying nefil's head.

Harvey's mouth opened in a silent cry. The red and blue colors of his aura deepened into purple spirals of pain. He gasped and fought for control, the battle written on his blunt features.

Rage flowed through Diago's blood. "Let him go!" He took three steps toward the mirror. There had to be a way to extract Harvey from that hell.

He was less than a meter away when Harvey finally pushed his last message through the radio: ". . . son . . . your son . . . th-think . . . of . . ."

Static drowned the rest.

My son. Terror washed over Diago and froze him in place. *How does he know about Rafael?* And then it hit him: his conversation with Karl. *And my phone call to Santuari . . . oh, Jesus Christ . . .* That was why Frauja had allowed Diago to move through the house with impunity. *I thought I was spying, but it's Frauja who knows everything about me.*

The realization must have showed on Diago's face, because Harvey smiled a crooked smile. With his free hand, he gave Diago the thumbs-up.

The angel's hand pressed harder. A thin line of blood squirted from Harvey's nose and his smile disappeared. The whites of his eyes flamed red as blood vessels burst. Dark sounds picked up the blood spatters and linked the mottled spots to form a sigil.

Diago realized the truth Harvey had known all along: *I can't save him by sacrificing us both. But I can make damn sure his death isn't wasted.*

Diago designed a glyph to seal the border between the mirror and the mortal realm. With a wild cry of desperation, he vocalized the sigil to life and charged it with the magic of Prieto's tear, and then he sent it across the glass.

Frauja's ward pushed against the barrier between the realms. Harvey's blood lent strength to the angel's spell. The air grew oppressive and the temperature dropped.

Diago's glyph shimmered . . . but held. *Barely. It's barely holding.* Hoarse with fatigue, he raised his song again to shoot his aura into the sigil. Viridian lines edged in black surged through the ward.

The thin hum of the dark sounds swept into the room, accompanied by the percussion of the bombs. The dissonance rose to become a single piercing chord that brought tears of agony to Diago's eyes.

The armoire shattered. Shards of wood flew through the room. The concussion sent Diago reeling. He stumbled over the settee and fell. The couch overturned and covered him. He huddled there, covering his head and shielding his eyes as the splinters rained down around him.

After the last board clattered to the floor, the silence grew so intense Diago thought he'd gone deaf. He counted ten heartbeats, then twenty, and then sixty. When he finally peeked over the lip of the settee, he saw scorch marks smoldered on the wood floor. The armoire's door hung by a single hinge, but the mirror was intact.

Frauja remained in his prison realm.

For now.

In the hearth, the fire burned low, yet the room seemed brighter. It took him a moment to realize that dawn had come, bringing with it another storm.

2
September 1932

free at last

[22]

STRASBOURG, FRANCE
PLACE DE LA GARE

At the train station, Guillermo entered the main concourse and soon found the tobacconist's shop. Inside, a young nefil with blond braids and a red bow tie worked the counter.

Based on Suero's description, she could be none other than Lorelei. He browsed the counter while he waited for her to finish with two young mortals who were flirting with her. On any other day, Guillermo might have enjoyed the show. Today his temper was as short as his time.

Taking off his gloves, he placed his right hand on the glass case. Lorelei's gaze flickered to Guillermo's gold signet of office.

He growled, "My train will be here soon. Can I get some service?"

The more ambitious mortal—or, as Guillermo thought of him, the one with a death wish—glared at Guillermo. "Wait your turn, old man."

His friend measured Guillermo's dark scowl and got the

message. "Let's go, Louis." He aimed a protesting Louis toward the door.

Once they were gone, Lorelei asked, "How was your train, Monsieur?"

"I drove."

She reached beneath the counter and withdrew a cigar with a gold band. "Then you're free to enjoy Strasbourg at your leisure. Enjoy your stay."

Guillermo paid for the cigar and returned to his car. Inside the vehicle, he removed the cigar's band and noted the address.

Twenty minutes later, Guillermo found the warehouse in a business district near the Rhine. He pulled up to the gate and gave the guard the cigar band.

"Very good, sir. Please follow the road to the right and someone will show you where to park."

"Thank you." Guillermo rolled up the window and turned onto the narrow lane.

A woman wearing work clothes and a heavy wool jacket gestured for him to park between two lorries. He grabbed his bag and left the car.

The woman was none other than Sabine Rousseau herself, the queen of Les Néphilim. She was a heavy-bodied woman and almost as tall as Guillermo. Her dark hair showed streaks of silver, and the wrinkles around her eyes had deepened since their last meeting. A thin scar ran from her right brow to her chin—a souvenir from the Great War.

"Madame." He held out his hand, which she shook with a firm grip. "Your graciousness knows no bounds."

"Don't make a saint of me, Don Guillermo. I have my

limits, just as you do." Her smile rounded the sharpness from her words. "I'm glad you arrived safely. We were hoping your man would be headed toward the Angel's Nest by now." At Guillermo's raised eyebrow, she explained, "It's a pub we own in Kehl. So far, we've managed to keep it off Queen Jaeger's radar, and we use it as a rendezvous."

"But Diago hasn't returned?"

"No." She guided him deeper into the warehouse. "I remember him from the war. He's cunning and quick. What makes you think he can't handle the situation?"

"He's up against a rogue angel."

"Then I won't keep you long," Rousseau said as she opened the door to an office.

A set of dirty workman's clothes were thrown across a chair. Scuffed boots and heavy gloves completed the outfit.

Guillermo took off his hat. "What do I owe you for all this, Sabine?"

She perched on the corner of the desk and answered his question with a question. "You know that the Nazis gained quite a few seats in the Reichstag this summer?"

He nodded. "I'm aware. We're keeping an eye on the situation."

"There's a nasty little piece of work by the name of Hitler, who is gaining political traction. A couple of years ago, the upper classes laughed him off, thinking him a clown. Now they invite him to their salons and make him the talk of the town. He tells the common people what they want to hear: that he's going to make Germany a great nation again; there will be jobs and prosperity and he'll achieve this by kicking all the foreigners out of Germany. In lieu of concrete plans, he offers them nothing but rhetoric, and he fills their empty minds with delusions of grandeur. The people are lapping it up like pigs at a trough."

The chills going down his back had nothing to do with the warehouse's icy air. "They want someone to come and solve their problems for them."

Rousseau's brow creased. "The angels are . . ."

"Uneasy?" Guillermo unbuttoned his shirt.

She frowned and glanced aside. "Something tells me the Great War was a dress rehearsal."

"You know I'll have your back regardless of what the mortals do." He put his pistol on the desk and asked again, "What do I owe you for this trip?"

"Answers."

"About what?"

"We followed the trial of the mortal general José Sanjurjo."

Uncomfortable with the direction the conversation had taken, Guillermo nonetheless feigned nonchalance. "Then you know he was convicted of treason and is on his way to the Dueso penitentiary."

She nodded. "Have you managed to tie the event to our affairs?"

"Nothing yet," Guillermo lied and thought of Jordi. Despite his bluster in front of the countess in Barcelona, Guillermo wasn't eager to admit to Rousseau that Jordi had murdered three of his nefilim. Rousseau would consider it a brazen act of war, just as Guillermo did. She would also question Guillermo's ability to cover her nefilim while fighting a war within his own ranks.

She frowned at him, obviously sensing that he held information he wasn't ready to divulge, but she didn't push the point. "I want a full briefing on your return from Germany."

"That I can do." *She's letting me slide today. Tomorrow might be another story.* As soon as he finished this business in Durbach, Jordi would become a top priority.

Rousseau stood and went to the threshold. "I'm sending you across underneath a load of hay. I hope you're not allergic."

He smiled and shook his head.

"Good. Once my drivers cross the border, they'll stop in a field. We'll have a smaller truck for you, and you'll have to go on alone."

"I couldn't ask for more. How long will it take me to reach Durbach from here?"

"Depends on the border crossing. Forty minutes to an hour? Any other questions?"

"May I use your phone?"

"Help yourself and good luck. We will watch for you." She shut the door and left him alone.

He picked up the handset and rang Santuari.

Miquel answered.

Guillermo waited for the operator to finish and then said, "I'm going to take care of our business now. Any news?"

"All bad unfortunately. Our good servant committed suicide, but he left a short message about Lisbon. We're following leads now."

"Shit. What else? Anything from Diago?"

"He tried to call but we had interference on the lines, sort of like what happened to your radio."

Jesus Christ. "Is everyone okay?"

"We're fine. Your teletype, not so much."

“What happened to my teletype?”

In the background, he heard Juanita’s voice. She said, “Tell him I’ll explain when he gets home. It was worth the loss. The new one will be here in a week.”

“Did you catch that?” Miquel asked.

“Okay—try not to break anything else. I’ll be there soon.”

“Listen, this morning . . .” Miquel hesitated.

Guillermo gripped the handset. “What?”

Another beat passed, and then Miquel blurted, “Rafael woke up hysterical around three this morning. He said Diago was digging through corpses and the dark sounds were getting in his papá’s eyes. We finally got him calm enough to go back to sleep at dawn. I don’t know if that means Diago made it through the night or if he’s—”

“He made it,” Guillermo said before Miquel could go on. *He made it and I refuse to believe otherwise.* “I’m leaving in a few minutes.”

“Bring him home, Guillermo,” Miquel whispered.

“I will.”

They rang off, and Guillermo finished dressing. He opened the door. The clock on the wall ticked steadily toward eleven.

[23]

DURBACH, GERMANY

It was midmorning by the time Jordi finally reached Durbach. Unable to tell whether his nervous energy stemmed from the amount of cocaine in his system or his apprehension at seeing Diago again, he ground his teeth and searched for the Griers' drive.

Diago had most likely arrived sometime yesterday. That gave him several hours alone with the Griers. *What lies had he told them? Or was he even still there?* Without thinking, Jordi touched the brooch pinned just over his heart. The action soothed him. *Everything is going to be fine. Frauja is with me.* The angel wouldn't have summoned him to judge Diago in vehmgericht if he didn't have a broader plan.

Calmer now, Jordi shifted gears and slowed for a curve as a Mercedes Tourer approached from the opposite direction. Both drivers were forced to move their vehicles closer to their respective ditches in order to pass.

The other man kept his attention fixed on the road but not Jordi. As they drew even with one another, he noticed that the Mercedes driver was none other than Karl Grier himself.

That left the other brother, Rudolf, at home. Jordi recalled the newspaper photograph of Karl standing confidently on the courthouse steps and Rudolf's miserable countenance. *Karl is the dominant brother, so he is the one I need.*

That meant delaying his meeting with Diago. Cursing, Jordi turned his car around and followed Grier. He consoled himself. If Diago was gone when they returned, there would be time to hunt him later. Right now, Jordi needed to find out how the Griers were tied to Frauja.

Careful to trail the Mercedes at a distance, Jordi wasn't surprised when Karl took the road to Offenburg. He followed Karl to the business district, where the mortal parked on the street. Jordi continued around the block to position his car out of sight. By the time he returned to the main avenue, Karl had disappeared.

A quick survey of the pedestrians produced no sign of his quarry. Jordi went to the Mercedes. Most mortals parked close to their destination, so in all probability, Karl had business with someone on this block.

A quick glance in a café's window revealed no one resembling Karl. Three doors down, Jordi noted the name OSKAR HENGELER, SOLICITOR on a metal plate.

Nico's Berliner mentioned a solicitor. Jordi's instincts hadn't failed him yet. He opened the door and walked upstairs. Hengeler's office was on the right. If Grier wasn't in the waiting room, then Jordi would pretend to be lost, retreat to the sidewalk, and monitor the car.

A woman's voice murmured from behind the frosted glass of the attorney's door. Jordi entered just as the secretary hung up the phone. He barely saw her. Seated in one of the stiff chairs was Karl Grier with a briefcase on his lap.

Karl's gaze flickered to Jordi. His eyes widened at the sight of the brooch.

Got you, you little fucker. If Karl recognized the pin, that meant he was the one who had sent it to Avignon.

Jordi flashed the secretary a brilliant smile. Someone had once told him the best lie was the simplest one.

Yago. Yago said that to me in our last incarnation.

"Good morning, Fraulein." He deliberately spoke his German with a slight Spanish accent. "My name is Sir George Abellio. I am seeking to invest in this area, and I was told that Herr Hengeler might know of properties for sale."

"Do you have an appointment, sir?"

"Yes." Jordi glanced at the clock, which showed ten forty-five. "It's at eleven."

She consulted a book on her desk. "I'm sorry, Sir Abellio, but I don't have you down."

"What?" He feigned indignation. "I don't see how that can be. My secretary assured me that she had secured an appointment with Herr Hengeler."

The secretary shook her head sympathetically and offered to put Jordi down for tomorrow. He pretended to be mollified and took the card she offered him. As he passed Karl, he nodded to the young mortal.

At the street level, Jordi walked slowly, pausing at a tobacco kiosk. He purchased a pack of cigarettes and lit one as he pretended to read the day's headlines.

Within minutes, Karl emerged from the building and scanned the street. He immediately strode in Jordi's direction.

"Excuse me!" Karl held out his hand and introduced

himself. "Karl Grier. I couldn't help but notice the brooch you're wearing. What an exquisite piece."

Jordi took the young man's hand and squeezed hard, drawing him away from the kiosk. "Why, thank you. It was a gift from an unknown benefactor. As a matter of fact"—he tossed his cigarette into the gutter—"the package seems to have been mailed from Offenburg."

Karl's face flushed a spectacular shade of red. Excitement radiated off him in waves. He lowered his voice to a whisper. "You truly *are* Sir George, aren't you? You've returned, just as it was prophesied."

One of the pedestrians gave them a raised eyebrow as he passed. He must have overheard Karl's statement.

Time to take this conversation off the street. "May I buy you a cup of coffee, Herr Grier?" Jordi took Karl's arm and steered him toward the café, making it clear the offer wasn't exactly a request.

Once they were seated in a back booth and had ordered, Karl said, "It's all right, Sir George. I know what you are."

What. Not who.

Jordi's lip twitched. "Excuse me?"

"You, sir, are one of the most powerful nefilim to walk the earth."

Not quite, but the compliment wasn't wasted. "And how do you know about nefilim?"

Their coffee arrived and Karl waited until they were alone again before he spoke. "Because I am a nefil, too. Surely you can see it in my eyes."

Jordi stared at the mortal in disbelief. *This day just keeps taking one strange turn after another.* He covered his confusion with a sip of coffee, and then decided: *What the hell? Play along.* "Ah, I see now." He touched the corner of his own eye and nodded. "You're a master of hiding your true nature."

"Well"—Karl glanced around the room and lowered his voice—"it wouldn't do for the mortals to know about us. Now would it?"

"Of course not." *Which is why I'll have to kill you, but not before I'm done with you.* Jordi smiled and tapped the brooch. "How did you find these brooches and know to send them to me?"

Karl leaned forward with the eagerness of someone who'd held a secret for far too long. "The angel Frauja has spoken to my dreams since I was but a boy. I cherish his wisdom and have followed his advice. He has asked for my aid in restoring him to this realm so he can cure the world of its evil. In return for helping him, he will give me my song." He waited a beat, and when Jordi made no comment, he elaborated, "He will make me a true nefil."

Jordi lit another cigarette and hid his contempt behind a screen of smoke. That was impossible. Nefilim were born, not made, but Karl had no way of knowing that. *Frauja is using him.* "And the brooches?"

"Frauja showed me where to dig so I could find them."

"Showed you how?"

"Through the mirrors."

A memory stabbed Jordi's brain. *I died in white light and fire, the sun burning like a thousand mirrors . . . not a thousand mirrors, but one . . . one mirror bound by Yago's song.*

"That doesn't explain how you found me."

"I found your address through a nefil by the name of Rainier Laurent. He gave me your business card."

Laurent, Laurent—the name rang a bell. Jordi rubbed

his temples with his thumbs and recalled a French nefil with a flashy jacket. *I courted him to join my cause and gave him a card with Nico's address. That is how this pretentious little fuck knew where to send the brooches.*

But why would a nefil as cautious as Rainier give Jordi's business card to a mortal? *He wouldn't . . . which meant Rainier was dead.* Intrigued now, Jordi leaned on his elbows and asked, "Do you know a man named Diago Alvarez?"

"He is at my house as we speak."

"And what do you think of him?"

"I think he's dead."

"What?" Jordi gaped at the mortal. *Diago? Dead?* Rather than jubilation, he found himself disappointed. *He was* mine *to kill.* "What do you mean you *think* he's dead? You're not sure?"

"We put him in our guest room. Any nefil who has slept in that room joins Frauja in the mirror."

"Of their own volition?"

Karl nodded. "We lure the rogues into the house with my father's Stradivarius."

He means Diago's Stradivarius, Jordi thought, getting a feel for how loosely Karl delivered facts.

"Then I find some pretext to get them to stay. I offer them food and drink . . . drugged, of course."

"Of course," Jordi muttered, liking Karl less and less.

"At first, I had to find some pretext to lure them to the ballroom, but as Frauja grew stronger, he was able to move from mirror to mirror in the house. Now I can give the nefilim the guest room with an old armoire. Deep in the night, Frauja lures them through the glass, and once they step into his realm, they cannot return to the mortal world.

The next morning, the armoire door is open and the nefil is gone. Frauja takes their song and makes it a part of him."

Karl obviously had no idea what that act truly entailed; otherwise, he wouldn't be so blasé. Jordi, on the other hand, stifled a shudder. *Frauja is murdering nefilim and eating their souls.* For a nefil to die in such a way was worse than the second death, the final death from which no nefil could reincarnate, because unless the angel was destroyed, the nefilim's souls were forever bound to him. *And angels are notoriously hard to kill.*

"Is that what this is?" Jordi tapped the brooch. "A lure to draw me into Frauja's mirror?"

Karl gaped at Jordi in shock. "No! Frauja loves you. He says you are the only nefil who can free him. It's why he instructed me to guide you here."

Maybe, Jordi thought. He didn't trust Karl, but he needed him for a little longer. *Besides, if he is trying to trick me, he wouldn't have related Frauja's techniques for ensnaring the nefilim. The cocaine is making me paranoid.* Which in and of itself wasn't a bad thing, because mortals were capricious creatures.

At the same time, this is *the opportunity of an incarnation.*

If he was careful, he could help Frauja escape the oblivion realm where he was imprisoned, and then use the angel to destroy Guillermo's soul. *Maybe in the end, Frauja would help me accomplish my original goal after all.* Taken by a soul-eater, Guillermo would never reincarnate, leaving Jordi's claim as king forever untouched. *It's just as good as locking him in a prison realm.*

Yet he could almost hear Nico's voice in the back of his mind, urging caution. *But a soul-eater . . .*

This wasn't the Middle Ages. The nefilim were more numerous now. If Frauja proved difficult to control once Guillermo was out of the way, Jordi could enlist the aid of Queen Jaeger to call down the Thrones on the angel.

Karl gripped his coffee cup. "Please, Sir George, you must believe me—I'm on your side." A note of apprehension crept into his statement.

Let him worry. Jordi crushed his cigarette in the tin ashtray. "What's in it for you, Karl?"

"I told you—Frauja will give me the song of a nefil."

Jordi stared at him.

It took merely a moment before Karl broke beneath the weight of that glare. "With the song of a nefil, I will be able to take over all the branches of Ordo Novi Templi and bend them to my will."

"And then?"

Karl leaned over the table, his eyes wild with hate. "I will show them what it means to be pure, and then I will force them to endure every humiliation they have given me."

"I see," said Jordi. Well acquainted with the desire for revenge, he finished his coffee and signaled for the check. "Then it's fortunate our paths crossed, because I can help you . . . if you like."

The rage faded from Karl's eyes but not the fanatical gleam. "I would be honored to fight at your side."

And I'll tolerate your presence until I don't need you anymore. "First things first then. If Diago isn't dead, you're going to have a very powerful, angry nefil on your hands when you go home."

"I am not afraid."

Jordi leaned across the table and hissed, "Well, you

should be. Frauja is where he is *because* of Diago." Again he saw the mirror bound by Yago's song. *Why in the hell can't I remember what he did to us?*

For the first time, the young man seemed uncertain. "What should we do?"

"Tell me, Karl, do you own a gun?"

Karl opened his jacket just enough for Jordi to see the shoulder holster he wore. It was clearly a German military issue Beholla from the Great War.

"Excellent. Now listen closely, because there can be no mistakes . . ."

[24]

KARINHALL

Diago awakened hours later to the sound of Rudi playing the piano. He recognized the music: act three of Wagner's *Götterdämmerung*: the burning of Valhalla.

He pushed himself free of the settee. Stiff muscles checked his every move. He felt like he'd been in a brawl. *Because I was*, he thought groggily as he stretched each limb, attentive to the slightest twinge.

Years of dancing attuned him to his body's signals. No bones were broken, no tendons torn. "Fine," he whispered. "I'm fine."

Okay, not quite fine, but limber enough to get moving. "And still in the mortal realm." *Thanks to Harvey and Prieto's tear.*

Rolling to his feet, he staggered through the debris and went to the window. Dust rained down on him when he pushed the curtain aside. In spite of the cloud cover, he guessed it was about midmorning, maybe noon.

Across the yard, wooden stakes marked the rectangular outline of a shallow pit. *That must be the chapel excavation Karl spoke of last night.*

As Diago's gaze roved the grounds, he knew that if Karl continued to dig, he would find foundations that belonged to other buildings. To his left and out of sight would be the bakehouse. To the right, the gate, which was beside the coarse wooden buildings where the soldiers were housed. Directly opposite would be the inn.

For one blurry moment, Diago envisioned the structures superimposed over Karinhall's grounds. He blinked and rubbed his eyes. When he looked again, the castle courtyard disappeared.

That's the past, a grave that never should have been disturbed.

Turning from the window, he assessed the room's destruction and tried to decide what to do next. *Stay and hunt for the violin or leave?*

He'd been through enough battles to know that winning was one part skill, three parts luck. In his current state, he doubted he could replicate last night's reflexes, and luck was a fickle diva who didn't always sing her part.

Staying would be a gamble, but insane risks weren't his to take anymore. *I promised my Rafael I would come home.*

The thought of his son led to the jagged memory of Harvey's agonized face behind the mirror. His old friend had given himself so Diago could flee. *And I won't squander his death.*

Besides, Guillermo had been adamant that Diago should take no unnecessary risks. Part of proving himself to Los

Nefilim meant following orders, and Guillermo would see this as a prudent move.

In spite of all that, leaving still felt like failure. *It'll feel more so if I get myself killed, though.*

Before he could find a reason to stay, he grabbed his bag and opened the door. A dagger's hilt almost hit him in the face. The blade pinned a sheet of paper to the door.

Diago ripped the document free. The rusty brown ink was the color of old blood. Written in archaic German, it was a summons to appear before the vehmgericht to be tried for treason.

Diago crumpled the paper and threw it in the mirror's direction. "Fuck you and your courts, Frauja."

Across the hall, Rudi's door was open. The radio still squatted on the night table, only now it was no longer a benign appliance.

A flush of rage hit Diago's chest as he once more saw Harvey struggling to speak. Striding across the hall, he picked up the radio and smashed it on the floor. The crystals shattered and one of the knobs flew beneath the bed.

Downstairs, the piano fell silent.

Diago struggled for calm. If he went down now, he wasn't sure he could control himself. Pacing back into the hall, he stalked into the lavatory and splashed cold water on his face.

Rudi is just a boy, a mortal, and Frauja is using him. He can't possibly understand the ramifications of Harvey's death. Repeating the mantra to himself, he waited until his breathing evened. Harvey was gone. Killing the Griers wouldn't bring him back or free his soul.

Getting to the border alive is the goal. Stay focused. He drank from the tap to soothe his sore throat and then left the lavatory to collect his bag. As he descended to the first floor, he noted the ceiling stains in the entryway had broadened. Eight lines were joined by two ligatures and overlaid the rune Fehu.

Just as Karl had drawn in the photograph.

Diago almost made it to the front door before Rudi said, "Herr Alvarez, you're—" He abruptly stopped talking.

Clenching the handle of his bag, Diago turned and met the boy's bewildered gaze. "Alive?"

Hysteria touched Rudi's laugh. "Don't be ridiculous! Of course you're alive." He twisted something in his hands and Diago noticed he carried his mother's compact. "I'm afraid there is no lunch for you. Karl sent Frau Weber home this morning as soon as she arrived."

I'm sure he did. He wouldn't want her to see daggers buried in the doors. "Where is Karl?"

"Offenburg."

"He was supposed to take me with him to use a phone."

"He must have forgotten. Karl gets like that sometimes. He has so much on his mind, he forgets things."

"I see." Diago debated how much longer he wanted to play this game.

"You have your bag. Are you leaving?"

Diago nodded.

"But you haven't seen the violin yet. Don't you want to see it?"

See it, hold it, take it away, yes to all those things. "Do you know where the violin is, Rudi?"

The youth shook his head. "Karl moved it."

Which meant Rudi had searched but hadn't found it. "You should leave, too, Rudi. Get out while you can."

Rudi twisted the compact in his hands. "I . . . I can't."

"Why not?"

"Because Karl will report me to the authorities. He said he won't let them take me to the sanitarium this time. He said he'll declare me incorrigible and that I will go to prison." Rudi shook his head. "I can't do that. I don't belong there."

"You could leave Germany."

"And go where? And how would I live? Can you see me working like a common laborer?" Rudi gave an incredulous laugh and shook his head. "As long as I don't . . ." He hesitated and fumbled with the compact.

As long as you don't profess your love for other men, Diago thought. *Come on, Rudi, say it. Give me an opening.*

Rudi's voice dropped to a whisper. "As long as I don't get sick again."

"You're not sick, Rudi. And I understand your fear—"

"You are a good person, Herr Alvarez, but I belong here. Karl will fix things. He's promised. He'll make everything right. He will."

Something about the hope in Rudi's expression diminished Diago's loathing. The boy truly felt that everything would be all right if he pleased his brother.

But Karl would never be pleased. That was the part Rudi didn't understand. If Diago had time, he would have shared some of the lessons Miquel had taught him: that change was frightening only at first; or maybe tell him that love was precious and shouldn't be squandered on abusers. But time wasn't his and he couldn't say any of those things without jeopardizing himself and his mission. And besides, even though the boy didn't believe his own lie, he was too afraid to change.

And there's nothing I can say that will alter his attitude.

In the end, he turned and walked away, listening in case Rudi decided to follow him. The youth remained by the music room door, clutching the compact against his chest.

Shifting his attention to the hall tree, Diago grabbed his hat and coat. He moved swiftly past the mirror, which reflected the room, as mirrors were meant to do.

Outside the icy air sucked the wind from his lungs. *It's far too cold for September.* He still didn't bother with either his hat or coat. A sense of urgency suddenly touched him and added speed to his movements. He'd delayed long enough. Every minute here was one minute closer to the next zero hour.

He tossed his things on the front seat and then slid behind the wheel. The engine hummed to life on the first turn of the ignition.

The sound of approaching cars caused him to glance into the rearview mirror. Karl's Mercedes roared down the drive, followed by a white Cabriolet.

Who is in the Cabriolet? Sturmführer Heines? Diago wasn't waiting to find out. He put his Citroën in reverse and wheeled it around. The sedan was about as responsive as a tank, but at least he was pointed in the right direction.

The driveway was just wide enough to allow his car room to pass. Hitting the gas, Diago picked up speed and shifted from first to second. The speedometer drifted higher. He shifted into third. He was going too fast for the rutted drive, but the thought didn't slow him.

As he neared the other vehicles, Karl edged the Mercedes into the Citroën's lane. The Cabriolet drew alongside the Mercedes. They gave him no space to pass.

Around them, then. Diago waited until the last possible moment before he swerved.

He saw the deep ditch too late. The Citroën's tires left the ground. The chassis bounced hard, wrenching the steering wheel from his hand. He grabbed it again and overcompensated.

From the corner of his eye, he caught the impression of a sigil flying toward the driver's door. Diago had no time to counter it. The glyph hit the Citroën, and the car skidded through the pine needles to broadside a tree. The passenger side took the brunt of the accident. The engine stalled.

Diago smelled blood. He touched his scalp and his fingers came away wet. A web of cracks intersected the driver's window. He didn't remember hitting his head. The steering wheel blurred and became two before merging back together again.

Reaching down, he groped for the keys and tried to start the car. "Come on," he whispered as the engine coughed and then died.

Two shapes moved toward him. For one horrible moment, he thought it was the corpses from his nightmare. Then he recognized Jordi.

Karl positioned himself in front of the Citroën's hood. He held his arms out stiffly and pointed a pistol at Diago.

A military issue Beholla. He recalled wondering what had happened to Joachim's guns. *Now I know.*

Diago didn't move. He sat with one hand on the steering wheel and the other on the ignition. His heart hammered against his chest. Karl blurred and turned into twins and then became one again. *I took a hard knock.*

Karl grinned like he'd won a prize. "Herr Alvarez. Why are you leaving? We haven't concluded our business."

Diago wasn't sure it was possible to hate Karl any more than he already did, but he found a dark part within himself that managed the task. *I'm going to kill him. It's just a matter of time.*

Jordi arrived at the door and jerked it open. He squatted beside Diago.

The first thing Diago noticed was the polished brooch pinned over Jordi's breast. The second was the Browning's pistol grip poking just over Jordi's hip.

Just as he knew I would. Their gazes met. *His eyes are like knives—like they were when he was Sir George.* He was thinner than Guillermo, hard and hungry and full of need. Anger radiated around him like a malignant corona.

Diago knew that rage, the kind that hovered just below a veneer of calm. When he was Yago, he'd felt it burn within his own soul. That was the difference between them in this incarnation. Jordi still held tight to his anger while Diago had conquered his.

Jordi kept his tone casual. "Car trouble, my friend?"

Diago noted a thin crust of blood rimmed Jordi's nostrils. *He's using drugs again.* The thought dropped into Diago's mind with the same banality as he sometimes recorded other everyday facts:

It's raining, the trains are running late, Jordi is using drugs again.

It would be funny except it wasn't. Coupled with his fury, drugs always increased the hostility in Jordi's song, making his magic unpredictable . . . and more dangerous.

Play his game until the world stops spinning. "I seem to have had an accident. Maybe you can give me a ride into town?" He drew his tarnished brooch from his pocket and offered it to Jordi as he switched to Spanish. "My friend."

Jordi's gaze flickered to the brooch and then back to Diago. He replied in Spanish. "We're not friends, Yago."

"And that's not my name."

"No. No, but it was. I've been thinking about you a lot lately." Jordi's smile was pleasant, as if they were two old comrades discussing bygone days. He placed his hand over Diago's and said, "I recall how we exchanged songs and passed the long cold nights with an angel between us. Do you remember that incarnation?"

"A little."

"A little." Jordi's hand tightened around Diago's until it became a vise. For Karl's benefit, he repeated the phrase in German. "'A little,' he says." A shrill edge tinged his laughter.

Even Karl seemed uneasy about Jordi's sudden glee. The barrel of the mortal's gun wavered.

Diago remained perfectly still. He had lived around enough abusive men and women to understand the hair-trigger tempers that accompanied a laugh like that—and that meant Jordi was no longer playing a game. *Don't provoke him.* Not that he could do much anyway—Diago was in no condition to fight. *Stall him until the vertigo passes.*

"How long have you and Karl been working together?" he asked in Spanish.

Jordi scoffed and replied in kind. "I don't work with mortals."

"Then he's using you like a whore to get what he wants."

Jordi leaned into the car and spit in Diago's face. "No one uses me."

But I *did, and that's what burns you, isn't it, Jordi? I used you and I won.* Except that was during their last incarnation. *A lifetime away.*

"It's cold," Karl said, nervousness raising his voice an octave. His gaze bounced from one nefil to the other. "Let's go inside." He nodded toward the house. "We can discuss the violin."

The violin. Does he still think that will work on me? And yet . . . how much does Jordi even know about it?

Diago looked down at the tarnished brooch in his palm. The angel leered at him and clenched the broken emerald as if to break it in half.

Then Jordi spoke Diago's fears aloud. "I understand Herr Grier has a Stradivarius for sale. A very special violin."

Here was Diago's nightmare come to life. The Griers possessed enough magic between them to rob Diago of sleep and ignite his fears. Jordi had the power and will to bring those terrors into the realm of reality.

That goddamn violin is a fetter around my soul. "They're killing nefilim, Jordi—"

"Let's go inside," Jordi whispered. His tone grew conciliatory again as he took the brooch from Diago's hand and pinned it over his heart. "My friend." He drew his pistol and stepped back. "Get out of the car slowly. Hands on your head. Good, now follow Karl."

Diago obeyed him. He was too weakened from last night's battle with Frauja to take Jordi in a fair fight. *Fight dirty, then.* And that meant waiting for the right moment to attack.

He considered the guns: Karl's Beholla probably held seven rounds, as did Jordi's Browning. *That's fourteen bullets too many, but Karl is overconfident with Jordi here, and Jordi is unbalanced by the drugs.* An opportunity would come. Diago just had to be ready to act when it appeared.

Because I will not give up. While there was breath in his body, he intended to do everything in his power to get home to his husband and son.

The beats of Siegfried's funeral march greeted them. Rudi had obviously returned to the piano the moment Diago left.

"Where are we going, Karl?" Jordi asked.

"Upstairs," Karl said before he shouted at his brother. "Rudi! Go up and turn on the lights!"

The piano fell silent and Rudi appeared at the music room's door, his mother's makeup case clutched in one hand. "What's going on? Herr Alvarez? What's happening?" He stared at Jordi. "Who are you?"

Jordi ignored the question. He stepped to the wall and ran an appreciative hand over the molding.

The barrel of his gun never wavered from Diago's torso.

He's testing me, expecting me to run, especially this close to the door. Patient as a cat, Diago made no overt sign that he noticed Jordi's feigned distraction. He kept his head bowed, his shoulders slumped.

Karl gestured for Rudi to move and only answered the last question. "This is Sir George Abellio, the rightful owner of the Stradivarius."

"And Karinhall," Jordi said, giving Rudi a wolfish grin.

The comment took Karl off guard. An expression of uncertainty flickered across his features.

Little fool, you've invited the devil into your house.

Diago seized the moment. "He's not joking, Karl. He's going to kill you." *And if he doesn't, I will.*

Karl didn't respond to the threat. Instead, he attempted to regain control the only way he seemed to know how—by ordering Rudi around. He turned to his brother and snapped, "What are you waiting for? Go upstairs and turn on the lights."

With one last desperate glance at Diago, Rudi turned and ran up the marble steps, his slippers whispering against the stone.

Karl followed him.

Jordi gestured with the barrel of his pistol. "Let's go."

Clenching his teeth, Diago climbed the stairs. Jordi kept several paces between them. Unbalancing him with a fast kick was out of the question. *Patience. The time will come.*

At the second-story landing, the pocket doors to the third floor stood open. A foul scent drifted on a chill draft. The ornate light fixtures that once decorated the ceiling were gone and replaced with naked bulbs. The walls were bruised and battered. The stains of more sigils bled across the shredded paper.

The next landing revealed an open area, much like a lobby. A door at the end of the hall, probably the servants' entrance from the kitchen, was shut. Rudi and Karl waited before a much more formal entrance that consisted of a pair of doors with brass handles.

Karl unlocked the doors and swung them wide. Inside, he touched a switch and a damaged chandelier blazed to life. The broken glass cast more shadow than light over the expansive ballroom with mirrored walls.

Diago's heart seized. Fissures ran through the glass,

cracks that spanned from one panel to the next to form sigils. As his gaze traveled from a broken line to a full ligature and then to three jagged lines, another wave of dizziness washed over him, but this episode had nothing to do with the blow to his head.

The design was made incomprehensible by disjointed glyphs that seemed to contradict one another. It was like trying to read a book with each word written in a different language . . . and out of order.

To further complicate the patterns, portions of the mirror were dented as if someone's head had been driven into the glass. Diago recalled the bits of hair and bone in Laura Howe's hat.

A savage flash of anger surged through his body. Karl. It had to have been Karl, getting the drop on her.

Diago dragged his gaze from the broken glass to a table in the center of the room. A modern violin case rested on it.

The Stradivarius.

Next to the table was a standing microphone, which was plugged into a huge homemade transmitter that stood against the back wall. Tubes and batteries lined the floor. More wires stretched from the transmitter to the baseboards.

There, the scuffed wax was darkened with veins of blood. They reflected the same designs that marred the ceilings and downstairs walls.

"Blood sigils," Diago whispered.

Even Jordi appeared uneasy at the sight of them. Maybe he wasn't as far gone into his addiction as Diago first surmised.

The glyphs formed lacy patterns on the floor and spread about two meters from the walls into the ballroom itself, like a boundary marking the line between two worlds. Wires erupted from the sigils and snaked across the floor to the transmitter.

Three thick cables ran from the transmitter to a wide pair of French doors on the western wall. The doors were cracked to allow the cables to pass through, probably to reach the electrical box on the side of the house.

That explains the power surges. Diago considered the doors and the balcony.

Although they were on the third floor, a nefil could survive such a fall if he anticipated the descent just right. The trick would be grabbing the violin as he sprinted past the table and then landing without injury.

From the door's position, Diago guessed they were over the haunted guest room he had occupied last night. If that was the case, a jump would lead him to a clear area.

And with the rain, the ground will be soft.

Jordi must have read Diago's mind. "Don't even think about it. I'll take you down with a bullet before you've gone three steps. Get on your knees and keep your hands on your head."

Once more Diago obeyed him. He caught a glimpse of Rudi's angry features as he did. *He promised he wouldn't help his brother anymore, yet here he is, helping Karl . . .*

Jordi waved the barrel of his gun at the transmitter. "What the hell is this?"

"I built it," Karl said proudly. "It's how we played the violin in your dreams, Herr Alvarez." He waited a beat as if hoping for a compliment on his ingenuity. When none came, he holstered his gun and went to the transmitter. "Allow me to demonstrate."

One less gun, Diago thought as he calculated the distance between him and Jordi. They were too far apart. *For now.*

Jordi kept his attention riveted on Diago but he addressed Karl. "I know how a transmitter works. Why do you need one this size?"

Karl flipped a switch. A hum filled the room as the tubes glowed to life. "To give Frauja his voice in the mortal realm."

The radio and the phone. Diago's eye followed the cord leading through the French doors. *Could it be that simple? Unplug him?* That would certainly stop Frauja from projecting his song into the mortal realm . . .

But those sigils. Diago scanned the dizzying patterns on the mirrors. There were almost enough cracks for Frauja to punch through, and if the angel freed himself, transmitters would be the least of their worries.

Blissfully ignorant of what he was about to unleash on the mortal realm, Karl returned to the table and removed the Stradivarius from its case. The wood gleamed in reddish hues, as well maintained as if it had never left Diago's care.

Diago's fingers twitched. He could almost feel the instrument in his hands.

"You see, Rudi stands here and plays the violin." Karl positioned himself in front of the microphone. Then he used the bow to point out the wires leading into the blood sigils. "Then Frauja adjusts the frequency before he sends his sigil into the power lines, where it interferes with the transmission from a local radio station."

Jordi's eyes lit up. "And from there, it goes from antenna to antenna until it finds its prey."

Karl glowed. "Yes! The transmitter never worked properly until my father died—"

"You murdered Father," Rudi blurted. "Just like you murdered Mother. Tell them the truth, Karl. You shoved her into that panel." He pointed to a starburst pattern on the opposite wall. "That's how all this started. When you murdered Mother!"

Because she was a lesser nefil, Diago thought. And when her blood seeped through the cracks, it nourished Frauja in his oblivion realm.

Karl didn't acknowledge his brother's outburst. This was his performance, and it was obvious he wouldn't be cheated of his moment. "But with Father's Stradivarius—"

My *Stradivarius*, Diago thought.

"—we were able to send the music into Frauja's realm." Karl replaced the instrument in its case.

It was like the perfect storm arrived: the resonances of the Great War damaged the glyphs; the Stradivarius retained enough of Diago's magic to alert Frauja that he had been reborn; and then Joachim stole the violin and brought it to Karinhall, where Frauja managed to possess first Karl and then Rudi to do his bidding; and so on and so on until one event led to another and now . . .

Here we all are.

"The violin was the solution to the equation," Karl went on. "Alvarez had carried it for so long his essence and the auras of nefilim who'd performed with him were entwined in the instrument. Frauja knows how to isolate the strands he needs. With the right frequency, one could take out an entire battalion of nefilim simply by targeting the one nefil who had performed with Alvarez."

"Or a town," Jordi murmured. "You could destroy a town." He smiled at Diago. "Like Santuari."

It was a nightmare. Diago thought of Rafael and Miquel, Ysa and Juanita and Guillermo. *Suero with his book of poetry and Bernardo with his little school.* They would never know what hit them.

Escaping the ballroom was no longer his priority. *I've got to smash that transmitter.*

"Karl, you promised." Rudi held out the compact.

Karl returned to the soundboard and lifted a pair of headphones, pressing one to his ear. Occupied with his work, he adjusted a dial on the transmitter. "Not now, Rudi."

"I've done everything you asked, Karl. Now you keep your promise. You said when Sir George returned, he would free Mother's soul."

Jordi's eyebrows shot upward, but he said nothing, waiting instead to see what Karl would do.

Karl glanced from Jordi to Rudi. "Sir George is busy right now."

Jordi met Diago's gaze and grinned. "Tell me about it, Rudi."

"Christ," Diago muttered. "You're still a bastard."

Jordi ignored the accusation. "Where is your mother's soul, Rudi?"

"Here." He opened the compact and pointed to its broken glass. "She had this in her pocket when Karl murdered her. Now I can see her in Frauja's realm. We have to get her out. She's frightened."

Jordi gestured for Rudi to go to Diago. "Show Herr Alvarez. He can see dark sounds. If she's there, he'll know."

The youth came and knelt beside Diago. Taking great care, he tilted the mirror at an angle. "See? There she is. You can see the top of her head." His features relaxed and he smiled at his reflection. “Don’t be frightened, Mother. This is Herr Alvarez, and Sir George is here. They are nefilim. They will help you.” Rudi touched the glass tenderly.

Diago looked into the mirror. The compact reflected only Rudi and himself.

His guilt places her behind the glass, and she will haunt him forever. “She’s not there.”

“No, you’re mistaken. Look, here”—he pointed in the lower left-hand corner of the mirror.

Diago shook his head.

Rudi’s expression dissolved from hope to anger. “You’re not trying. Or maybe Karl’s right: you are one of the weaker ones.” He rose and went to Jordi. “What about you, Sir George? Are you strong enough to see her?”

Go ahead and look hard, Jordi. Diago remained relaxed. *And while he’s distracted, I’m going to make my move.* He peered through his lashes and gauged the distance between him and Jordi. *Go low, take him at the knees. This might be my only chance.*

Much to Diago’s disappointment, Jordi barely glanced at the mirror before pinning his gaze back onto Diago.

And why wouldn’t he? The angel-born couldn’t see the dark sounds.

Jordi winked at Diago as if they shared an inside joke. “Of course, I see her. She’s in the lower left-hand corner.”

Rudi smiled. “Then you can help her?”

“Certainly.” Jordi circled the room until he was behind Diago.

“You will?” The hope in the youth’s face broke Diago’s heart.

Diago whispered, “Stop lying to him, Jordi.”

"I'm not lying. I'm going to help him free his mother." He pointed to the mirrored wall beyond the blood sigils. "Rudi, I want you to go over there and stand with your back to the glass."

Karl pushed a switch on a cannibalized radio. A low whine squealed through the room.

"A little to the right." Jordi motioned the youth into position between two starlike indentations in the mirror. "That's it, stop there."

Diago followed the pattern, noting how the lines connected. "Oh, Jesus." *When Rudi's head hits that section, the broken lines will enjoin.* His blood would seep into the cracks and charge the sigil with power. "Rudi, he's going—"

Jordi fired the gun.

Karl's transmitter hummed to life.

The bullet ripped through Rudi's skull and smashed his head into the mirror. The blood seeped into one long line, connecting the other starred patterns.

Rudi's body slumped to the floor. He fell on his right side. The compact skidded across the floor and stopped at Diago's knees. He barely noticed it.

The dark song of Rudi's death rode a trickle of blood that slipped through his parted lips. Pale and blue, like the icy irises of his eyes, the song rose, delicate as a moth. The sound floated around the room, calling out in anguish: "Herr Alvarez? I'm blind! I can't see! Help me! Are you here?"

Diago wanted to close his ears to the plaintive cries, but he couldn't. Nor could he answer the dead youth. His gaze was locked on the blood sigils throbbing along the baseboards. The wires connected to the glyphs pulsed like veins. The transmitter crackled.

From a crack in the mirrored wall a tendril of fog seeped through one of the clefts.

Not fog, Diago thought. The smell of cordite was too strong in the air. "It's smoke."

Rudi's soul paused and then dived toward Diago. "Herr Alvarez? I heard you speak. I am here. Help me, please."

Diago barely breathed. "Hush, Rudi. Stay close to me and be quiet."

"You can hear me! Am I dead, Herr Alvarez? Is this death?" Rudi's aura hovered near Diago's shoulder.

Pinned under Jordi's eye, Diago couldn't answer. He merely bowed his head and watched the mirrors through the fringe of his hair.

All around the room, the mirrors darkened until the walls no longer reflected the occupants. A power surge blew more of the chandelier's lights to dust, leaving the room deeper in shadow.

Not the least concerned that his brother lay dead on the floor, Karl adjusted dials and monitored gauges on the soundboard. On the other side of the mirrors, magnesium flares dropped from a black sky. Bombs burst in the distance.

Diago's nightmare rose up to throttle him with terror. *Only this time it's real. And it's coming for me.*

A figure emerged from the smoke. Frauja. The tail of his trench coat flapped and hitched with each limping step. Burned during the angelic wars, two of his wings were missing: the one that once covered the left side of his face and the lower left at his ankle. Without those limbs, he couldn't fly.

So he became an earthbound angel full of hate . . .

Thick keloids marred his left cheek and ear, as well. The

German officer's uniform that he wore hid more scars—blemishes that covered his body from shoulder to heel.

When I was Yago, I gave him a Persian mirror to assuage his vanity. In the small glass, Frauja could turn his face so that his scars were hidden and he was perfect once more. Delighted with the gift, the angel had spent hours admiring his snowy hair and alabaster skin.

But he's changed, Diago realized. His flesh, once so white, is now darkened and bruised. Colors writhe under his skin, giving him the same mottled look Karinhall's mirrors wore. His long snowy hair had turned brassy and yellow. Eyes once the color of tourmaline were now muddy and gray.

Diago stared at the angel in horror. *It's the dark sounds of the souls he's taken.*

Rudi's soul cowered near Diago's hip.

Although Diago couldn't see Jordi's face, the uncertainty in his voice was loud and clear. "Frauja?"

"My beloved," the angel growled with the voices of the dead pouring through Karl's speakers. His gaze swept first over Jordi and then Diago.

Jordi moved back into Diago's line of vision. His face was pale, but that old familiar determination also reigned supreme in his eyes.

He's having second thoughts about Frauja, but he won't admit he's wrong. Diago knew the nature of both beasts all too well.

From his place by the soundboard, Karl crowed, "Our court is convened!"

The gun spasmed in Jordi's hand. His head turned and the barrel twitched upward before zeroing in on Diago's chest again.

He almost shot Karl. If the mortal is smart, he'll shut up. Diago's tension locked his fingers on the top of his head. He forced himself to relax. He'd need to be limber to move fast.

Jordi's grin was more like a grimace. "Yes," he echoed the mortal. "Our court is convened. Let us begin."

Frauja pointed at Diago. "Name his crimes."

Narrowing his eyes, Jordi glared at Diago. "I remember: after Guillaume summoned me to vehmgericht, we devised a sigil to lock him away into another realm. The plan was simple: lure Guillaume and Michel into the courtyard. Once their guard was down, Frauja and George would sing the oblivion sigil."

Diago remembered the glyph rising between the two groups of men with angelic lightning flashing through the complex series of lines and ligatures. The ward was designed to create a new realm, one that magnified and reflected all of earth's wars, hence its name: the oblivion sigil.

Jordi continued, "Yago's job was simple: he was to remain in the chamber overlooking the courtyard so none of Guillaume's people could kill him before he finished his song. When the sigil rose, Yago was to sing Guillaume's death so that his soul would be taken into the new realm. But you didn't." Jordi's eyes narrowed. "What did you do?"

He could stall them with lies, but for what? The sooner he told them the truth, the sooner they would decide his fate. *And if Jordi allows me to stand, I will have to fight or die.*

Feigning defeat, Diago said, "After you left Yago in the room, he took the Persian box he'd given to Frauja and wrenched the mirror free of its casing. By the time Frauja and George reached the courtyard, Yago was back in his assigned place. He positioned the mirror facedown on the windowsill.

"When the moment came, Yago drew on the darkness of his soul. He reversed the chords of Frauja's song and threw the mirror from the Persian box into the oblivion sigil. The glass reflected the fire of the angel's glyph back on him, reversing the ward."

Except Yago's trick wasn't enough. Frauja maintained a tenuous hold on the mortal realm with his song. Like Heines's tracking sigil, the shimmering streams of light gave him a pathway back into the earthly realm. No matter how Yago sang, he couldn't shatter those gossamer threads.

Then Guillaume's troops attacked George's nefilim. Mortals were caught in the crossfire. The dark sounds of their terror and death rose into the air. They blinded Yago's vision and clung to his throat.

In a flash of inspiration, Yago wove those dark sounds into a piercing sigil. He cast the ward at Frauja's song and severed the notes holding the angel to the mortal realm.

The maneuver took Frauja off guard. His song faltered, and when it did, the mirror shattered into a million shards, and the wards snapped shut, locking him in the oblivion realm.

Then I died with those dark sounds still ringing in my voice, and I managed to forget . . .

Diago had buried the trauma of those dark songs deep, hoping never to experience the touch of them again. And he'd been successful until the Great War—with its terrible destruction—resurrected them.

Because no matter how I try, I cannot escape myself.

Jordi took a step closer. "And then?"

He doesn't remember what I did. Diago glanced at

Frauja. The angel leaned forward, watching intently. *And Frauja suspects but doesn't know for certain either.*

Diago chose his words with care. "Instead of Guillaume and Michel, the ward takes Frauja. By the time Guillaume kills George, the sigil has closed, so that your soul"—he nods to Jordi—"remains in the earthly realm."

With the memories came another realization: Yago didn't compose the Key. While Frauja had allowed Yago to assist him in writing the song, the composition itself belonged to the angel. Likewise, it was Frauja's ethereal voice that opened the realm, not Yago or his music. *I merely reflected his song back at him.* It was an act of mimicry, like Rudi playing by rote.

Frauja's tainted voice filled the ballroom. "I sentence you to death, Yago. But you are mine. I will take your life with my hands." He reached out. "Come to me, Yago. Come to me of your free will and I will make your death quick. If George must push you through the glass, then you will suffer for eternity. You decide."

When Diago didn't move, Jordi took two steps toward him. Diago rolled to his feet.

Jordi halted.

Frauja smiled. "Quickly now."

Diago walked toward the mirror.

Rudi's soul fluttered by his ear and whispered, "Don't go, Herr Alvarez."

Diago picked up his pace, snapping his heels against the floor. As he drew parallel to Jordi, he executed a vuelta quebrada, a broken turn—a rapid flamenco step that spun him toward the other nefil. His right leg crossed behind his left and then he whirled hard to the right.

Surprised by the sudden move, Jordi jumped backward, but he wasn't fast enough.

Diago kicked at Jordi's knee. His blow landed low and caught the taller man's shin, but it was enough to send him to the ground.

Karl fumbled for his pistol, accidentally discharging it before he cleared the holster.

Six bullets, he is down to six bullets, Diago thought wildly.

Frauja lifted his hand and released a sigil, charging it with his voice. The ward oozed through a crack in the glass and sped across the ballroom to hit the brooch over Diago's heart.

He stumbled backward. The sweater smoldered and he remembered dying. When Frauja knew he'd lost, he retaliated against Yago with a final murderous ward. The spell struck the brooch over Yago's heart and ate through his flesh.

In that incarnation, Yago couldn't stop playing. Lost in the depths of his spell, he'd sang while the brooch chewed through muscle and bone, to wrap itself around his heart.

But this incarnation was different. Diago wasn't singing a spell, and Frauja's glyph was weakened by its journey through the mirror.

The past doesn't have to repeat.

Diago ripped the brooch from his chest and flung it away. It struck the mirror and rolled against the wall.

Jordi regained his feet and aimed his pistol in one fluid motion. Karl finally freed his gun. The mortal squeezed off a shot. Diago heard the bullet whiz by his ear.

[25]

Guillermo gunned the truck up the hill. It was midday, but there wasn't a car in sight. Clouds the color of steel suddenly opened and dumped rain onto the road. The truck's windshield wipers scraped his nerves raw.

The Griers' driveway had to be close. He glimpsed a flash of silver in the ditch. *It's a sigil.* Guillermo pulled the truck off the road and got out.

Jogging to the spot, he kicked the pine needles aside and found the fading lines of a glyph designed to detect traps. It smoldered in hues more black than green. The curl of the glyph ended in Diago's signature flourish.

Guillermo followed the direction of the ward and saw the drive. He hurried back to the truck and climbed inside. Within moments, he'd maneuvered the vehicle between the stone pillars. Pine limbs, heavy with ice, lowered their arms before him and slapped the cab as if to say: *Turn back, turn back, turn back.*

The storm grew heavier, the rain churning the warmer ground to mud. The driveway widened and he picked up speed—which was how he almost rear-ended the white Monastella Cabriolet parked on the road. Slamming on the brakes, he drew the truck to a halt. Then he saw the Citroën against the trunk of a pine and the Mercedes parked just beyond it.

Rousseau said she'd given Diago a Citroën.

He left the truck and went first to the Cabriolet with French plates. A bag rested on the seat. Guillermo checked it and found Jordi's papers.

Becoming increasingly nervous, he moved to the Citroën. The remnants of the sigil glowing on the door carried his brother's amber aura. Jordi had obviously struck the car with a glyph to give the wreck a little extra force.

Diago's bag had been thrown to the floorboard. The cracked driver's window and the blood on the glass alarmed Guillermo even more.

It took him only a moment to ascertain that the Mercedes belonged to Grier, which meant the mortal was most likely working with Jordi. Guillermo returned to the truck and parked it beneath the ice-heavy limbs of a pine. He designed a quick sigil to hide the truck from the casual observer, sang it to life, and then walked toward the house.

A great gust of wind rushed through the trees. Guillermo removed his gloves and drew his gun. He hunched low and circled the yard to approach the house at an angle. The lower level appeared deserted. The lights spilling through the entrance were the only illumination. The other rooms were dark.

The front door was unlocked. Guillermo squeezed inside to find the entryway from his nightmare.

In spite of the electric lights, the room seemed to be full of shadows. The wallpaper rustled and then quieted. The hair on Guillermo's arms shot straight up.

All I'm missing is timpani playing a death march, he thought as he sidled past the hall tree. Fear gave his stomach a hard bite. *Fear is good, though. It's a warning.*

That said—I'm thoroughly warned.

Moving slower now, he reached the marble stairs.

The percussion of a distant bomb striking the earth sent Guillermo into an instinctive crouch. The lights remained steady. The earth didn't shake. *It's like an echo from another time. Another realm.*

He stood and climbed swiftly but no less cautiously. It was evident that the second landing was as deserted as the first.

A gunshot rang out. It came from somewhere above. He recalled his dream of Diago clutching the banister with blood spreading across his shirt. Guillermo hugged the wall and climbed, hoping he wasn't too late.

[26]

Diago fashioned a sigil. He whirled and snapped his heel against the floor, throwing the glyph at Jordi with all his might. Hoarse from last night's battle with Frauja and exhausted beyond measure, Diago's hurried spell misfired and Jordi easily deflected it.

From the corner of his eye, Diago saw Karl take aim again. *He won't miss this time.*

Then the small dark sound of Rudi's soul left Diago's side. It flew toward Karl with the savage energy of an angry bee.

Diago heard Rudi's shriek. The frustrated scream was the screech of iron against rock.

Karl flinched and slammed his palm against his ear.

How can he hear his brother's dark sound? The question ran through Diago's mind with the speed of light. *They're angel-born.*

The answer came almost immediately. They were also

mortal, their auras tied through their blood. *Jordi won't hear the noise, but Karl will.*

Rudi's aura easily streamed into Karl's ear canal. The screeching resumed. Seventeen years of frustration and hate poured from Rudi's aura in a cacophony of rage. The sound increased in pitch, rising until it became a siren wail.

And that noise must be a direct hit on Karl's auditory nerve.

Karl's eyes went wide. He dropped his gun and beat the side of his head with his fists. "What is this? What's that noise? Can you hear it, Sir George? Frauja! Help me! Get it out of me! Get it out!"

Karl was right, Diago had time to think. *Rudi is the more powerful of the two.*

Shocked by Karl's sudden contortions, Jordi backed up a pace.

That was all the distraction Diago needed. He dived for Karl's gun, grabbed it, and spun. His double vision returned. He staggered sideways.

Karl's screams turned into inarticulate howls.

Two reports ripped through the room in rapid succession. Karl dropped like a stone, his cries suddenly extinguished. The dark sound of his soul shot through his lips and flew straight into Frauja's realm.

The angel opened his mouth and swallowed Karl's soul.

Rudi's aura emerged from his brother's ear and joined Diago once more.

"Thank you," Diago whispered.

The faint blue light touched his cheek.

Diago blinked his watering eyes and squinted at the new

threat standing in the ballroom's doorway. He expected to see Sturmführer Heines and his Brownshirts. Instead, he found a big man in workman's clothes.

It can't be. But it was. "Guillermo?"

Rudi's voice shouted in Diago's ear. "Herr Alvarez! Look out!"

Diago whirled to find himself looking down the barrel of Jordi's gun. He raised his own weapon and fired. The shot went wide. The bullet hit the mirrored wall and further shattered the glass.

Jordi ducked and rolled. When he rose, he faced his brother. "Guillermo! You're just in time!"

He could only mean one thing. Diago looked at the mirror.

Frauja worked on the other side. He took his time, designing a sigil with ligatures Diago now recognized. *He's going to free himself while we're distracted with each other.*

A quick glance in Jordi's direction assured Diago the other nefil was focused on his brother. Keeping his body low, Diago moved to the transmitter.

While Guillermo and Jordi faced each other, Diago examined Karl's creation. The profusion of switches and dials bore no resemblance to the soundboards he knew. He might shut off Frauja's voice, or he might accidentally end up amplifying the angel straight into the mortal realm.

"Show me how to kill the sound on both sides, Rudi," he pleaded.

Rudi's aura hovered over a dial before it flitted to a switch.

Diago switched off both connections. A subtle change washed over the mirrors. The glass partially reflected the room while still showing a dimmer version of Frauja's realm. It was like looking through a two-way mirror.

Rudi's dark sound hovered by Diago's shoulder. "Is that better, Herr Alvarez?"

No, but Diago didn't say so. That pallid reflection between the worlds was the worst sign, because it meant the glyphs were too damaged to completely shield Frauja from the mortal realm. Fear gnawed Diago's gut. How long those wards might hold against Frauja's assault was anyone's guess.

Red light flashed in the glass as Guillermo sent a fiery glyph barreling into the room. The sigil headed straight for Jordi. The nefil ducked and rolled, coming to his feet after the ward flew over his head.

Jordi aimed his gun at Guillermo.

Diago raised the Beholla, but even as he did, he saw he was too late.

Jordi's finger squeezed the trigger. The dry click was loud in the sudden quiet. The Browning had jammed.

Guillermo trained his revolver on Jordi. "Drop it."

From behind the mirror, Frauja forced his sigil against the barrier. The house shook from the furious blow.

Just as it did last night, Diago had time to think.

Splinters of glass trickled to the floor.

Guillermo gave the enraged angel an uneasy glance. *Shit. I don't remember him looking like that.*

"Guillermo!" Diago shouted again. "He is close to breaking through!"

"We'll get to him," Guillermo growled. But first he had to deal with the more immediate threat of his brother. "Damn it, Jordi. Don't make me kill you."

"Then give me what's mine." He nodded to the signet on Guillermo's finger. "It's *my* birthright."

"See, this is why you keep fucking up." *Why can't he stop this madness?* "You're locked in the past, Jordi. Birthrights and kings and queens—these things are dying before our eyes. Let's look to the future."

"What future?" Jordi sneered as he backed toward the balcony. "That little socialist enclave you've carved for yourself in Spain? Is that the future you want for me? To be a worker among workers when I am meant to rule them all?" His voice rose on the last question, belying his rage at the unfairness of it all.

Diago moved away from the transmitter. His finger tensed ever so slightly on the Beholla's trigger.

Guillermo lifted his hand, palm up. "Don't do it, Diago! He's mine!"

Diago didn't lower the gun, nor did he fire.

Focusing on his brother again, Guillermo said, "We can make a different future, Jordi. One in a world without war."

Jordi's laugh came as harsh as a blow. "Have you forgotten what you are? The nefilim were bred to be soldiers." He gestured at the demented angel behind the mirrors. "Why do you think I sought Frauja in our last incarnation? He is the Destroyer. He offers us the one thing that gives the nefilim meaning: eternal war."

As if in answer, Frauja struck the mirrors again. The floor shuddered beneath them. It was all Guillermo could do to keep his feet.

Jordi threw the useless pistol in Guillermo's direction. He traced a hurried glyph and tossed it after the gun. Then he ran for the French doors.

The pistol exploded midair. Guillermo gave a roar and charged a sigil to shield Diago and himself from the shrapnel. Jordi's chaotic spell died without harming either of his targets.

He's going to jump, Guillermo had time to think. *After he murdered three of my nefilim—damn near four with Diago—the son of a bitch thinks he can just walk away.*

"I made you an offer of peace. You've slapped my hand. We are at war." Guillermo aimed his pistol at his brother's back. "This is for Valeria Soto and Enrique Rosales," he whispered as his finger tightened on the trigger. "I will watch for you, my brother."

Frauja struck the mirrors again.

The tremors hit just as Guillermo fired. His arm jerked to the right. The bullet struck Jordi and took him down, but it wasn't a clean kill. Rolling to his feet, Jordi formed another sigil and gave it jagged edges, charging it with his pain. He flung the ward in Guillermo's direction.

With barely enough time to counter it with a glyph of his own, Guillermo worked fast to produce a ward. The sigils struck each other in a blaze of crimson and orange, like a dying sun. When the light evaporated, Jordi was gone.

Guillermo ran to the balcony. The rain lashed the ground and stung his face, or maybe it was tears. When it came to his brother, he no longer knew.

The yard was empty. A trail of bent grass led to the woods. Guillermo considered following him. He wanted to end this—he couldn't afford a protracted battle with his brother.

A concussion shook the ballroom. Guillermo crouched and covered his head. Pieces of the mirror fell from the wall. An icy wind blew through the cracks.

Diago shouted, "Guillermo!"

His brother's reckoning would have to wait. Guillermo whirled and hurried to Diago's side. *He looks ready to collapse, and his voice is almost gone.* Reaching into his coat, Guillermo retrieved a flask of liquor and handed it to Diago. "Take a drink."

Diago took three long swallows, and then he passed the container back to Guillermo.

"Jordi called him the Destroyer." But Guillermo knew how to sing a more intimate name for the angel. "He is Abaddon."

The angel paused before a break in the mirror. He ran his fingers over the fracture and smiled. Although Guillermo couldn't hear him, the angel's lips moved as he formed another glyph on the glass.

Guillermo quickly assessed the ballroom floor. The two mortals were dead. He recognized the Grier brothers from their photographs. "Bring me up to speed." He gestured at the body nearest the transmitter. "Karl's death looked supernatural. What happened?" *And can it kill us?*

"Jordi shot Rudi"—Diago gestured to the body of a youth with hoarfrost hair—"and Rudi's dark sound murdered Karl."

That isn't good. Guillermo scowled. "I thought mortal dark sounds couldn't kill."

"The mother was a lesser nefil. Rudi apparently inherited her power. They were bound by blood."

"Where is this dark sound now?" Guillermo scanned the room even though he knew he wouldn't see the manifestation of Rudi's death.

"With me," Diago said.

He couldn't help but raise an eyebrow. "You made a friend."

Diago nodded and gestured toward Abaddon. "And a very powerful enemy." He tucked the Beholla in his belt.

His voice is stronger, but not nearly where he needs to be in order to defeat Abaddon. Guillermo studied the transmitter. "How does it work?"

"Rudi would play the violin, and as he did, Karl channeled the sound into Frauja's realm. Once there, Frauja manipulated the frequencies until he found the right pitch for his sigils. Then he would send the sound back through the speakers and into the wiring. He can reach Santuari."

"He already has," Guillermo muttered as he evaluated the wires hooked into the blood sigils, and then followed them back into the transmitter. "Juanita is protecting them." He examined the dials and meters and soon found the homing circuits. "Okay, I think I see how he accomplished it." *That doesn't mean I can reverse it.*

"We're beyond using mortal means to stop him."

A flash of light accompanied the latest crash reverberating through the room. They turned to see Abaddon's ward throwing sparks over the glass. When the last of the fire died, the crack had lengthened by a meter.

Diago whispered, "I never knew the Key, Guillermo. I reflected Frauja's song on him. That's all. I can't stop him."

The defeat on his friend's face tore Guillermo's heart. He gripped Diago's shoulders. "We're going to get out of this. Now listen to me. This is what we must do." He pressed his mouth close to Diago's ear and whispered.

Diago listened carefully to his friend's instructions. "Okay." He nodded. "I can do that."

Guillermo turned him toward the violin. "Get to it."

Rudi's aura remained by Diago's side as he went to the table and lifted the Stradivarius from its case. The instrument felt like an old true friend in his hands. He tucked the chin rest beneath his chin and ran through the scales. The bow felt unbalanced in his right hand with its missing pinkie. He adjusted his grip and played again. *Yes, that's better.*

Everything suddenly felt right and familiar. *I kept thinking the composition was written for a violin, but it wasn't. The music was written for a lyra.* Like the violin, the lyra had no frets, but instead relied on the musician's muscle memory.

Whether or not he possessed the ability to carry the memory of those movements from one incarnation into another remained to be seen.

There is only one way to find out.

He lifted the bow to the strings and faced Abaddon. Playing through the scales a second time, slower now, Diago evaluated the glyphs. Suddenly he understood why they seemed so strange.

When Yago threw the mirror into Frauja's original ward, it shattered and sent glittering variations of the spell to surround and imprison the angel. It became not one oblivion realm, but millions. Because the glass fragmented, no two pieces were alike. Each time Abaddon destroyed one variation of the mirror, he was met with another. To break free of the oblivion realm, he had to decipher each shard separately and then formulate a new ward to shatter Yago's spell.

And he's almost succeeded in finding each piece. Only a few shards prevented him from reaching the mortal realm.

Diago had to find one of the original slivers of that Persian mirror and break it again. *Pulverize it to dust, so that Abaddon must decipher each particle, like the legends of witches who must count each grain of salt before entering a house.*

And he had to do it before Abaddon reached the mortal realm.

While Diago worked through the puzzle of glyphs, Guillermo went to the blood sigils Abaddon had created on the floor. He hummed a sonorous note and formed a banishing glyph with his knife. At the final flourish of the ward, he used his blade to open a wound on the palm of his right hand—the same hand on which he wore his signet. With a snap of his wrist, he sent spatters of his blood across the floor and sang his sigil to life with an ominous chord.

The fire of the Thrones joined with the blaze of Guillermo's aura. A scorched odor filled the ballroom as Abaddon's sigil was extinguished. Guillermo moved to the next one.

The falling rain and Guillermo's song gave Diago his beat. He rapped a series of steps in three-quarter time and spun. Halting himself with his right foot, he lifted the bow to the strings.

As Abaddon's blood sigils died, the lines and ligatures on the mirror became clearer. Diago began to play—*three quick jabs of the bow: strike, strike, strike*. The power of his aura thrummed through his hands and into the violin.

With his own voice ragged from exertion, he let the violin sing for him. Executing a pull to slur the chords, he lifted the bow so that it barely touched the strings—*softer, softer*—he sent vibrations of green and black to sweep across the ballroom's walls.

Watching for a matching spark among the profusion of

glyphs, he performed a slow turn. The toe of his shoe brushed close to the fading blood sigils.

Rudi's aura stayed with him, spinning around the bow and across the strings as if he could somehow join the nefilim's haunting duet. The brightness of his aura lifted Diago's flagging spirit.

Behind the glass, Abaddon brought another glyph to life. He threw it at the wall, and when it struck, the colors in the ballroom became faded and gray. Diago smelled cordite and the wet sharp scent of death. The muffled thunder of a bomb exploded in the distance. Magnesium flares fell like stars.

Abaddon's sigil swept over Rudi's corpse, drawing Diago's gaze to the body. Shadows played over the cadaver's face.

Diago remembered another battlefield of the Great War. A mortal boy, no more than seventeen, writhed in the mud—*gut shot and dying*. No one could reach him. The boy begged someone to kill him . . . anything to end the pain.

I shot him, Diago thought. *With Harvey's hand on my shoulder.* A head shot.

Just like the one that took Rudi's life.

The bow faltered over the strings.

The next explosion sounded nearer. The ballroom floor rumbled beneath their feet. The air turned pallid and gray as Abaddon dissolved the barriers between the oblivion realm and the mortal world.

Guillermo's head came up. A glimmer of light caught his pupils and turned his eyes into twin embers. "Stay with me, Diago!"

With a gasp, Diago jerked free of the memory and pulled the bow across the strings. The Stradivarius wailed.

I'm too tired. I can't focus and Abaddon knows it.

The angel smiled as if acknowledging the thought.

"Herr Alvarez?" Rudi's voice suddenly spoke next to Diago's ear. "Do you remember you said that we couldn't unmake hell but we could work toward repairing the damage?"

"Yes," he murmured as he fought to find his way back into his song.

"How do nefilim say good-bye?" Rudi asked.

"We say: watch for me."

"Watch for me," Rudi echoed, and then he shot toward the mirror. The dark sound slithered through a crack still wet with his blood. He disappeared into Abaddon's realm.

Rudi's small spark of courage reawakened Diago's resolve.

I can do this. Summoning his son's face into his mind, he reminded himself of his promise to return to Santuari. *I* must *do this.* He struck his heel against the wood and left a spark of silver in his wake.

Guillermo nodded and went back to his work. He formed another glyph. This one he threw at the mirrors. His aura's fire crackled with the celestial light of the Thrones and burned across the glass, eroding another series of Abaddon's wards.

The ballroom brightened and the colors deepened, becoming true once more. As the war sounds faded, Diago increased his tempo. He found the beats again—they came harder, faster, as he gazed at the profusion of sigils writhing over the mirrors.

One spark finally answered his violin's call. It came in a single flash. *There.* Diago glared at the juncture of stars where Rudi had died. A thin sliver of the Persian mirror glittered and turned.

Abaddon saw it too. His ward was already formed. He only had to sing it life.

Terror settled in Diago's chest. *There is no way I can beat him. His ward will disentangle the spell before I form the first line to break the mirror. We've lost.*

Then Rudi's pale blue light buzzed into view. He flew straight into Abaddon's ear. The angel opened his mouth in a silent scream. He clamped his hands against the sides of his head.

Rudi must have used the same banshee wail he'd used to destroy Karl, because Abaddon went to his knees.

Except Rudi wouldn't find the angel so easy to kill. *Maybe not, but he has bought me time. Don't waste it.*

"Guillermo! I found the sigil!" Bending his body into the music, Diago made the violin weep with long, sweeping strokes. The notes lingered in the air as he used the violin's bow to make four straight lines intersected by eight vertical links and enjoined them all with a crescent stroke.

In desperation, he channeled the sigil to shatter the fragment of the Persian mirror. Silver fire from Prieto's tear followed Diago's magic, spinning the glass into splinters of light, rejuvenating the old wards and giving them new life. They multiplied and spread across the borderlands between the realms.

Diago gave a savage cry and tasted blood in the back of his throat. Guillermo sang with him. Their voices moved together, merging their songs as one.

Guillermo sent rays of golden light from his signet into Diago's glyph. The Thrones' celestial tones filled the room and enflamed the wards with a bank of light, like an aurora borealis flowing across the glass.

Diago continued to play. The chords floated over the room, deeply, sadly, moving into a dirge. Then he resumed his attack and punch against the strings *(strike, strike, strike)* and the Stradivarius shuddered in his hands, the body buckling, sending viridian glyphs spinning into the mirrors, shooting like lightning across the glass, and as the light died, the notes faded, softer and softer, shifting into a quiet that yawned throughout the room, a terrible sound that was no sound, interrupted only by the occasional crackle of sigils before they faded into the glass . . .

The mirror solidified. No longer did it reflect two worlds. Not a single crack marred the ballroom walls. Abaddon's war-torn world had disappeared.

A spark of light hit the silver brooch and sent it spinning across the floor.

The emerald rolled free of the angel's grip.

Free at last.

[27]

Diago swayed on his feet.

Guillermo caught his arm. "What the hell happened? Abaddon was winning."

"It was Rudi." Diago gently extracted himself from his friend's grip and searched the floor until he found the compact. Taking it over to Rudi's body, he placed the makeup case in the corpse's hands. "He flew into the oblivion realm and entered Abaddon's ear. Just like he did with Karl."

"Dark sounds can't kill an angel . . . can they?"

"Probably not. But Abaddon took the auras of the daimon-born. Because of that, he could hear the dark sound of Rudi's voice through their souls, and that was something an angel wouldn't expect. It didn't hurt that Rudi was a lesser nefil." A white lie, but the youth had certainly died bravely in the end. *Let it rest.* "We should honor his song."

"We will," Guillermo said as he turned back to the transmitter. He formed a sigil of destruction and sang it life. The ward struck the soundboard. Sparks flew through the wiring and the odor of burned circuitry filled the room.

Turning to Diago, he said, "Come on. We've got to get out of here before someone comes and sees this mess. And let's not forget my brother is still out there somewhere."

Diago gathered the brooch and the emerald and placed them in the case with his broken violin. "I don't think Jordi is near," he said. "I'm sure if he was, he would have come to Abaddon's aid, or burned the house down around us."

"We're still going downstairs carefully." Guillermo drew his pistol. "You got a gun?"

Diago drew Karl's Beholla.

Guillermo reloaded his revolver. "You look like a strong wind will blow you down. I'll go first."

Diago didn't move. "We talked. We said this assignment was about trust . . ."

"No, *you* said this was about trust and *you* were worried about what the others would think."

"Why did you come?"

Halfway to the door, Guillermo halted but he didn't turn. "We had intelligence that you were up against a rogue angel. You're one of us now. We watch each other's backs."

All that was fine and based on Miquel's constant assurances, Diago expected no less, but Guillermo was king. Diago pressed the question. "Yes, but why did *you* come?"

Guillermo turned and met Diago's gaze. "Because you're my friend." He shrugged and looked away. "Besides, even tough guys need saving sometimes."

Diago nodded and whispered, "Thank you."

"You're welcome." Guillermo motioned to the door with the gun. "Now be quiet and keep your eyes open in case Jordi is waiting for us."

"I've done this before, you know."

"Ya, ya, ya, come on, tough guy."

[28]

OFFENBURG, GERMANY

By the time Jordi made it to Offenburg, the bleeding had almost stopped. Thanks to Frauja's intervention, Guillermo's shot had torn through the flesh at Jordi's hip and missed the bone.

It was a bleeder, though. The Cabriolet's seat was slick, but the wound had already started to heal.

Jordi parked the car near a public phone. Pulling his dark coat around him to hide the bloodstains, he limped to the booth and stepped inside. The rain and cold kept most people in their homes, so he wasn't worried about being seen.

Lifting the handset from the hook, he dialed the operator and gave her Nico's number. Counting the rings, he watched the rain cry down the booth's glass doors.

Nico finally answered and accepted the charges. "Jordi? Where are you?"

"Offenburg." He peered through the rain and gave Nico the street name. "I have a problem, and I need some help."

"Are you all right?"

Jordi leaned against the booth's wall to take the weight off his injured leg. "I'm functioning. I need a place to rest for a few days."

"Erich Heines is nearby. I'll call him. He'll take you to a safe house. I'll be there as soon as I can."

"Call Heines, but you stay in France. I'm coming home. I'll contact you as soon as I know my train schedule." He licked his lips and bowed his head. "You wanted to go someplace warm. I want you to find us a house in Estoril, Portugal. It's on the Portuguese Riviera with a close proximity to Lisbon." General Sanjurjo would see it as an exile worthy of his status. More importantly, Nico would love it.

"Is that all?"

A couple ran past in the rain. They huddled close beneath their umbrella. The man's arm was around the woman, and they laughed as they jogged by the phone booth.

Jordi licked his lips and wished Nico was close. *He is the safe harbor I need after a storm.* "Have I told you how much I appreciate you?"

"Every chance you get. Ring off now so I can call Erich."

Jordi hung up without another word. He stumbled back to the car and got inside. As he sat watching the rain fall, he held the brooch in his hand and formulated a plan.

An hour passed before a car parked in front of him. A large nefil with white-blond hair exited his vehicle and came to the driver's door of Jordi's Cabriolet. The man's right cheek was pitted with shrapnel scars, which disappeared beneath his collar. He knocked on the window.

Jordi noted the heavy ring with its dominant glyph and angel's tear. *One of Queen Jaeger's Inner Guard.* He rolled down the window. "Herr Erich Heines, I presume?"

"Herr Abelló, please come with me." He signaled to someone in his car. A young nefil with reddish hair hurried toward them. "This is Julius. He will follow us in your car."

Jordi allowed Erich to help him. Erich's driver, an older man wearing a cap favored by the Brownshirts, held the door as Erich maneuvered Jordi into the backseat.

Once the driver put the car on the road, Jordi allowed himself to relax. "I am in your debt, Herr Heines, but I fear I must ask one more favor. Can you arrange a meeting between me and Queen Jaeger?"

"I can assure you, sir, Queen Jaeger is already on her way. She is very interested in what happened today."

"What happened today, Erich, is that I was forced to forfeit the battle in order to win the war."

[29]

KARINHALL

Guillermo took the lead as they went downstairs.

Diago insisted on stopping at the second floor. "There is something I have to get."

Guillermo didn't have the heart to tell him no. He guarded the landing while Diago went down the corridor and into the room next to a lavatory. When he returned, he carried a red silk scarf, which he slipped into his pocket.

"We are alone," he said as he joined Guillermo. "I can feel it. Can't you?"

He's right, Guillermo thought. Nothing stirred. *Jordi's fled. I'm sure of it.* He relaxed somewhat but still wanted to be on his way.

Diago wasn't in as much of a hurry. "I need to check one more thing."

Guillermo sighed and nodded. "Let's do it together."

In the opposite wing, they investigated the rooms. As they did, Diago told Guillermo about the previous night and his discovery of the dead nefilim's clothing. The first two rooms contained dusty furniture. The third held the dead nefilim's instruments.

Diago searched until he lifted a battered violin case with a thick strap from the pile. "This was Harvey's." He opened the case, brushing his fingers across the strings. "We fought together in the Great War."

It's almost like he's in shock. Determined to keep him moving, Guillermo put his hand on his friend's shoulder. "Bring it with you. We'll honor his song, too."

Diago nodded and lifted the case. He almost toppled from the weight of the two violins. Guillermo took the Stradivarius from him and led him outside.

Jordi's Cabriolet was gone.

So much for the hope that he'd crawled into the woods to die. "Aw, fuck," Guillermo muttered. "He's on the move."

The cold air must have rejuvenated Diago, because he seemed more aware of his surroundings, less lost in dreams. "Were you hoping to find him dead?"

"I'm hoping he didn't sabotage our vehicle, smart guy." To his relief, the truck started without a problem. He retrieved a screwdriver from under the seat. "Get your things and the papers for the Citroën."

"What about the car?"

"We're leaving it. If it's traced back to Rousseau, she will claim it was stolen." He went to the bumper and removed the license plate.

"She'll give the car up that easy?" He gathered his things and took the papers from the glove box. His movements were slowing again.

He's exhausted. "No, I'll have to pay her for the goddamn thing."

"This is a newer car. That's going to be expensive."

"Stop trying to make me feel better." He gave the plate and screwdriver to Diago. "Wait for me in the truck. I'm going to start a fire."

Returning to the house, he found a couple of kerosene lamps and broke them in the library. A single match set the room ablaze. Then he rejoined Diago, who waited beside the truck.

Guillermo asked, "How are you holding up?"

"I'll be fine."

He didn't look fine. As Guillermo passed the Citroën, he retrieved the blanket from the backseat.

Diago got in the truck, cradling Harvey's violin case in his arms.

Guillermo draped the blanket over Diago's lap before he took the wheel and cranked the truck.

Behind them, the flames glowed through the house's windows. Guillermo pulled onto the drive, alert for any sigils Jordi might have left for them. Fortunately, there were none and within minutes, they were on the main road, headed toward Kehl.

They had traveled less than a kilometer when Diago said, "I remembered something, from my death as Yago."

"What was that?"

"I died in George's bedchamber. I remember you came into the room and grabbed me. Why were you angry?"

"I'd wanted to leave earlier to get you out of there, but I'd promised you three weeks. I waited too long. You died in my arms."

"I'm sorry," Diago murmured.

"It's okay, just don't do it again."

Diago gave him a weary smile. "I'm just tired. My throat hurts, and I'm cold. Christ, but I'm cold."

Because his mortal body has been stressed to the limit. Guillermo drove down the mountain as fast as he dared. The Angel's Nest would have a doctor familiar with a nefil's physiology.

"Was he upset with me?" Diago asked.

"Who?"

"Michel. We never got to say good-bye. Was he upset with me?"

"No, no, he wasn't. But something in him died with you that day."

"He said I took his heart."

And mine, too, Guillermo thought. "Don't take it again."

[30]

SANTUARI, SPAIN
9 SEPTEMBER 1932

As Guillermo guided the battered Suiza up the drive to his house, Diago clutched the box of watercolors he'd purchased for Rafael in France. Excitement stirred in his stomach and soon reached his breast. They were finally coming home.

"Do you think he will like the paint?" Diago asked as he glimpsed the children playing fútbol in the yard.

Guillermo chuckled. "He'll love whatever you bring him."

Ysabel looked their way. She turned and said something to Rafael. He beamed and waved at the car as Guillermo parked.

Diago grinned at the sight of his son. He barely got the door open before Rafael was in his arms. He embraced the child, inhaling the familiar scent of the Catalonian sun in his hair. "I missed you so much."

"I missed you, too, Papá." Rafael pulled back and gave Diago's face a critical examination. "You got in a fight, didn't you?"

"Yes, but I'm okay." From the corner of his eye, he saw other nefilim were coming into the yard to greet Guillermo. They surrounded him and chattered like magpies. No one seemed to notice either Diago or Rafael.

Which was just fine with Diago.

"Look," he said, suddenly remembering the gift. "I brought you something from France." He presented the watercolors to his son.

Rafael ran one finger over the metal case. "Oh, Papá, they're beautiful."

Glancing at the crowd around Guillermo, Diago whispered, "Let's sneak home and you can paint me a picture."

The car door widened, and Miquel looked down at them. "There will be no sneaking home."

His husband's face was like cool water after a drought. Diago stood and Miquel embraced him. Rafael pressed himself close to Diago's side, and he reached down to put his palm on his son's head.

Someone patted him on the back. "Welcome home, Diago."

He turned to find Suero grinning at him. Carme walked behind the young nefil. She gave Diago a nod in a rare display of acceptance.

As his small family moved away from the car, more nefilim paused to speak to him. For the first time since he'd taken his oath to Guillermo, Diago finally felt that he was a part of the community.

Bernardo gave them a ride home. All the way, Rafael regaled Diago with the adventures of living in Guillermo's big house for a week. Diago nodded and made all the right sounds, barely listening to the words as he enjoyed the happy music that was his son's voice.

Miquel sat beside him, holding his hand with a grip that promised he would never let go.

At the house, they unloaded Diago's bag and the two violin cases. While Miquel paused to speak with Bernardo, Diago carried Harvey's case into the bedroom and placed it on the bed.

Rafael followed him, hugging the watercolor kit to his chest. "Is that your violin, Papá?"

"No. It belonged to a very special friend."

Miquel came into the bedroom and put Diago's bag on the bed. "What are you going to do with it?"

"Give it to Bernardo. Guillermo said we will honor Harvey's song. I saved it for the service."

Rafael asked, "What happened to your violin?"

"It got broken."

"Ysabel said there was a soul-eater angel. She said they are very evil and strong. But you fought it, didn't you, Papá?"

"Don Guillermo and I both fought it. We worked together, like a team."

Rafael leaned on the bed. "Did the soul-eater attack you? Is that how you got in a fight? Were you scared?"

Diago nodded and only answered the last question. "Oh, yes. I was very scared."

"How did you stay brave?"

Diago looked down into his son's eyes. "I thought of you."

EPILOGUE

SANTUARI, SPAIN
2 DECEMBER 1932

Diago sat at the upright piano and considered the heavily revised intro. The dark emerald rested beside his pencil on the music stand. Taking the jewel in his hand, he closed his eyes, and thought back to his past incarnation as Yago when an angel sang to him of shifting realms.

I might not have mastered the Key in my last incarnation, but that doesn't mean I can't try in this one. Replacing the gem on the piano, he played the movement again, more softly this time. "Quiet now," he whispered.

Someone knocked at his door, startling him. Miquel was in Barcelona and Rafael was in school.

With a sigh, he left the composition and went to the door to find Guillermo. He carried Diago's old violin case.

"Got a minute?" Guillermo asked.

"Sure, come in." Diago stood aside. "Can I get you something?"

"No." Guillermo dismissed the offer with a wave. "I'm

fine. I felt bad about your Stradivarius, so I . . . um . . . brought you a gift." He thrust the case at Diago, giving him no choice but to drop it or accept it.

"You didn't have to do that," Diago murmured as he set the case on the couch and opened it. The violin's body gleamed in golden hues. He stroked the strings. The sound was pure. "It's beautiful." Protective sigils glittered along the sides, warding the instrument so that no one could ever use it against him. "Thank you."

"It's the least I could do." Guillermo went to the upright and pressed two keys. "I heard you burned your Stradivarius. We could have repaired it."

Diago shook his head. "I did the right thing. The instrument was tainted by Abaddon. Too many nefilim died because of it. If he used it against me once, he or someone else might do so again."

Lifting the emerald from the music stand, Guillermo tilted the stone in the morning light. Then he withdrew the jacinth from his pocket and placed the gemstones side by side on the top board.

He walked his fingers across the keys. "There is no easy way to say this. Rousseau's spies have reported that Queen Jaeger purchased the Grier estate for one of her lieutenants. A nefil named Erich Heines."

Sturmführer Heines. "I made his acquaintance in Kehl on the way to the Grier household."

"I heard about that." Guillermo treated Diago to a fleeting smile. "Anyway, that's the bad news. The good news is they are finding it difficult to free Abaddon."

"I take it Jordi is somehow involved in all this?"

Guillermo nodded. "He's maintaining contact with them."

That explained why he left them so quickly at the Grier house. He'd sacrificed a short-term victory for a more abiding gain. *Classic Jordi.* "Even if they free Abaddon, do you think they can control a soul-eater?"

Guillermo shook his head. "But that won't stop them from trying." He didn't bother with platitudes. "We're not out of options. I'm petitioning the Thrones. Based on what happened, we're hoping they will remove Jaeger from command, but we're not counting on them doing it soon. Jaeger has a great deal of support. It doesn't help that petitions before the Thrones aren't evaluated in what we would call a timely fashion."

No, because the angels didn't experience time in the same manner as either the mortals or nefilim. A mortal year was but a minute to them.

Guillermo sat on the bench and read Diago's score. His fingers danced through the scales as he warmed up, and then he played the intro on the piano. "This is beautiful. What is it?"

"The intro to the Key."

Although he tried to hide it, that old hungry light sparkled in Guillermo's eyes. "You've found it?"

Diago hedged. "I don't know if it will work."

Guillermo examined the score more closely. He played it again, but the music sounded flat.

Diago joined him at the piano and tucked the violin beneath his chin. "Together."

"On three," Guillermo whispered as he counted them off.

They played the song, and suddenly the chords, which

never seemed quite right when Diago played alone, took on a new life. The music fell with the hush of an angel's voice, or the sound of stars falling. Everything grew still, like the world held its breath.

Then the colors shifted and grew brighter. The walls were still warm and golden, the leather of the couch deep and red, but the hues seemed somehow brighter and more intense. As the last note faded, the air shimmered as if dawn's soft light flowed over them. At the end of the song, the colors dulled and became plain once more.

Diago let the bow fall from the violin's strings. His pulse hammered in his ears. *We did it.*

"That was a glimpse into another realm." Guillermo sat with his fingers poised over the ivories.

They exchanged a look.

Diago nodded at the score. "Frauja sang me his beginning in our last incarnation. I remember how he wove the sound of anguish into all his sigils. His music encompassed the sorrow of the angels driven from their homes and all that they knew. Had they not been banished, they never would have learned to shift the realms as they did."

Guillermo took up the pencil and made a notation on the stave. The note's tail wavered beneath his trembling hand. "So interpreting the Key begins with understanding loss."

"Yes. We must begin at the ending, and then go forward."

Guillermo experimented with a series of chords and then stopped. He kept his gaze on the keys. "I've missed composing with you."

"And I with you," Diago whispered.

A moment passed and then two. Guillermo said, "Okay." He stared at the score. "What comes after sorrow?"

"Healing. Trust. No. Wait. I'm going too fast." Diago lifted his bow to the violin's strings. "Before those things can come, one must first surrender."

Guillermo met his gaze. "Surrender is hard. It's lonely."

Diago shook his head. "Not when you have friends."

ACKNOWLEDGMENTS

Writing a novel is rarely a solitary endeavor. People help in ways both big and small. Special thanks always goes first and foremost to my family, especially to my husband, Dick, who does so many things to make sure I have time to write.

To Courtney Schafer and Lisa Cantrell for all your help and numerous suggestions. To my fabulous first readers: Rhi Hopkins, Glinda Harrison, Vinnie Russo, and Sarah E. Stevens. To Josep Oriol for his early assistance on Barcelona and his beautiful photography. To Ollivier Robert for help with French addresses. To my copy editor Laurie McGee, who filled in my missing words and kept me from looking like an idiot with her mad editing skills.

To the Extraordinary Fellows of Arcane Sorcery: you know who you are. You probably don't know how many times you saved my sanity. Also, to Beth Cato, John Hornor Jacobs, and Dan Koboldt for riding to my rescue more times than I can count.

To Mark Lawrence, Ed Ashton, and Andrew Hopkins for helping me understand basic physics, which I'm still not sure I entirely understand, but that's okay. Special thanks to Michael Mammay for firsthand information on howitzers and trenches and for reading Diago's nightmare scene for technical assistance. If I made a mistake in the facts, it's mine, not theirs.

To Lisa Rodgers, who is one powerhouse of an agent and who always has my back. And to David Pomerico and the team at Harper Voyager, who believed in this series and made it happen.

My deepest gratitude goes to my readers. This book couldn't have happened without you and your support. Thank you for giving this story your time. I hope you enjoyed it. Read on . . .

ABOUT THE AUTHOR

T. Frohock has turned her love of dark fantasy and horror into tales of deliciously creepy fiction. She currently lives in North Carolina where she has long been accused of telling stories, which is a southern colloquialism for lying.

www.tfrohock.com

Twitter: @T_Frohock

Instagram: tfrohock

ALSO BY T. FROHOCK

WHERE OBLIVION LIVES

A LOS NEFILIM NOVEL

A lyrical historical fantasy adventure set in 1932 Spain and Germany that brings to life the world of the novellas collected in *Los Nefilim*: Spanish nephilim battling daimons in a supernatural war to save humankind.

LOS NEFILIM

Collected together for the first time, T. Frohock's three novellas

In Midnight's Silence, Without Light or Guide, and *The Second Death* brings to life the world of Los Nefilim, Spanish nephilim that possess the power to harness music and light in the supernatural war between the angels and daimons. In 1931, Los Nefilim's existence is shaken by the preternatural forces commanding them…and a half-breed caught in between.